Three Seasons of Sadie

RICHARD MASEFIELD

THREE SEASONS OF SADIE

Red Door

Published by RedDoor
www.reddoorpress.co.uk

ISBN 978-1-913062-01-9

A CIP catalogue record for this book is available from the British
Library

Cover design: Clare Shepherd

Typesetting: Fuzzy Flamingo
www.fuzzyflamingo.co.uk

Printed and bound in Denmark by Nørhaven

For Lee as ever

*... and for Margaret, to make up for my
behaviour when we were seventeen*

Dramatis Personae

Abigail Compton: imperishable star of stage and screen
Cordelia: her daughter and dresser
Barbara Bayliss: her toxic understudy
Nigel Hughes-Milton: a 'Who's for tennis?' type
Crispin Blake: total tosser
Lumsdon Gould: Old Vic luvvie
Yvonne Hayes: character support
Primrose ('call-me-Primmie') Allan: gullible pekinese-owner
Nanki-Poo: said pekinese
Tom Allan: Primmie's solid, real-life husband

Oh, and me, Sam Ashby: Assistant Stage Manager and dogsbody

Prologue

Do you ever wish that brains were like computers, with some sort of delete facility for things we'd rather not remember? I know that I do. And one youthful memory I'd be happy to consign to a black hole on the far side of the universe involved my very first pair of Levi jeans.

I don't suppose there's anyone these days who's too important, fat or ancient to own a pair of jeans – except perhaps the Pope, or possibly the Queen. But back in the early 1960s they were strictly for the young and trendy. The fashion for them started with James Dean, the doomed young film star famous for his blonde quiff, moody scowl and well-worn Levi's. One of the posters in my bedroom at the farm showed him in his final movie, *Giant*, just before he killed himself in a car crash at the age of twenty-four – James Dean leaning on the mudguard of a black Cadillac Tourer, with a rifle slung across his shoulders and Liz Taylor kneeling at waist-level gazing at his denim crotch. On him the jeans were skin-tight with strategic creases radiating from the vital bulge.

Which of course was what I wanted as soon as I was old enough to bulge convincingly myself. To look like the dead Adonis all the girls considered the last word absolutely. To look like Jimmy Dean.

'I suppose you've *half* a look of him in a dim light from a distance, Sammo,' my cousin Mag conceded while I was staying with her one half-term. She narrowed heavily mascaraed eyes to look me up and down. 'You'd need a T-shirt, a leather jacket and a pair of jeans. I can do the hair.'

Mag worked as a hairdresser at Antoine's Beauty Salon in Eastbourne, and followed her advice by pushing me through to her kitchen, to leave me with my head under the geyser spout while she fetched towels, tubes and bottles and a bright green Pifco hair dryer. The result an excruciating half-hour later was a quiff rearing from my eighteen-year-old forehead in a stiffened plume, before folding at the back into the then obligatory duck's arse. Photos of me at the time look less like James Dean as a teenage rebel than someone who's just met Anne Boleyn without her head.

I bought the T-shirt at Bobby's Department Store a few doors up from the Eastbourne art gallery where my mother sold her paintings. A red plastic zip-up jacket was the closest thing to leather I could afford. But as the main ingredient of Jimmy Dean-ness, the 'blue jeans' as we called them then, had to be the best on offer – had to be by Levi Strauss, imported from the States complete with metal rivets and brass-button fly.

'You'll want the shrink-to-fit 501s, Sir,' an unctuous menswear assistant told me while he nudged my scrotum with his tape. 'You're a Medium 34-inch, Sir.' (The 'Sir' pitched short of genuine politeness and quite a long way from respect.) 'Medium for everything but length, Sir. With your legs you will have to have them taken up.'

I didn't care, rushed back to Mag's to put them on and view them in her bathroom mirror. On Jett Rink in the *Giant* poster they'd been tight as eel-skin. On me they hung completely straight – baggy, sexless, creased only where they concertina'd at my feet – being as the menswear assistant had asserted, far too long. 'You'll also have to shrink them, Sir,' he'd told me, pointing to the label on the Levi's.

He couldn't have been more than five years older than me, but made a point of staring at my quiff while smoothing his own sleekly Brylcreemed Cary-Grant-style hair. 'Shrink-to-fit, Sir,' he repeated. 'You'll need to wear them in the bath to give them something to fit *on to*, if you take my meaning – and make sure the water's hot, Sir.' He'd smirked unpleasantly.

* * *

First thing the next morning, as soon as Mag and her live-in lodger, Len, had left for work, I nipped down to the bathroom we all shared, took off my clothes, and while the bath was filling pulled on my brand new Levi's and buttoned up the fly.

I think it must have been the first time I'd worn any kind of trousering without pants on underneath, and have to say I liked the way it felt. There was another thing, it occurred to me, that I might do in Mag's pink bathroom while I was on my own. Besides taking a bath, I mean. I glanced at the pink toilet roll beside Mag's pink porcelain lavatory and locked the door.

When I'd run the water as hot as I could bear, I climbed in gingerly one foot at a time to watch the fabric covering my shins begin to darken. When my backside hit the water, it felt as if a pair of hot and eager hands were reaching up to grasp it; another if I'm honest not unpleasant feeling. Then, as I extended them, I felt the denim mould itself around my legs like greedy anacondas swallowing their prey. I ran in more hot water and lay back to let the shrink-to-fit 501s do what they'd done for Jimmy Dean, albeit with a little more to work on in the leg-department.

Mag's bath was pink inevitably, to match the walls, the toilet, basin, bath mat, towels and scented soaps – although below the water line, reflecting as it did the colour of the saturated denim, it appeared less pink than mauve. That was what I thought. Until I saw it wasn't a reflection.

I should have let the water out of course the moment I realised that the jeans weren't colour-fast, and can only think that I was mesmerised by the sheer speed with which it changed from lavender to purple and then navy blue – or else immobilised by the prospect of my nether regions vanishing beneath the dye? Either way I left it too late to react, and by the time I pulled the plug, my cousin's bath was stained, half pink, half blue.

Well I panicked – tried to stand, but finding that my legs, shrink-wrapped in boiling denim, refused to bend, sank back on to my knees inside the bath. Then made a wordless sound a bit like *ooouccch!* as something very tight and cruelly studded gave my testicles a violent squeeze. It wasn't so much that the jeans had shrunk-to-fit, as shrunk-to-strangle-me-alive from the feet up.

Working slowly, painfully unbending, whimpering a little as I scissored one leg then the other over the bath's pink flank, I landed on the lino in a roughly upright posture, in the middle of a spreading pool of dye. There was no question of attempting to wipe round the bath's now two-tone interior before I could move freely – or actually at all. So, concentrating all my efforts on the top button of the Levi's, I struggled manfully to force it through its shrunken button hole.

Then the second button.

Then the third and fourth, and finally the fifth... which was when my genitals burst through the open fly, parboiled, flat-packed, stained bluish-grey and frankly looking at their least appealing.

But if I thought the worst was over, I was wrong. Despite the welcome outbreak in the front, the shrunken fabric of the Levi's still clung tenaciously to my clenched buttocks and cramped thighs. My first attempt at moving it felt less like peeling a banana than skinning a live rabbit. The blood trapped round my shrink-wrapped knee joints had puffed them up to twice their normal size, and however hard I pulled, the jeans refused to budge. Until it dawned on me that I would have to tug them from the bottom. Not too adroitly as it turned out. Because it was when I stooped to get a grip on one wet cuff, to give it a sharp yank, that I crashed over backwards – hit the bath, slid heavily on to the floor and lay there moaning.

'Sam, is that you up there?' I heard Mag yelling from below me in the kitchen – having come home I suppose for something she'd forgotten. I never did discover what. 'Sammo, do you hear me? What the devil do you think you're up to?'

Somehow I scrambled to my feet to snatch a hand-towel from the basin as I heard my cousin thunder up the stairs – calling out that I was fine, had just slipped and fallen, nothing broken, I was perfectly OK. By then she'd reached the landing, trumpeting like a herd of elephants and pounding on the bathroom door.

'But I'm not decent, Maggie.'

'What the hell has that got to do with anything? OPEN UP THIS INSTANT, SAM, before I call the fire brigade!' Which left me you must see without a choice.

The first thing I saw when I'd unlocked the door and hopped back awkwardly to let her in, was Mag dressed in the mauve overalls she wore to work, one hand still balled into a fist, her face a picture of suspicion. I watched her gaze move slowly downwards from my blue-streaked torso, to the blue fingers and pink scrap of towel that did more to draw attention than to hide what they contained, on down to where the Levi's double-clamped my swollen knees, then slowly up again to meet my eyes.

'I think I am in trouble, Mag,' I muttered feebly.

'Good God, boy!' She goggled at me, open-mouthed.

'Now I've seen it all, I really have!' my cousin gasped between unseemly shrieks of laughter, 'Bill's going to kill herself when I tell her, she'll absolutely *die!*' (Auntie Bill was Mag's best bosom buddy, whom we'll come to presently.)

I expect you've heard of people laughing so hard that they have to hold their sides? Well I'm telling you, I watched Mag do it while I made some furtive readjustments to the towel. Until finally she took a grip, first on herself and then on me, ordering me to lie flat on the lino while she fumbled for a purchase on the Levi's slippery hems. At the first hard tug, my unappetising manhood was unavoidably displayed. The second must have moved me several feet across the floor. At the third great heave, with Mag still honking like a goose and the mascara running down her cheeks, I found myself freed of the jeans, the towel and every last vestige of human dignity, as I shot naked through the bathroom door to hit the wainscot on the far side of the landing.

* * *

Luckily the blue stain didn't prove indelible, while Mag had been so anxious to ring Auntie Bill with all the gruesome details that she'd simply left me with a mop, a scrubbing brush and strict instructions not to leave the bathroom until universal pinkness was restored.

'Your bum and legs and whatnots will probably stay grey for weeks,' she predicted (accurately as it turned out), 'and serve you bloody right, you berk.' Mag can be pretty awful but she's family, which means we care about each other but pretend we don't – and probably makes this as good a time as any to introduce the rest of us, and tell you how I came to be in Eastbourne in the first place.

ACT I

Scene 1

But let's not start this with the opening passage which resulted in my birth, or a description of the kind of slippery customer I was at the time. No, let's fast forward shall we to the day that I was christened in the village church at Sellington, objecting stridently to being doused in tepid water from the font. Samuel Patrick Ashby were the names they gave me; though no one from that day to this has ever called me anything but Sam, or Sammy. Or in Mag's case, Sammo – or something ruder by Miss Compton, come to think of it. But we'll get to all that in due course.

Meanwhile, the sooner I tell you the better you will understand that I'm in love and always have been with Sellington and the Bury Farm, and hope to love them until I die. These days the village isn't quite so peaceful, with the sound of traffic from the main road so often carried down the valley on the wind. But the old farm is still as beautiful as it ever was, with its gabled farmhouse, byres and barn, its outbuildings and hanging woods. We Ashbys have run sheep up there for centuries. Dad used to say our fortune rested on the woolly backs of Southdown sheep, although Grannie always claimed her dairy Shorthorns boosted profits through the war.

There were cows and sheep at the Bury Farm all through my childhood. The milky smell of Grannie's dairy, the bleating chorus of the ewes and lambs down in the dig yard, the games my sister Caroline and I played on the stacks when we brought in the hay, are my most treasured memories. But nothing lasts for ever does it. The fashion for synthetic fibres along with a demand for bigger crossbred sheep eventually put paid to our fat, mousy little Southdowns. They've joined the rare breeds now on show at Sellington, competing for attention with our Clydesdale horses, Lop pigs and Bagot goats.

You'll find us with the other ads and leaflets at all the Sussex tourist sites. We call ourselves 'The Sellington Rare Breeds Centre' promoted recently as: 'Ashby's Ark: A rare day out for all the family'. My granddaughter Amelia thought that one up, clever girl.

But back to my own childhood. I'll try not to dwell on it for longer than you need to understand what kind of boy I was – the main point being that I was lucky, really lucky to grow up in the Sussex downland with its open skies and boundless space. All our schoolfriends envied Caroline and me our freedom, and in our turn we pitied them for their restricted lives. They lived in town, in Seaford or in Eastbourne, in street houses with postage stamps for gardens and hardly any space at all. Their mums cooked joints on Sundays. Their dads trudged in from work at six, and at the weekend took them all out in the car if they possessed one – or if they didn't, walked them to the beach. Their lives were neat and tidy, unlike ours.

Cue David Attenborough: 'The whole tribe pitch in to care for new additions in the meercat family.'

Which is rather how things were for me and Caro, with a tribe of relatives and friends to bring us up. It wasn't that our parents didn't love us. Just that they left our care to those who had more time for us than they did – people like our grandparents and Sim, our cousins or our schoolfriends' mothers. Or really anyone to hand.

I was conceived in wartime, if you want the record straight, in 1944 while my father, Patrick Ashby, was home from France on leave; and although unlike *his* father, Dad returned uninjured from his war to spawn Caroline in 1946, he'd had to fight another battle in the post-war years to wrestle back the farm from Grannie. I don't suppose he ever felt the place was truly his again, poor man, so long as she was there to tell him how to run it. He mostly coped by staying out of doors all day and in all weathers, knee-deep in something smelly – bouncing in to snatch a bite of toast and marmalade for breakfast with barely time to comment on the weather, or stroke Caro's hair, before bouncing out again to turn the hay, or plough the bottom field, or do whatever needed doing on the farm.

As an artist who sold her oil paintings through a gallery in Eastbourne for a good deal more than Dad could hope to clear at livestock sales in Lewes or in Hailsham, my mother, Pamela, spent all day every day up in her studio – painting seascapes which looked identical unless you saw them side by side. And to call Mummy inattentive as a parent would be a bit like calling Einstein bright, or Atilla the Hun a little on the bossy side. So it was Grannie in her sky-blue Austin Cambridge who drove us to the bus stop up at Gibbet Cross; our cousin Nancy on her bicycle who met us from it after school and walked us down for tea in Sellington with Auntie Helen.

It was Grannie who decided what we wore and ate, and how we looked and spoke; Grannie who dosed us with malt extract every morning and wielded the nit comb when we got infected. Grannie managed most things at The Bury – Grandpa, Dad whenever she could pin him down, the house, the garden and the dairy herd until we had to sell it. A bustling little person with a tight grey perm that looked like some sort of crenulation from the back, she'd learned to manage in Australia where her father managed coal mines, and later on in South America before she married Grandpa.

Grannie hurried everywhere as fast as her short legs would carry her, told everyone exactly what she thought and how she thought they should behave before they thought to ask. But of course we loved her, Caroline and me. Partly for the thrilling stories that she told us of her adventures as a girl in Queensland and Colombia, and partly because we knew she'd flatten anyone who threatened us without a second thought. It's how she was with those she loved, particularly Grandpa. Even while she scolded him and told him what a fool he was and always would be, you could see the way that Grannie's shining eyes behind her glasses lighted on the ruin of his face, that there'd be nothing left worth mentioning of anyone who dared to stand in Grandpa's way.

And now I've got to Grandpa, how shall I describe him? How *do* you paint a portrait of a man without a face?

Other people's grandpas showed how they felt by smiling. Other people's grandpas spoke. With the facial injuries he'd suffered in the First War, you might think communication would be hard for Grandpa. But it's amazing how expressive hands can be – and eyes; even one of them if it can wink. And Grandpa's hands were wonderful. So big and sensitive and strong. He sometimes spun his signet ring for Caroline and me; to look like a tiny, golden goldfish bowl gyrating on his desk. He taught us card games with those hands; canasta, snap and whist. You could even say that Grandpa's big, strong hands and Grandpa's kind blue eye made up for all the things he didn't have. Because he'd come back from that dreadful war a shattered man, without a chin or nose or mouth or a left eye.

Grannie never spoke of it. But Sim did when we asked

why Grandpa's face was always hidden (and I'll get to Sim in just a sec). He wore a pair of spectacles with smoked glass in one lens – and tied to them a sort of scarf; a piece of dark blue fabric, which he tucked into the collar of his shirt. When he went out with Grannie in the car, Grandpa wore a trilby hat with under it a painted metal mask.

Yes, you heard that right, a *painted metal mask* – a thing that from a distance made him look as he had looked in photographs before the war. Its enamelled surface seen close to was crazed with tiny cracks like an old plate. Yet it was still the image of a young man's face, which made it slightly creepy. I don't think Grandpa can have liked it anyway, because he never wore it in the house. We weren't allowed to see him eat. He did that in the Bury flat with Grannie or with Sim, or sometimes on his own – and in all the years I knew him, I only once saw Grandpa's face – I mean the real one underneath.

One morning, when I was quite a little boy of five or maybe six, I ran into their bedroom in the flat, to find Grandpa with his back towards me sitting at the dressing table brushing his white hair – and in the mirror, just for the briefest instant, I saw… I saw a kind of fleshy crater the colour of boiled gammon, with no more for a nose than a flat blob with holes in it above a twisted gape where a mouth should have been. With one wide open, pale blue eye, staring – staring back at me before he covered all the rest with the blue scarf. It *can* only have been an instant before I turned and ran, but even after all these years, the image is still there inside my head.

I never said what I had seen, not even to my sister, and no one spoke of it to me. But I remember thinking Grandpa's hands when he next pulled me in to see the spinning ring, were even gentler than before.

***

7

The other member of our household at the farm, who I've already mentioned, was Sim – and if we're talking of importance to us children, I should have put her first; and would have done if she had only lasted through our childhood. 'I think that God's a lucky man to have Sim up there helping Him in heaven,' was how Caro put it at the age of nine when Grannie broke it to us that she'd died – and we ran off into the barn for our first good cry.

'Why couldn't she have waited for us to grow up?' Caro sobbed into the hay.

'Because she would have had to live to ninety-five at least,' I pointed out, 'and that's too long for anyone to last.' (They didn't tend to in the fifties.)

Her real name was Beatrice Sims; a *Miss* because she'd never married. Dad and Grannie called her Simmie. But she was always Sim to us. Looking back, I still see her as the sweetest person in the world. Everybody loved her everywhere she went – and if she wasn't blood-related, we knew her as the person who had introduced Grandpa to Grannie when they were young, which had to make her one of us. Sim always claimed she'd come to Sussex in the first place to help Grannie with her boys, then never had the heart to leave.

'I didn't have a proper family myself, you see,' she told us once. 'That's why I came to live with yours.'

The flat she shared with our grandparents was really just a suite of rooms in the old farmhouse that had its own front door; and although our own rooms were quite a way along the corridor and up a flight of stairs, Caro and I ran in to Sim most mornings in the week before we dressed for school, and at the weekends carted piles of books into her bedroom for cosy cuddles in her big brass bed. She read us fairy stories. Then everything by Enid Blyton, the *Just So Stories* and *The Jungle Book*, *Black Beauty*, *Treasure Island*

and *King Solomon's Mines*, propped with one of us on either side, tucked in beneath the knitted wings of her bed-jacket. Sim's bedroom smelled of lavender and so did she – and even now whenever I catch a whiff of that distinctive perfume, I can picture her with reading glasses halfway down her nose, doing all the voices in the books and keeping us enthralled.

Then she would make us tell her what we did at school, and made us see that even horrid children, even teachers, needed friends. Sim helped us practise the piano. She taught us 'Sweet Lass of Richmond Hill' and 'By the Light of the Silvery Moon'. Then made us sing them for the family downstairs and clapped the loudest when we did. Sim always saw the best in everyone – and when not long before she died first heard about four-letter-words, refused to think that they were half as bad as everyone had told her. She made us spell the worst one out for her, one letter at a time.

By the time we reached the final K, Caro and I were both as red as poppies. But Sim opted to pronounce the word aloud, repeatedly while we tried desperately to shush her – before declaring that she thought it: 'Quite a cosy little word dears, surely? Like duck or tuck or luck?'

It's another image I still have of her, with her white and wispy head a little to one side, pronouncing an obscenity. 'I really can't think what the fuss can be about,' she told us, gently smiling at our scarlet faces. Dear, sweet, other-worldly Sim. How we missed her when she died.

* * *

Which really only leaves the odd spare aunt and cousins to complete this sketch of what amounted to an Enid Blyton country childhood of the 1950s. Auntie Helen and her daughters lived in the village halfway up the hill between our farmhouse and the road. She was Grandpa's sister who had married Uncle Dan Goodworth, the farm cowman, in between the wars. Her cottage was the neatest in the village; its little garden crammed with phlox and stocks and hollyhocks and asters. Another small grey person, she'd managed to produce two daughters, Mag and Nancy, before their father died; both of them as loud-voiced and enormous as he'd been. How the three of them squeezed into quite so small a space for quite so many years was then and still remains a mystery. Both girls stayed on in Sellington well into their thirties, when Nancy finally departed to set up a tea shop in Tunbridge Wells.

Mag found a job and house to rent in Eastbourne, and I've more to say about her later. Let's just add here before I end the story of my childhood, that to describe my elder cousin as a burly redhead would have to be an understatement on both counts.

Scene 2

The public school they sent me to was Grannie's idea, claiming as she did that boys of thirteen needed a firm hand to stop them wasting everybody's time. I have no memory of whether my parents offered an opinion as to whose firm hand was needed, but do recall the glossy brochures I was shown for Lancing, Hurstpierpoint and Ardingly, with the latest increase in their fees inserted at the back. Grannie said that no one in their senses would pay for even half a term at such outrageous rates, and told me that I'd have to go to St Edgar's School in Eastbourne as a weekly boarder. She'd drive me in herself she said on Sunday evenings and let me take the Seaford bus back home on Fridays. That's what she decided; and it might have been because I shrank from the prospect, or would have shrunk if Grannie had allowed for shrinkage, that my marks in the St Edgar's entrance exam were considered borderline-to-fail – by everyone but Grannie.

As it was, she telephoned to fix an interview with the headmaster, put on the Marks & Spencer raincoat and pork-pie hat she always wore outside, and drove to Eastbourne. In the HM's study she accepted an armchair, crossed her sturdy legs implacably and told the luckless man that:

a) his Common Entrance marking system was a total farce,

b) a minor public school like St Edgar's could be grateful for the slightest chance to educate a Sussex Ashby, and,

11

c) she'd pay the first year's weekly boarding fees in total, there and then.

She'd rummaged in her handbag for a chequebook and a fountain pen (remember those?). 'He tried to make some feeble kind of an objection before I got to d),' she told us afterwards. 'But I just sat and stared at him until he took the cheque and offered you a place in Ramsdon House.'

I knew that terrifying stare of Grannie's; the one she used on me the time she caught me peeing on her peonies. 'Firmness is all that's ever needed,' she concluded. 'That and a readiness to shout your head off and smash the furniture, if all else fails.'

***

Oh super! isn't what I thought at any point during my first term at public school, because it wasn't what you might call a success.

What can I tell you? It was a time when horse-troughs were still in evidence at roadsides, when inner space was free of satellites and *Top of the Pops* had yet to reach the airwaves – and when at public schools like St Edgar's, boys of thirteen were made to feel as small as possible by being made to work as 'fags' for prefects who could beat them when they chose with gym-shoes bulked up with metal spoons and heavy bars of soap. (I'm not claiming we new boys were blameless. But still!)

Ours was the school that time forgot. In sparse Victorian classrooms, case-hardened teachers past retirement age instructed us with ill-concealed disgust. We called them Sir. They called us halfwits, wore black gowns, threw chalk and bellowed things like: 'Wake up you cretins!' when we failed to satisfy, which was pretty often. Most afternoons the younger masters who'd survived or somehow missed the war, donned

12

baggy shorts and dashed about the playing fields blowing whistles, driving flocks of boys like spindly sheep between white-painted goals.

Not that I myself could ever be described as *spindly*. Built more for fieldwork than athletics, with short, inelegantly rough hewn, oak bench-type legs, I found I could be useful in a rugby scrum, or on a cricket field if we were batting. But lacking any sort of killer instinct, generally lost the will to win before the final whistle; a tendency that kept me firmly in the B teams.

On Mondays, we were trained for military service, to polish boots and buckles, stamp about in uniform and learn to shoot with guns left over from the First War. We showered in tepid water, slept on metal beds in dormitories that offered all the comforts of Tibetan monasteries, and were herded into chapel every morning to beg forgiveness for our foolish ways and pray for manly virtue. The hymns they made us sing involved Steep Pathways, Swords and Spears, Fighting the Good Fight and Going on to War. The school motto *Per actionis vinco* (roughly translated as 'By action I conquer') encouraged us to act decisively in any crisis, regardless of the cost. It wasn't quite the educational equivalent of a five-year stretch in Wormwood Scrubs. The food was worse for one thing. But the pursuit of happiness, it was brought home to us, was not for St Edgar's boys unless achieved through selfless service, or by winning trophies.

Nor was there privacy of any kind. Used to the wide-open downs and even wider sky, at school I found myself boxed in with brick and concrete, never on my own amongst the teeming hordes, pushed forward constantly towards an idea of life I neither recognised nor wanted. Yet I swore blind to Grannie every Sunday when she drove me back to penal servitude that everything was fine. 'Fine Grannie, absolutely fine.' For when the chips were down, I knew I'd rather lie than disappoint her.

In fact not everything about the five-year stretch was totally unpleasant. If I couldn't care how many joules of energy you'd need to push a ton weight up a ramp inclined at thirty-six degrees, or want to know what Archimedes did when he was in the bath, I made friends readily enough with other disenchanted boys, and still had my pony Jack for weekend rides with Caro on the downs. If I was less than brilliant at maths and science and not much more than average on the sports field, I was good at English, having always read a lot – adventure stories mostly by Rider Haggard and John Buchan, or whodunnits by the triple queens of crime; Christie, Marsh and Sayers.

Oh, and acting, did I say that? Rather to my own surprise I found that I was good at that as well. St Edgar's had two drama socs; a Junior and a Senior. I joined them both in the course of time, assuming parts before my voice broke which ranged from Mrs Malaprop, to a stocky sort of Cleopatra. In one end-of-term production of *The Lady's Not For Burning* I played 'The Lady' as a busty blonde with rolled up football socks stuffed into one of Mag's old bras – and recited a gloomy version of *The Wasteland* that was booed consistently throughout.

Yet nothing could deter me. Not even the ill-fated stab at *Romeo and Juliet* attempted by the Senior Drama Soc. while my voice was still see-sawing between Olivier's strained tenor: *For God, for Harry and for England!* and Edith Evans's double-bassed: *A haand-baaaag?*

I played The Chorus; the boy who comes on first in breeches and a feathered hat to introduce the story of: 'Two houses both alike in dignity in fair Verona', followed by a dozen lines of convoluted monologue which mention, worryingly for spectators on unyielding chairs, 'two hours' traffic on our stage'. In actual fact the famous play begins with: *Two households*, not *Two houses*. But I had houses on the brain, and in rehearsals kept repeating: 'Two houses both alike in dignity', until the exasperated English teacher who directed told me to go away for pity's sake and practise, Ashby, until you get it right!

So I did. I practised in a droning monotone through prayers in chapel, in time with every panting press-up in PE – sitting on the toilet, last thing at night and first thing in the morning – until eventually I had it nailed and planned to act my socks off. Which meant that no one was more surprised than I was, when at the opening performance I strode centre stage, to sweep my feathered hat off and declaim: 'Two HORSES, both alike in dignity in fair Verona...'

But there was worse to come when I attempted to correct myself in character and Jacobean idiom with a falsetto: 'Nay...'

Cleverly you see, I'd planned to save the day with 'Nay, forsooth I am in error', but barely got beyond the 'Nay', before predictably the audience to a boy was neighing, whinnying and clopping heavily shod feet. Falling off its seats and rolling in the aisles.

CRIKEY! as I might have put it then. I mean, have you ever woken suddenly to find yourself completely naked in the middle of a toyshop and on Christmas Eve? I didn't think so and no more have I, although at the time I found that I could well imagine how that might have felt. Sidling from the stage in a big hat and inflated breeches was not an obvious option. But in the end, I managed to unstick my slashed Tudor slippers from the boards – revolved on my own axis and shot off sideways, to press myself into the nine-inch space behind the curtains that we student actors liked to call 'the wings'.

The director wisely cut the remainder of my prologue from that first performance, which jerked along as these things do until the last scene of Act III – when the Star Cross'd Lovers dreamily emerge from Juliet's chamber and out on to her famous balcony.

The first problem with that iconic scene was that Romeo had been cast largely for his good looks and brilliant reputation as Captain of the First Eleven. But he couldn't act for toffee. The second was that Juliet was played by an anaemic fourth-former called Lucas, in a wig that years of school productions had worn to the consistency of raffia. The third problem, and the clincher, was W. Shakespeare's second hobby as an ornithologist.

Enter ROMEO with JULIET aloft.

Jul.: *Wilt thou be gone? It is not yet near day.*

Rom. accidentally skipping four lines of dialogue and getting the wrong bird: I hear the cock, the herald of the morn.

Johnson-minor, loudly from the prompt corner: *It was the lark!*

Jul. gulping none too girlishly and by now in obvious panic: *I say it was the cock and not the nightingale that pierced my fearful hollow.*

Rom. freezes, bites back a grin that's starting to lift sharply at the corners.

Jul./Lucas retreats as far as possible into his lifeless wig.

After the first sharp intake the audience in the school hall holds its breath and strains its ears for dropping pins. Until someone's purple-faced great-uncle bellows: 'FILTHY!' and 'DISGRACEFUL!' and a tidal wave of laughter engulfs the hall.

(Exeunt.)

Which rather neatly brings us (well, doesn't everything at some point) to SEX; the force that turned the tale of Star Cross'd Lovers in our play from tragedy to farce. The need that runs like a live current through our adult years. The urge that's subject to more provisos and taboos than any other aspect of our lives. The cart that's constantly before the horse. The thing which, allegedly, makes beasts of company directors, footballers and film producers, and victims of the unprotected or unwary.

And now we're on the subject, I'm hoping that memories of how you felt yourself through adolescence with all those yeasty hormones sloshing through your system, will help you to spare a kindly thought for young men faced as I was with that age-old challenge of how to function biologically without becoming beastly. It's a trying time for all of us, to put it mildly; although I'd like to state that I'm with D H Lawrence in his rosy view of the activity, as opposed to those of Mary Whitehouse, or the Catholic Church, for instance.

The other day I heard a new word, *pollulation*, to describe the whole sticky procreative process – an alternative which begs the question as to whether even the all-too-ready-to-be-affronted Mrs Whitehouse could take umbrage at the friendly invitation: 'How about a spot of pollulation, darling?' Or to 'Pollulate off, you creep!' as an expletive?

But I'm rambling off the point, which is that by the time that I'd reached an age when pollulation was an issue I had

17

no reason to suppose that I was helpfully good looking. For a start I had protruding ears, and too much, too sandy-coloured hair that tended to keep losing sight of its own parting – while no one, as I've said, could claim my legs to be designed for speed or beauty (though by and large they've served me well and personally I like them). By the age of thirteen in common with most adolescent males I'd grown randomly and out of scale, with huge hands and feet, a splurgy sort of mouth, and glands of course, a lot of those. My oily skin attracted pimples, chiefly to my bum – and then within a year or so, more hair began to sprout like pallid moss, not as I'd hoped around my chin and upper lip, or even on my chest, but out of every humid crevice of my body.

I wouldn't go so far as to say I was a freak; and yet looking back at the old photos – well I'm only stating facts, but if you can visualise some sort of an unlikely cross between, say Eddie Redmayne and Paddington Bear, then you've got the general picture. My sister Caroline was similar at her most lumpen stage (although with plaits and much less body hair). She turned out better later.

* * *

You could be forgiven by now for thinking that a spotty youth who intends to make himself the hero of a story, would be advised to start with at least *some* redeeming features. So on the plus side, I can offer you what has been called an honest face, and I was a kind boy really; loved animals and children, liked adults in small doses and generally tried to help out where I could. But then again, I must admit that that was all above the belt. Below it, things were happening beyond all reason or control. The eagerly awaited male equipment had put in an appearance relatively early. But while I was as proud as any boy of what I'd managed first to grow and later to grow hairs on, let's face it the part with the main starring role can hardly be described as beautiful exactly (I simply mention it in passing). There are TV shows these days in which men's bits and pieces are sorted for attractiveness; and no one ever dares to say they aren't especially; looking as they tend to for so much of the waking day less like proud and mighty prongs than inverted toadstools – without the gills and spots (well mostly).

As a country lad I'd been aware of livestock humping one another for as long as I could remember. For them the act was commonplace, boring even in the case of sheep. Which meant the first discovery in my bedroom of the equipment's projectile possibility had come as something of a big surprise – no really. The amazing pod-to-rod in twenty seconds trick of an erection was one thing, to find that it could also act as a bazooka rocket launcher, quite another!

Too much information? Untoward, distasteful? I expect you're right. But if you're male, do make an effort to remember how it felt to be a teenager yourself, with seismic spasms off the Richter scale – and if you're female, well feel free to laugh at me and all the rest of us for being led for so much of our lives, not by the nose as bulls are, but by something that in the average man is twenty inches lower.

There was of course a lot of it about at school. Sex I mean, despite rumours that Matron regularly dosed our tea with bromide. The boarders at St Edgar's sometimes offered one another help, on the friendly principle of all hands to the pump. But for my own part (and I won't rephrase that), like Galahad in quest of the True Grail I felt the need to search for relief alone, with heavy-breathing concentration in the college toilets, or in weekend expeditions to deserted outbuildings round about our farm. Poker, as Omar Sharif is famously said to have observed, is not the only game you need a lucky hand for.

These days people seem to think two sexes aren't anything like enough. Back then the choice was simpler – and believe me I was ready, more than ready, for a transition into manhood that involved a willing female in place of a moist palm. The only problem, you could say man's eternal problem, was how and where to find one – and if I'd known at thirteen that I would have to wait for as many as *six years* for bona fide sex?

Honestly?

Well honestly, I can't say *what* I might have done. Created my own woman, like Pygmalion, who clearly shared my problem? Joined the Foreign Legion? Emigrated to Tahiti? The year, for heaven's sake, was 1957; the year it's generally agreed when teenagers were invented – when Sophia Loren emerged from the Aegean wearing nothing more than steaming cotton and salt water; when Eartha Kitt purred through 'Let's Do It' by Cole Porter; when Tennessee Williams wrote *Suddenly Last Summer* and Elvis flexed his famous pelvis to the frantic beat of 'Jailhouse Rock'.

By 1957 we knew all about Joe Lampton and James Bond; hard men who treated women like London buses, hopping on and off again at will. By 1957 we'd seen Sinatra in *Pal Joey*, witnessed the torrid goings-on in Peyton Place, tried and failed to visualise the more advanced positions in the *Kama Sutra*, read *Sons and Lovers*, *Forever Amber* and all the rude bits from the *Canterbury Tales* in Middle-English and translation. By then the post-war sexual revolution had arrived in Paris and in Hollywood – had even got as far as Brighton, where the first X-rated cinema had opened on the seafront.

But dodgy body parts described in anything but Latin? Pouting sex-kittens and pounding pelvises? The dawn of youth culture, *in Eastbourne?*

Are you mad?

Scene 3

Eastbourne's exclusive reputation rests on the tailored shoulders of the Seventh Duke of Devonshire, who on inheriting a mansion and a stretch of shingle on the Sussex coast, decided to build Kensington-on-Sea there. His ambition was to found a town 'built *by* gentlemen *for* gentlemen' – a concept that in a snobbish era appealed to those Victorians who were, and those who liked to *think* they were, and even those who knew they weren't but wanted others to believe they *could be* gents. The Duke sent his architect abroad for inspiration from the boulevards of Paris, the timbered gables of the Norman coast and terracotta roofs of Florence; to blend ideas from all of them into an elegant resort which he called Burlington, and later Eastbourne. A pleasant place of tree-lined avenues and substantial villas, with swimming baths, a golf course, tennis courts and several well-appointed theatres.

Cue mewing seagulls, oompah bands in bandstands, ladies with parasols and men with brass-topped canes.

The godlike Duke decreed that ornamental gardens should be planted on the seafront, with promenades and carriage drives and several grand hotels. Its resolutely stony beaches were somehow made to seem more gentlemanly than common sand.

By the time we knew Eastbourne, its elegance had somehow managed to survive two generations of cheap rail excursions and heavy wartime bombing to be the best place anyone could think of for keeping pubescent youngsters out of trouble, in schools like mine at St Edgar's, or Caro's at the girls' equivalent of Wimborne House a short way up the hill. For years before we were incarcerated, Grannie drove us into Eastbourne to watch her bully the assistants at Elliott's, her favourite grocers, or buy us ice creams by the pier – and by then the place was surging with old ladies walking little dogs on leads. The old gents who limped along the promenade wore blazers with cravats. The last horse-drawn vehicles, the rag-and-bone man and the butcher, still clopped along the back roads, and apart from shop assistants scarcely anyone you met in those days looked less than eighty-five.

A decade later things were stirring down the coast in Brighton, but in Eastbourne barely changed. If there were less ancient and less gentlemanly folk in evidence along the seafront, the few girls we college boys encountered in the town were all as closely supervised as we were; only to be seen outside their penitentiaries in prim columns of pudding hats and clumpy lace-up shoes. (Caro told me, and it could be true, that Wimborne House girls' shoes were left unpolished quite deliberately to avoid inflammatory reflections of their dark blue knickers.)

We sometimes passed girls on the way to the St Edgar's sports fields, or on sweaty runs along the seafront, when we looked at our least attractive and they refused to look at all. But hope springs eternal. By 1960 the old Gaiety Cinema in Eastbourne, out of bounds to school boarders but not to day-boys at weekends, not only screened films like *Slave Girls of Sheba*, and *Fast and Sexy* with the pneumatic Gina Lollobrigida, but had thoughtfully installed two rows of double-seats for 'courting couples' in the nether regions of the stalls; to give the concept of 'sex in the movies' a new and altogether more exciting meaning.

It was in the double back row of the 3/9s that, two years later with what I can only describe as dogged determination, I first managed to kiss Sally, a larky schoolfriend of Caro's – and would have tried to kiss the red-haired Irish girl who worked at Boots the Chemist, if in a previous encounter I hadn't bought my first experimental pack of Durex from her on the outside chance of getting lucky.

But free love, enjoyed supposedly in Scandinavia in saunas or beneath the midnight sun, was still unknown on the Sussex coast except by reputation – while if according to John Braine and D H Lawrence even nice girls could be sexy underneath, in my personal quest for sexual enlightenment I was still a long way from *getting underneath* one. Until… well, it was when Mag told me that a trainee beautician at the salon by the name of Joanne was looking for a boy to take her to the cinema, that I went for the main chance.

The film Joanne was mad to see was the A-Rated *Splendor in the Grass* – spelled the American way and starring the American Sensation all the girls were crazy over: Warren Beatty. To get her in without embarrassment, Joanne required an escort who could pass for a male adult, more or less. The stars were in alignment, so I thought. Our date was on a Saturday; and when I boasted of it to my schoolfriends in the concrete alley behind the St Edgar's fives courts two days later, they demanded details.

'Did she let you kiss her?' (Smithson Senior.)

I nodded.

'And touch her boobs?'

'Of course.'

'DECENT!' (A favourite word of ours, in this instance meaning the reverse.)

23

'Bet you didn't get inside her skirt?'

'How much do you want to bet?'

'Crikey!'

'Strewth!'

'Ooh missus!'

(three boys in unison, equivalent to three rousing cheers.)

The fact that they seemed so eager to be titillated was my excuse for representing failure as a triumph. It seemed unkind somehow to disappoint them – was what I told myself. (Come on, you've stretched the truth yourself like that sometimes, you know you have.)

But to tell it as it happened. I'd seen Joanne just once before the date, when Mag pushed me through the door of Antoine's to ask her if I'd do. She was a very pretty girl in a done-up sort of way, with little conversation and a nervous laugh. Her hair was nice (it would be wouldn't it), ash-blonde with a thick Dusty Springfield fringe and French pleat at the back.

I used Dippity Do hair gel to reinforce my own quiff for the date, cauterised my shaven pimples with Old Spice aftershave, put on the T-shirt and faux leather jacket combo and essential Levi's (having replaced the shrunk-to-fit-a-child-of-ten originals with something prestretched from the Oxfam shop), and set off, looking as I hoped if not the living image of James Dean then at least more like a rocker than a schoolboy. Joanne met me at a coffee bar ambitiously called Maxims, and from there we walked down to the Gaiety in Seaside Road to squeeze ourselves into the back row 3/9s, talking all the way in careful platitudes.

The movie started exactly as I'd hoped, with Natalie Wood as Deanie thrust deep into the front seat of a sports car by a rampant Warren Beatty; both of them enlarged to something like ten times their actual size through a fog of cigarette smoke from the stalls. A waterfall exploded with orgasmic violence behind them, as Deanie writhed and Bud pressed his advantage, his free hand working busily just out of shot.

Emboldened by Joanne's offer of a Rowntrees fruit gum, I followed his example, easing a stealthy arm around her narrow shoulders. At which point in our different ways we both went rigid. Onscreen, Deanie's moans were rising to an inevitable crescendo. Offscreen, through her mac and twinset I could feel Joanne begin to tremble.

Things it seemed were going nicely, when suddenly the word 'No!' cut through the gasps, the moans and sounds of crashing water.

Onscreen, Natalie (aka Deanie) fought her way free of the American Sensation in the very moment offscreen that I'd reached tenderly to stroke Joanne's blonde hair. Which was when Warren Beatty in the role of Bud behaved, not at all as I'd intended but as the censors thought he should, by leaping out to leave his not unwilling girlfriend in the car and stare blankly at the waterfall – before, *unbelievably* from where I sat, offering to drive her home.

Offscreen, my hand made contact with the unyielding surface of the spray-on lacquer Joanne used to keep her hair in place, while it dawned on me with a sinking feeling (and you can take that literally) that *Splendor in the Grass* was going to be a lot less splendid than I'd hoped.

The next scene in the movie unhelpfully showed Deanie's mother in her bedroom warning her that no boy would respect a girl he could go all the way with (thanks a bunch!) – and while the frustrated couple on the screen abandoned all idea of sex, in Deanie's case to go right off the rails eventually with unrequited lust, offscreen Joanne stopped trembling, shrugged off my arm and turned like Lot's wife into stone.

I knew by then that if I cared to investigate I'd find her

breasts encased in the latest bullet brassiere. It would be a Maidenform and mean it, underwired and inaccessible without a set of pliers. I could already tell from the adhesive way her knees were rammed together, that under Joanne's skirt there'd also be some kind of surgical appliance; an uninviting heavy-duty roll-on girdle, panelled at the front, elasticated at the sides and vicious as a snapping turtle. With under that in place of frilly lace, some kind of a portcullis?

Thanks to Messrs Wood and Beatty, and despite what I said behind the fives courts, I accepted that our date was doomed. As far as the double seat allowed we sat apart for the duration, and walked apart to the door of Joanne's flat in South Street without the glimmer of hope on my side of getting any further. Her flat was Jericho, and I was what's-his-name outside its walls without a bloody trumpet! To ease the strain we shook hands gravely, like Bud and Deanie in the final scene of *Splendor in the Grass*, when he hoped she would be happy and she gave a hopeless shrug.

***

I left St Edgar's the following summer, unschooled still in so many ways, with an unhelpfully posh set of vowels, a half-formed character that veered between inferiority and self-obsession, and no real idea of what on earth I wanted to do next. I had some pretty clear ideas admittedly of what I *didn't* want to do (e.g. join the army or any other service, military or civil). I didn't want to go to university, or move in city squares or diplomatic circles. I saw the word 'career' less as an occupation than an effective means of locomotion, for careering out of Eastbourne and back into the downlands where I'd started. Which more or less is what I did.

I knew, had always known, that whatever else I tried, I'd

end up running the Bury Farm as Dad had done, and Grandpa and all the Ashby men before them. 'So why not just get on with it?' was what eventually popped up into the vacuum between my ears. I'd long since learned to drive Dad's Fordson tractor and was familiar with the round of tasks involved in farming – could see myself beneath an open sky, outside like him in every sort of weather, using the strength I had developed on the school playing fields, the energies I seemed to have no better use for, to help with dipping, shearing, stacking hay and later on with lambing. It came as a relief in many ways to put the theory into practice, and it was good I thought for Dad.

'It's good to have you out here with me, Sammy,' is what I think, in an unusually loquacious mood one day, he said when we were working together to repair a fence one misty autumn morning at the edge of Bury Wood. Or did he say, 'It's good for you to be here, Sam'? Not quite the same thing. But at least we talked.

I celebrated my nineteenth birthday during lambing the next spring. I say 'celebrated', but can't remember much about the day itself, beyond the feeling when I woke that I'd reached a watershed of some kind in my life – which admittedly may have had more to do with what was going on below the cord of my pyjamas than anything too much above it. Because we're talking still of course of the much-anticipated loss of my virginity. If you can call a youth so devoted to his time alone in bathrooms and farm outbuildings, a virgin? Technically I mean.

I'd long since accepted that state-educated boys, who sat with girls in class and chatted to them at the bus stops, were already skilled by my age in the dark arts of seduction. I knew that *they* knew just how to make a pass, how far to go and if or when to stop. Whereas I knew nothing of the female mind and how it worked (sisters obviously don't count). The only locally unattached girls were either too young, like the vicar's daughter Alice, or already spoken for like Mandy-in-the-Post-Office who was walking out with one of our young farm hands. The upshot being that increasingly I found myself back in Eastbourne with my cousin Mag, sleeping in her attic spare room, and trying when I could to pick up girls along the seafront. (Don't make that disapproving noise, in my shoes you'd have done the same.)

I passed my driving test at first attempt and would have liked to drive off round the country to explore, if only I'd been able to afford a car. Instead I took a job at Stacy-Marks, the gallery where Mummy sold her paintings, packing up their artwork for dispatch. Then the weather changed, the talent left the seafront, and I was back at the Bury Farm again by Christmas for the coldest winter in 200 years.

The snow began on Boxing Day, giving us barely time to get the sheep into the yards before a blizzard cut us off completely from the outside world. Grandpa felt the cold most terribly and spent whole days in bed. Grannie bustled up and down the stairs with hot-water bottles and tureens of soup. Mummy managed to continue painting dressed in an overcoat and mittens, with her oil paints set to warm on trays beside the fire, while Dad and I worked outside with the men to feed the stock and keep the yards clear of fresh snow.

* * *

Which brings us to the crucial year of 1963 – when, driven by intense frustration, and more by luck than management of any kind, you may be glad to hear my sex life finally jerked (if I can put it that way) into something like first gear. It's surprising, looking back, how many of the details I remember. Or maybe not when you consider what they were?

Scene 4

By mid-January the sea had frozen for a stretch of two miles off the coast of Eastbourne, with fears the Channel could be blocked with ice. But by then the roads down to the town were open, and when Mag drove up to Sellington in her new Morris Mini to whisk Caro back to school, she'd offered me a job that I was totally unable to refuse. One of her lodgers working in the theatre down the road had fallen on the ice to break something he needed to perform with. It must have been an arm or leg I think, because they'd sent him home in plaster, to leave the company an actor short for the last two weeks of panto – and by now you will have guessed where this is going.

In my last term at St Edgar's I'd taken on the title role in the Senior Drama Soc's production of *Julius Caesar*, with my smooth young face criss-crossed with ageing lines. Or as the *Eastbourne Gazette and Herald* unkindly put it: 'displaying more crows' feet than you'd find in a fair-sized rookery'. Reviews otherwise were pretty good, and Mag who knew the pantomime's producer, had seen me play the part. 'So I've told him you'll be ready to audition at eleven,' she announced on her arrival at The Bury. 'You've half an hour to pack.'

Which as it happened was twenty minutes longer than I needed, as I'd seen the pantomime, *Dick Whittington*, on Christmas Eve; and having watched a line of bare-legged chorus girls high kick their way across the stage, believed I knew a good thing when I saw it.

My character had been given the show's opening lines to deliver – both of them. Dressed as a medieval butcher in striped apron and felt hat, twice a night, three times on Saturdays, I strode out from my canvas shop in Babblebrook Village, to pitch my rhyming couplet at the unevenly matched students of the Babette Stevens School of Dance from Polegate, who'd just crashed through their opening number.

'Away with you all, you rowdy young brats! You make enough noise for fifty tomcats!' was what I bellowed in a vaguely rural accent, before striding off as manfully as my short legs could manage to change into another costume.

For my next appearance, in *The Court of Morocco*, I wore a turban with pair of baggy Turkish trousers, displayed a wide expanse of chocolate-coloured torso – and thought that I looked pretty dashing too, until I saw my character described as 'Sultan's Second Eunuch' in the cast list. With the outside pipe to Mag's pink bathroom frozen solid, the *dark Egyptian* pancake make-up of the torso presented its own challenge; forcing me for the last two Sundays of the run to use the public baths to wash it off, and leave behind a stain (not blue this time, but chocolate brown), which for the bath-attendants must have raised some interesting possibilities. Was I a mud-wrestler perhaps, or someone more disgusting from a sewage farm?

Most of the chorus girls as it turned out were aged sixteen or under; to set them well beyond the pale as far as I was concerned, even if their dragon of a dance instructor wasn't constantly on patrol. Mag's lodger with the broken arm or leg wrote in to say that he'd decided to abandon acting for safer work as a firefighter. But by then I was in thrall to all the magically chaotic onstage/offstage business of provincial theatre, and gladly filled the vacancy he left.

The job entailed a fifty-three-hour week as second assistant stage manager, with bit-part acting roles thrown in; and the reason why I wasn't trampled in the rush to take it was the salary it offered – a next thing to invisible £4 a week. 'Slave labour,' Grannie called it when she came to see me play the butler in *Black Coffee*, the first whodunit that we staged to follow panto. But all things are relative. Mag only wanted £2 for my attic bedroom, charged nothing for my keep and fed me like a fledging cuckoo.

When it wasn't hosting provincial tours of one kind or another, the Meads Theatre's stock in trade was weekly repertory; a killing routine which demanded new plays, new sets, new casts of actors every week. That's why no one does it these days. But back then in 1963, with TV in ill-focused black and white and videos, DVDs and iPads no more than glimmers in the eyes of fledgling boffins, the residents of towns like Eastbourne were very much in the market for live entertainment.

Six days a week and twice on Saturdays, the Meads staged melodramas, comedies of manners, and whodunits involving trivial characters who motored up and down from London committing adultery or murder, and sometimes both. Their sets were drawing-rooms with wobbly French windows opening on to hazily painted gardens, in the days when everyone wore hats outside, lilac flowered all year round and servants popped up on demand. Their scripts, full of words like *topping*, *ripping* and *most awfully*, were penned by Terence Rattigan or Somerset Maugham, Oscar Wilde or Francis Durbridge, with an occasional Noël Coward or an Agatha Christie murder mystery inserted every second month, as a sort of theatrical suppository to keep the audiences regular.

As second ASM, I was responsible for props; for finding,

assembling them and placing them correctly for each scene. They sent me out to Bobby's for the vases and the china, up to London on the train for things like goblets made of sugar crystal that could be smashed without injuring the actors. For firearms, they sent me to a West End gunsmith tucked away behind the National Portrait Gallery, where a lady who looked like a Bond villainess (viz. Rosa Klebb) provided the pistols, shotguns and revolvers for our thrillers. Each came with a certificate to prove that it was hired for stage use. But can you imagine sending off a nineteen-year-old these days to fetch a shotgun back on foot through central London to Victoria? Seriously?

I doubt that he'd get further than Trafalgar Square before being flattened by a brace of dutiful policemen.

* * *

By March, the beginnings of a thaw to end that arctic winter made life a little easier in Eastbourne. Each morning after Mag had left for Antoine's, her live-in lodger, Len, and I splashed through the slush to work. Len was the lighting director for the Meads, the 'sparks'; a gloomy bloke with a hunched posture and scrawny neck that reminded me of a tortoise I once had. He seldom spoke (Len I mean, the tortoise never did), but had a key to the stage door. So, while he turned the working lights on and stoked the boiler in the basement, it was up to me to fetch the milk in for the first of umpteen cups of tea, and to climb the ladder in the opposite prompt (OP) corner to winch up the safety curtain.

During that first season, at around the time John Profumo was denying any kind of hanky-panky (as the tabloids liked to put it) with pert model Christine Keeler, I was cast in half a dozen walk-on roles, all of them unmemorable – as a policeman with a geordie accent, as a cockney window cleaner, a curate, a snooty butler (twice), and in ageing make-up with a wig like a Brillo pad, as the decrepit waiter in *Peril at End House*. It wasn't real life or anything approaching it; that was up at the Bury Farm with Dad and Grannie and the sheep. And yet appearing with professionals, hearing the applause, still had to be the most exciting thing I'd ever done.

***

Three Seasons of Sadie was the revival of yet another comedy of manners, penned in the 1930s by Neil Craven as a vehicle for his own comic talents and those of his best girlfriend, Florence Girton. Its run at the Meads Theatre was scheduled for the last two weeks of June at the end of a provincial tour which had begun at the Oxford Playhouse, played to capacity audiences in Birmingham and Bournemouth, and following its stint at Eastbourne was due to transfer to the West End. As a smallish house that seated just 900, the Meads was booked solid for the fortnight.

'And you know who's in it, don't you, Sammo?' Mag was full of it, could hardly wait to tell me. 'Abigail Compton, that's who, and this is her big comeback!' But then when I looked blank: 'Gawd help us, don't you know anything? She was The Business! Broadway, West End, Hollywood; box-office dynamite! Don't tell me that you've never seen her in *Dear Emmeline* or *Maytime in Mayfair*, or *The Parkers of Pimlico*,' she demanded. 'Or in any of those soppy musicals with Michael Wilding?'

I hadn't obviously; although each time Mag pronounced Miss Compton's name it did sound more familiar. 'How many husbands has she had?' I hazarded, remembering I thought one thing about her.

'Dozens I should say, if you count other people's.' Mag gave a bark of laughter, then estimated four. 'I can't believe she's coming here to Eastbourne. That you'll be working with her, lucky sod! We saw her as Camille in London when I was just a kid. I cried into my hanky on the train the whole way home. Ask your Auntie Helen if you don't believe me – then *Private Lives*; she was a hoot in that at the Apollo. Anyway, you'll see her on TV this Sunday,' my cousin added in a tone of voice that left no room for an excuse. 'It's in the *Radio Times*. They're showing *Great Expectations*, the one she made her name in. We'll have an early lunch and watch it through.'

We did as well. But not before the first member of the revival's cast arrived to take Mag's double bedroom for the fortnight. The stage-name she used was Primrose Malory, although Mag introduced her as Mrs Allan – a motherly little person with fluffy hair, beige skin like chamois and a breathless way of speaking which made it sound as if she'd just been running. Her husband, she was eager to impress on us, was the actor and stage director T G Allan, who would be driving down from Manchester to join us all on Sunday.

'*Hay Fever* at the Theatre Royal, dear, that's what my Tom's been up to. Nanki-Poo and I decided we'd come on ahead.' Mrs Allan did the panting for me while I lugged her cases up the stairs to Mag's lime-green guest room at the front. 'One step closer and my Nanki would have had that disobliging ticket collector's hand off on the train, dear – courageous little man!'

The pekinese she cradled in her arms had runny eyes and the worst dog-breath I'd ever smelled. 'A *Cancer* dear you see, that's Nanki, loving and protective. We bought him from that nasty Abanazar at the Lyric when we saw how much he hated pantomime.'

'But do you think astrology applies to dogs?'

'But *of course* dear!' Mrs Allan made a vague attempt to smooth her hair. 'Dogs, every creature, even beetles. We had a goat you know in Dorking, born in April, Aries through and through. I can't begin to tell you how many times she had the postman baled up against the gate.' She paused on the landing to examine me with luminous brown eyes, like Olivia de Havilland's in *Gone With The Wind*. 'You're Miss Goodworth's cousin, aren't you? Sam, is that your name, dear?'

I nodded.

'So tell me, Sammy darling, when you were born exactly?'

'Nineteen forty-four.'

'No dear, not the year. I mean the month and date. You're a Virgo if I'm not mistaken?'

Standing in the bedroom doorway Mrs Allan watched me blush my standard shade of post-box red. 'February,' I told her, 'I am a Pisces.' I really hope I didn't stammer. But she caught me off guard with the Virgo, and what I took to be a stab on her part at the shameful truth.

'Of course you are dear, *lovely!* Sensitive and sympathetic,' she enthused, reminding me quite painfully of Sim. 'I'm sure I knew that all along, dear. Fish you see and water.'

'I... I'm not at all sure what you mean?'

'Water dear; that's me, Aquarius, you are the fish. So you see we're bound to swim along together splendidly!' Mrs Allan beamed – then as I put her cases down beside Mag's tangerine bedspreaded double guest bed, 'But look, DO look, a SIMPLY GLORIOUS view of the allotments! Don't you just *long* to go out there and dig and dig for Britain!' She spun back from the window with another delighted smile. 'Talking of fish, dear, where's the bathroom? Can you show me?'

'It's just down there along the corridor Mrs Allan. Shall I... ?'

'Just be a love and hold Nanki for me, will you dear? But do try not to let him bite you, it's so bad for him you know. And do call me Primmie; everybody does, dear!'

Scene 5

Opens on an evening sky backlit through trailing clouds. All below is dark and indistinct.

As the bright sphere of the moon emerges, the ruins of a house move into view. Light streaming through an empty window projects the shadow of a man across the broken flags to where the girl awaits him. She pushes back her bonnet to reveal a luminously heart-shaped face that's startling in its perfection. A breeze sighs through the trees to ruffle her blonde curls. Her eyes are brilliant and unblinking. The man approaches, older in the moonlight than he first appeared. His hair is fair like hers. She looks down as he nears her, can't seem to meet his eyes.

For a long moment they remain in silence. *You have returned,* he says at last, as if he has just noticed.

I have, she tells him, dead-pan with a sideways movement of her head which frees a curl to catch the breeze and blow it fetchingly across her cheek. *And yet I've thought so often of this place, for it is all I have now in the world.*

Abruptly she looks up with all her heart and soul exposed in her wide and beautiful blue eyes (you somehow know they're blue despite the lack of colour).

No my dear, not all, he tells her gently, placing a long-fingered hand on her white satin sleeve and turning slightly. His best angle. *You mustn't think that this is all you have.*

But you? You live abroad still? She tries and fails, perhaps deliberately, to tuck the errant curl back into place.

At present, yes.

And have done well? She speaks with clear precision.

You could say that. I've done the best I can.

Whereas, I have suffered at the hands of one who's used me in ways that I cannot repeat. She pauses for his sharp intake of breath to register, and for an almost too agonised expression to distort his famous face. *He's changed me out of recognition. I have become so bent and broken, I wonder that you knew me.*

But now he's dead; an accident. They told me on the marsh that he was trampled by his horse.

Yes, oh yes. It was so dreadful, horrifying! She turns away affectingly.

Yet now you're free?

Free to regret all I have done, what I have thrown so heedlessly away! Her eyes when she turns back to face him are tragic, sparkling brilliantly with tears.

And did you think of me through those unhappy years? A sound like music surges and recedes behind their words; pulses with emotion, strains with passion.

Yes often – oh so often! But I never thought that when I came to take my leave of this sad place I would be taking leave of you as well. She smiles through lips gently parted to retain their shape. *It seems appropriate, do you not think?*

That I do not! His educated very English voice is pitched to something which is almost, but not quite a shout.

But you've forgiven me for all I've done, and we are friends at last. I see it in your face!

You think us friends?

Please say we are.

No never! I will never call us friends, when THIS is what

I feel! He sweeps her up into his arms, to kiss her hands, her lips, the white skin of her shoulder, from which her scarf has artfully descended to show a generous expanse of cleavage.

Pip calls her by her name – once, twice, and then again – enunciating every syllable. *Estella, Estella! Oh my God, Estella!*

They kiss again in close-up and soft focus. It is too early for a sunrise. But their glowing image flickers in the gloom. The camera tracks back on silent wheels for a long shot of the pair of them framed perfectly within a ruined archway, before it angles upwards to the moonlit sky-cloth, and the word in florid type:

The End

All right, *two* words, but linked by trailing clouds across the shining circle of the moon.

That's when the music rose to a crescendo, to set all the little ornaments on top of cousin Mag's twelve-inch Philips TV jiggling several inches to the right.

'Out of this world, just *heaven* wasn't she,' exclaimed Mrs Allan from where she sat on Mag's purple G Plan settee with Nanki-Poo inert across her lap. 'Did you see the way she tilted her face up into the spot? I should imagine that was Len David's doing, wouldn't you – *such* a good director! Our darling Abi is a Gemini you know, and even if they're superficial, they generally manage to show themselves in a good light. It's why so many of them make it in Hollywood – like Marilyn, and poor dear Judy Garland.'

'Corny old film really.' Mag heaved herself up from her chair to switch off the TV (mauve-screened and minuscule compared to the enormous things that we go in for these days). She paused to right the plastic cactus, painted seagull and plaster fish with 'A Present from Lowestoft' printed on its scaly flank, that she'd knocked over with the front room curtains as she wrenched them back to let the light in. 'But then it was her first.'

'Abigail Compton's?'

'No Sammo, Arthur Askey's playing Widow Twankey – what do you think?' Reversing heavily on to the settee, my cousin blew a thin stream of blue smoke into the air. 'Lewis Hayward was more than twice her age, and looked it even with the hairpiece. He took her out to California you know, and found that famous part for her soon after she found his.'

'His what?'

'His famous part, Sam, do keep up – hung like a carthorse so they said. It beats me what she saw in him, but then again that could be it.'

***

Later on that evening, Mrs Allan's husband Tom arrived to join her in Mag's lime and tangerine front bedroom; and the next morning, Monday, I walked down to the theatre to see the set erected for 'The Three Seasons', as everyone was calling the sequence of one-act plays Miss Compton had selected for her comeback.

'Only the greatest comeback since the Resurrection,' according to my cousin Mag.

The previous afternoon, a team from Hall Stage Equipment had driven the new set up from Bournemouth in three huge pantechnicons; and although we'd been instructed to leave them to it at least until midday, I sneaked in soon after ten to watch them assemble the revolving stage. It was total bedlam. The dock doors were open, to illuminate a small army of large men in overalls disentangling what looked like a giant Meccano kit of perforated girders welded into triangles and squares, some of them with wheels attached.

With our own staff quietly chilling in the stalls while this was going on, I nipped back to watch the action from the circle. One of the Hall's technicians held a blueprint centre stage. Others argued, swore and whistled through their tasks – until within a shorter space of time than you'd think possible, all the girders had been bolted into the shape of an enormous wheel that filled the whole stage and backstage area of our little theatre. With equal speed the whole affair was covered with a timber cladding, and by the time the last plank had been screwed in place, everyone in sight was eating sandwiches. Mine were cheese and pickle, I remember.

New plays are always tricky for stage management, with sole access to the sets demanded by the crew until the last flat has been braced. So, while the stage crew were being briefed on the revolving stage controls, we'd had to wait to dress the sets with props, tack down the carpets, put up pictures, hang curtains and fill bookcases with books. Which meant that we were running late that Monday, and I was up a ladder wrestling with a set of curtains when we heard the pass door open to the sound of laughter.

I don't believe that eyes can bulge, not really. But if they could, I'm sure mine would have done in the moment that Miss Compton swept up from the prop room corridor on to the stage.

'Bless you, angel!' The voice came first, bell-like, melodious. Then the entrance in a pungent cloud of scent that smelled of lilies, Persian harems, the Ritz Hotel and God knows what besides. (It was *JOY*, I discovered later, by Jean Patou.)

Well I hardly need to tell you the advance publicity had been terrific. Weeks earlier, the largest of the dressing rooms had been repainted with a stonking great gold star stuck to

41

its door – and from first thing that morning, Trevor-on-the-stage-door had been dashing in and out of it with cards and telegrams and cellophaned bouquets of flowers.

In cinematic terms Abigail Compton's was the face that launched a thousand clips. She must have known that everyone who'd seen it (i.e. everyone) expected it to remain unchanged, and in a way it had. But in another hadn't. Even after all these years I can still see that entrance; so vivid was the first impression – phenomenal, too glamorous for words? Maybe, but I'll try.

The once flowing yards of blonde hair had been reduced and styled, to sweep back from Miss Compton's forehead in a faux-careless wave with perched behind it like a saddle a blue velvet crescent of a hat. To describe her figure as *disciplined* sounds artificial and a little scary. However it was managed, all I can tell you is that there was nothing out of place. The young face of *Great Expectations* might have blurred a little round the edges. But not enough to dim its brilliance. All the qualities of the bona fide, five-star star were there still and in spades – the trademark open smile, the flighted brows, the long-lashed bright blue eyes, expressive ballet dancer's hands and legs like flower stems.

After all I'd heard by then about her, I was ready to be impressed – and was immensely. She exuded practised charm, and something... would it sound odd to you if I said *gallantry*? A kind of brave refusal to let her own legend fade?

Behind Miss Compton, sucking up like mad, was our theatre manager, Eric Benson. Behind him, an attractive girl in a candy-striped blouse.

'But how *simply marvellous!* Just as I remember it, Mouse, a *darling* little house!' the great star fluted. 'We staged *The Scottish Play* here with that frightful ham who did things with his claymore.'

42

All actors hate a silence unless it's in the script, and still talking solidly, Miss Compton glanced about the set, to spot me on the ladder (staring at her I imagine with my mouth ajar). 'Someone's ghastly dog barked backstage on my damned spot line. *Out damned spot. Out I say... woof, woof!* It got the laugh but fucked the sleep-walk scene, my dear. But *utterly!*'

She moved into the thin beam of the working light to flash the expensive dentistry at me – at ME, perched on the ladder grinning back at her inanely! Turning up the wattage for an instant, she made her exit cleanly through the wings, stage left in the direction of the dressing rooms; to leave a technicoloured ghost behind her dancing on the dusty air.

I can't help it if it sounds ridiculous, but I very nearly clapped.

* * *

First nights in provincial repertory are at best nerve-racking experiences to be got through with the minimum of fuss and then forgotten. Normally, although not as I'm about to tell you in this instance.

Having lived in Rome for several years with her fourth, possibly her fifth, husband – an Italian count with a name that sounded like some kind of pasta – Miss Compton had decided to divorce him and return to England for her comeback in her friend Neil Craven's celebrated triple-bill. According to Mrs Allan, the famous playwright had at first refused point-blank to consider a revival of 'The Three Seasons', declaring from his tax haven in the Virgin Islands that he'd never been in favour of reheating his best dishes. But then, following a series of extravagantly pleading letters from his would-be star, and the offer of a generous percentage of the box office, he had allowed himself to be persuaded.

In a press interview the week before, Miss Compton was quoted as insisting that her darling Neilly *simply worshipped* the idea of her breathing new life into his best loved character, Sadie Swanson. 'He's tickled pink,' she claimed, 'the precious lamb!'

Once the set was dressed and I'd checked the props against my list, Andrea, the other ASM, an overweight girl with her hair pulled back into a bun, was settled with the prompt script, while I shadowed the sound-effects man with his tape bell-ring apparatus, in case he needed cover through the run. We had a little table in the wings on the OP (from the actors' viewpoint, the right side of the stage), which gave a clear sight of the action.

You could say that first night was technically the fourth; the first having been in Oxford six weeks earlier at the beginning of the out-of-London tour. And if you're wondering why anyone as rich and famous as Miss Compton would risk her reputation on a tour of under-funded theatres in a series of provincial English towns, I'd think that she was tempted from retirement by the thing all actors feed on, by applause – and then some more of it, as much as she could get – applause, applause, applause!

Having surged in from all points of the compass, the audience were nicely settled with the house full of nervous energy on both sides of the proscenium, as it doubtless would have been in Oxford, Birmingham and Bournemouth, on all the other first nights of the tour.

'Front of house clearance,' sounded on the tannoy speaker backstage.

'Stand by,' from our stage manager. 'House lights... curtain up!'

And up it went without a sound.

Scene 6

As the curtain rises the orchestra is playing the 'Moonlight in Mayo' waltz. The stage is empty for a moment, then Sadie Swanson dances out on to the moonlit veranda of Raffles Hotel in Singapore, before returning to the embrace of her young husband, Max. They are both still in their twenties and waltz divinely, despite their youth.

That was the stage direction for Miss Compton's entrance in the first play of the triple-bill, 'Spring in Singapore'. And it was no mean feat I have to say, to waltz divinely despite their youth from wings that seethed with lighting cables, through a typically unstable set of French windows, dead centre without glancing off either jamb – and then twice around a cambered veranda; avoiding amongst other things a wrought-iron table and four potentially bruising cast-iron chairs. All of it to thunderous applause.

Miss Compton, partnered by the actor Nigel Hughes-Milton, youthful and divine at every turn, completed the assault course with aplomb. In those days, the use of floods and footlights demanded full stage make-up. Miss Compton's, shaded carefully along the jawline, made her look about eighteen and ravishing. She wore a long blonde wig, which in the next scene would escape its ribbon tie, and a gown of floaty stuff (it might have been white chiffon, I'm not too good on fabric). Anyway, it all worked beautifully. The audience applauded them for what seemed hours, while in the words of our effects script: *THE MUSIC STOPS. So do the dancers, centre stage, their arms around each other in an extended kiss.*

* * *

In the second play, 'Summer in St James's', most of the action revolved around the telephone and doorbell; which, considering how frequently he had to press the buttons mounted on his board, was hard on the sound-effects man's index finger. Based on Neil Craven's own frenetic social life, the piece was set between the wars in an approximation of his luxurious London flat. In a bobbed ginger wig, long beads and lots of swinging fringes, Miss Compton quickly had the audience in stitches, taking advantage of the phone's long flex to tie herself in physical and verbal knots. Her comedy technique was faultless. Using everything to hand including her bead necklace, she'd worked in sufficient business to upstage the other actors. No one could outplay her, or was prepared to try. It was her comeback after all, with its success or failure resting on her shoulders.

I let down the safety curtain for the interval, and while they projected on to it the usual faded slides of Eastbourne's premier attractions, brewed tea for the management and crew in the vast enamel prop room teapot.

* * *

The final play of the triple-bill, 'Autumn in Antibes', was thought by everyone to be the jewel of the production. So with nothing for the moment to distract me, I settled down to watch it from the prompt corner with Andrea. The pretty girl in the candy-striped blouse was there as well, standing by for the quick change at the end of Scene 1 – having turned out not only to be Miss Compton's dresser, but her daughter by an earlier husband. Don't ask me which.

SCENE 1: ANTIBES. The curtain rises to reveal Sadie Fawcett in bed with her Riviera playboy husband, Freddie, in an ornately decorated bedroom of the Villa Bianca. A door at the back wall leads to a passage and the rest of the villa. Another, up right, leads to the bathroom. Morning sunlight streams through a window down left. Sadie has a breakfast tray across her knees. Freddie is reading from the Continental Daily Mail.

As Freddie, the actor Crispin Blake's hair was ruffled in a moody Heathcliff sort of way. Miss Compton's wig was this time an outrageous red in keeping with the 1950s setting and her advancing years, and to set it off she wore green silk pyjamas.

I think I can safely say that's one of the worst nights I've ever spent. (Her opening line, with an exaggerated yawn.) *I'm black and blue from all the bits of you I had to wrestle with, not one of them remotely pleasant.*

It serves you right for being such a pest, said Blake as Freddie from behind the Continental Daily Mail.

Then afterwards you lay back snoring like a grampus.

What's a grampus?

Something loud and hairy one imagines, with hard knees and horny hands and a maximum attention span of forty seconds.

47

You'll be riveted to know that amongst those attending Saturday's masked ball at the Hotel Victor Hugo were Princess Rimscoff, the Duke and Duchess of Brentwood, read Freddie from his paper, *with Mr Bud Solomon the London impresario, and the Contessa... Oh my giddy God – and the Contessa di Castioni, who has recently returned to the Villa Rosa at Juan les Pins!*

YOUR Contessa, duckie? The one you sponged off for three solid years then dropped like a hot potato?

I can't think Claudia would see herself as a potato, dear. Hot or otherwise.

She'd never call on us at any case, my sweet. She wouldn't dare.

D'ye want to bet? I tell you that she calls on everyone for miles around incessantly. She's as ruthless as Genghis Khan about forced entry, and the Villa Rosa's only round the corner.

Well if she calls, you'll only have yourself to blame. Damn it Freddie, the Riviera is awash with your discarded inamorata.

That's when the end of the brass bed fell off with a resounding crash.

And blast these damnable French beds, remarked Miss Compton from the floor, where she and Crispin Blake continued to play out the scene in a welter of bed-sheets and jammy croissants.

The audience laughed like drains of course, and I was beginning to wonder if the whole thing had been intentional after all when the girl in the candy-striped blouse burst into tears. I can't remember what she said exactly, because we were right beside a sign that read: STRICT SILENCE, and most of what she managed between the sobs was pretty indistinct in any case. But the gist of it was that the show would flop, her mother's new career would flop, the whole thing would be ghastly – A TOTAL ABSOLUTE DISASTER!

I passed her the hanky Andrea was waving at us with the hand that wasn't covering her ear; and while she dabbed her eyes with it, the candy-striped girl asked me for my name. Then called me by it several times.

'I have this feeling, Sam, that you are going to help us.'

'You have?'

'I think I knew immediately I saw you that you'd be someone we could trust.' (Strangers do tend to actually; maybe because I smile a lot and don't look threatening, what with the hair and ears.)

'Please say you'll help us, Sam?' The girl by then was giving me her full attention, which, considering her age and sex, was definitely something. Presently she laid a small hand on my arm. 'Please Sam, please!'

I met her searching eyes and nodded. Not just because she was about my age and appeared receptive. But because she was obviously upset and needed help – and leaving aside the hormones, I am as I have said quite nice. 'I'm not sure what you're asking. But yes of course I'll help you if I can,' I said. Superfluously as it turned out, because without auditioning it seemed I'd got the part.

***

As soon as they were out of make-up, Miss Compton and the others had commandeered the saloon bar of the Ship

49

Inn along the road from the stage door. It sounded like the opening of *West Side Story* down there. So for the quiet chat we needed I took the girl to a coffee bar I knew stayed open through to midnight.

The Cosmopol stood at the junction of three roads across the street from the Town Hall. They pulled it down some years ago to build a modern office block. But back then it was run by a Greek family from Thassos, whose ideas of modern decor involved chrome-plated furniture, Vista Vision photographs of Florida on all four walls, and orange plastic stalactites for lighting.

The stripy girl was eighteen I discovered, tastefully upholstered to front and rear (if I can put it that way without sounding beastly). Her face, viewed in the plastic lamplight as I set down her coffee on the table we had taken in the window, was round and pink with clear skin and an undecided nose. Her eyes were muddy-green. Their lashes, like her hair which fell poker-straight to well below her shoulders, were brown and thick. Her lips were free of lipstick. She spoke in a high register, sounding younger than she was and making jerky movements of her hands while she constructed ridges with her coffee spoon in a bowl of demerara sugar on the table.

Her name was Cordelia, by the way, and I'd just noticed that she bit her nails when she stopped speaking and looked up for a reaction. So then of course I had to coax a replay, pretending to be deafened by the jukebox.

'Well listen this time cloth ears, and I'll tell you,' she said with a small Mona Lisa smile. So I listened and she did. 'Abi calls me "Mouse" because she thinks it's what I'm like. But that isn't true at all.' Again the hand on mine, a little sticky this time from the sugar. 'She's no idea of all I have to do to keep her safe.'

What could she mean? I wondered.

'What do you mean?' I asked.

'I watch for her. I notice things and try to warn her. Abi's so focused on herself and what she's doing, it makes her blind to so much else.'

'To you? She's blind to you?'

'Yes, and to other people's feelings,' Cordelia said, staring fixedly into the sugar.

So then I told her that my grannie was a bit like that. Kept getting people wrong.

'But you're not, are you, Sam? Like that I mean? I've seen you watching us. I think you notice things.'

What I'd just noticed actually was that her skirt had ridden up to reveal an alluring little mole just above Cordelia's left knee, so rather missed the next bit.

'Sorry, what did you just say?'

'I said I thought that you could help me find out who's being doing all these dreadful things to Abi.'

Which was my cue to remember the catalogue of misadventures she'd been parading for me – the things Cordelia believed had jinxed the triple-bill through its first six weeks on tour; the green filter on her mother's spotlight for their second night at Oxford; the stolen wig in Birmingham which forced Miss Compton to wear her own hair in a chignon; the smashed pier glass in her dressing room at Bournemouth.

'But she refuses to be worried.' Her daughter made a hopeless gesture. 'Keeps telling me they're accidents and nothing she can't handle standing on her head.'

'Or the work of some joker with a warped sense of humour?' I offered.

The espresso coffee machine on the counter made a hissing sound that seemed to fit the situation. But Cordelia was unconvinced.

'JOKES? You can't be serious!' She shouted it so loudly

51

that the young couple at the next table both looked up. 'Can't you see that someone's trying to sabotage Abi's come-back?' (Which was when I noticed that she always used her mother's Christian name, never called her Mummy.) 'It's why we need your help Sam, to stop him from doing something dangerous.'

Cordelia stirred another spoonful of brown sugar into her coffee, and this time I noticed that her khaki-coloured eyes were filled with unshed tears.

'Ah.' I said it as a sort of substitute for a reaction. But by then unable to *stop* noticing, noticed that despite her bra the outline of her nipples showed clearly through the fabric of her blouse while she was talking. My eyes just fixed on them. (Sorry, couldn't help it.)

'That's it then really...' we both said next in unison before relapsing into silence.

That's it. That's how it started, with a protest and appeal for help; with the sticky little hand, the pink skin and the mole – and OK, with the nipples if you must; with on my part sympathy and rampant lust in roughly equal measure. Then Elvis took things to another level by trading on emotions I hadn't bargained for with his new 'Can't Help Falling in Love' hit record on the jukebox.

After we had heard that through and downed another coffee each, I walked Cordelia back to her hotel (the Excelsior in keeping with her mother's billing) – and there'd been something in the way she turned to say goodnight in the shadow of its backstreet entrance which gave me the confidence to kiss her. Admittedly she turned away at the last moment. But I was Elvis; couldn't help it, rushed in like a fool to offer – if not my whole life through, then at least the part of it she'd activated. Don't ask how much was sympathy and how much rampant lust by then, or what it made me at the time, because I've absolutely no idea.

'You're a very nice boy, aren't you,' was what Cordelia murmured with my lips still tenderly exploring the soft curve of her neck, where semi-accidentally they'd landed. 'So nice, not really like a man at all.'

Excellent.

Scene 7

For no better reason than I felt like it – with a camembert cheese moon above me and the scents of ozone, tamarisk, warm brick and tarmacadam in the air, I left Cordelia at the Excelsior, to jog uphill towards the village. A cat appeared and disappeared at twice the speed. Headlights of passing cars cast moving shadows from the elm trees on the pavement, and I consoled myself by leaping them as they swung by.

If the Duke of Devonshire planned swathes of his new town for gentlefolk at leisure by the sea, he'd had Meads Village built to house the humbler types whose duty was to serve them. Twenty or so pairs of gabled, Arts-and-Crafts-style cottages were ranged around a central square of gardens; divided like a feudal field into allotments with a plot for every cottager to grow what cottagers were meant to: cabbages and lettuce, onions, runner beans and carrots – or, for those more fancifully-inclined, sweet peas and roses. Mag's cottage was on the north side on an unmade lane with its allotment facing it across the track, and although it must have been well after midnight by the time I reached it, the light was on in its front room.

Then I spotted Auntie Bill's Harley-Davidson propped against the porch, and remembered it was Monday. I knew exactly how they'd look before I used my key to open the front door, and was right. The room was full of smoke and reeked of beer. Mag's card table had been set up under the standard lamp as usual to reveal three figures in a yellow pool of light. Len, like an undernourished Robert Mitchum, sat hunched in vest and braces. Auntie Bill, a dead ringer for Al Capone, wore shirt sleeves and green eyeshade. Even Mag projected decadence in a Size 20 puce silk blouse that fought her orange hair and lost.

On no other weeknight would my cousin tolerate disorder in her house; not even in my attic bedroom which she inspected after work on Fridays. But this was Monday, the night that Auntie Bill came, and the baize cloth between them bore all the squalid evidence of gaming: an overflowing ashtray, bottles, peanuts, crooked stacks of coins. They all looked up when I came in, then all looked down again.

'Sorry Mag,' I mumbled. 'Forgot that it was Monday.'

'Had other fish to fry more like. Oh, we know all about our Sammo and his women, don't we Bill; he's like an animal when roused – but ooh look, we're colour-coordinated!' Having made her move, she braced back to deploy the blouse and stare me into blushing; a favourite trick of Mag's and my Achilles heel. (It's not so much that I'm so easily embarrassed, just that I am susceptible to people thinking it, and then thinking that *they'll* think I am about to blush, I do. Ridiculous but there it is.)

'They seek him here, they seek him there,' said Auntie Bill with both eyes on the game still. 'Pay no attention Pimpernel, Maggie's only jealous.'

If Mag was large, Auntie Bill was around the size of a small principality, with a voice like a bassoon. They'd been fast friends since kindergarten when Mag was Margaret and Bill was called Belinda, and neither the eighteen stone of rock-hard muscle nor the narrow black moustache that Bill developed later had ever come between them. Least of all on Monday nights when Auntie Bill, who worked as a policewoman, slept over in Mag's mauve-sheeted double bed, with no questions asked or answers given.

'Len tells us that you're sniffing at the daughter's skirts, but what's the mother like these days?' Bill punched the purple settee with a hefty fist. 'Come over here and tell your auntie all about it.'

So I told them all I knew about Miss Compton; what she'd said and how she looked, how brilliantly she'd played each scene that night and how she'd managed when the bed collapsed. I told them everything, except the way I felt about Cordelia. (How the hell did Len know, anyway?)

'*Vanessa*,' Auntie Bill boomed suddenly. 'Remember the scene when she's standing on the hillside Maggie, looking drop-dead gorgeous? Those fabulous blue eyes – and she says, *Farewell!* – one word, with the tears running down her face, and it can't be glycerine or anything because she is in close-up all the time. *Farewell!* like that. Then that famous music… what was it? Yehudi thingummy played it at the proms, remember?'

'*Cumberland Theme*,' snapped Mag, doubling her stake. 'But if you're going to stand there looking gormless, Sammo, do us all a favour will you and stop *wittering*. You're giving me the pip!'

'Better still, come in and win some rent back, lad,' suggested Auntie Bill, pointing to the fourth side of the table. 'We've had to play three-handed since we started.'

I would have too. But it had been a long day one way or another, and I wasn't in the mood for Ludo.

***

I didn't sleep a lot that night. Len must have come to bed at some stage in the early hours; to be followed by heavier footsteps on the stairs, a spate of mezzo and bass giggling, and finally a joyful blend of voices, with percussion and sporadic Tarzan jungle yells that I'd really rather not have heard. To take my mind off what was going on below, I entertained myself in my own bedroom with an elaborate fantasy in which I unmasked the actor, Crispin Blake, as Miss Compton's evil saboteur, before – to everyone's astonishment and deafening applause – stepping in to take his part in the Antibes play and rocketing to stardom. With one hand beneath the bed covers (just to keep in touch you understand), I was looking forward to a graphic scene in which Cordelia was about to express her gratitude in various explicit ways I planned to imagine in some detail – but missed completely when it came to it, by dropping off to sleep.

You could say that real dreams, as opposed to bedroom fantasies, are like out-of-sequence rushes for a movie. At least that's what mine are like. So it hardly came as a surprise to me when the audience I'd invented to rocket me to stardom quite suddenly became a fairground crowd; or when the carousel behind them morphed into the bandstand halfway down the Eastbourne promenade; or as I climbed its steps became my grannie's dilapidated summer-house above Bury Wood, with a yapping Nanki-Poo instead of a brass band inside it. And that was just for starters.

I've long since forgotten what came next, but do remember how the whole thing ended – with a sunlit tableau featuring a pair of curiously familiar-looking huntsmen lounging on a woodland tussock, with bunches of dead hares and bright pink pheasants at their feet and somewhere in the background Nanki-Poo still baying shrilly... then two more pairs of huntsmen, four brace of pheasants, and the same again diagonally printed on my bedroom wallpaper – as I emerged from slumber to the yapping of an only too real pekinese from the Allans' bedroom on the floor below. You could even say dreams were ingenious, if they weren't so bloody stupid!

* * *

As luck would have it, Mrs Allan's husband Tom turned out to be very much Mag's type. Built roughly on the same expansive lines as Auntie Bill, he'd not only managed to convince my cousin that Nanki-Poo's dawn chorus was a one off and unlikely to recur, but by breakfast time had charmed her into such a pitch of affability that Mag cooked eggs and bacon for us all – even took out her rollers to prowl around the kitchen with her hair backcombed into an orange mane that would have done a Masai Mara lion some credit.

The producer called a meeting of the entire Three Seasons company onstage for eleven o'clock that morning, on the St James's set because it had more seats; and having raised the safety curtain, I'd just hopped off the metal ladder to the flies when Miss Compton and her understudy, Barbara Bayliss, swept in from the stage door with Cordelia in tow behind them. Miss Compton wore a trouser suit of turquoise silk to sensational effect (by Dior or Chanel for all I knew). Even in street make-up, her entrance made all the rest of us look like the walking dead. Except Cordelia who still looked pink and freshly scrubbed, to the point of *edibility* I rather thought.

'It was Marie Lloyd,' Miss Bayliss was saying as they advanced. 'I'm sure as sure of it, my dear.'

'Lights!' Miss Compton interjected, and then, 'I think you'll find, my love, that it was Florrie Forde. I have the record somewhere.' The two actresses continued with their argument while Len obligingly switched on the battens, arranging themselves artistically on the largest sofa with

Cordelia squashed in beside her mother, and Miss Bayliss on her far side. The other members of the cast grouped themselves around them, instinctively facing out across the empty auditorium.

'No Abi darling, it was Lloyd. It simply had to be. No one else but Marie would have dared,' declared Miss Bayliss.

'Florrie Forde,' Miss Compton snapped with clear precision, emphasising both the Fs. 'I sang it at an ENSA concert for the troops out in the woop woops and caused some sort of a riot.' She glanced around her to assess her audience, onstage, in the wings and up above her in the rigging. 'I could sing it for you now,' she offered with her wide blue eyes wide open.

The famous smile embraced us – and I believe that must have been when I first registered the trick Miss Compton had of holding her vivid carmine lips apart a little at the end of every line she uttered; as a sort of facial semicolon to let you know that there was more to come. Which in this case you can bet there was.

'Oh she sits among the cabbages and peas, and she talks to all the little bugs and bees,' she sang out suddenly in cod stage cockney. 'They climb her legs and arms, and all round her other charms, and they see lots of things nobody ever sees!'

I already knew by then what we were likely to be in for – felt the blood surge up into my ears, and in a mounting state of panic began to stare intently at my running shoes.

'Oh she sits among the cabbages and peas with her little dress a way above her knees,' sang Miss Compton, just a fraction out of tune. 'All the boys that pass her way stand and stare and wish that they were that pretty little peapot 'tween her knees.' She paused, reverting to a speaking voice. 'The lord chamberlain's office complained of course and said she'd have to change the "sits among the cabbages and peas" line. So she did. For Florrie's next performance of the piece, she altered it to…'

Miss Compton paused again, this time for two breaths timed within a fraction of a second.

'But what she changed it to was, "I sits among the cabbages – and leeks."'

The cast, or shall we say, 'supporting cast', were too well trained to emit so much as a titter during the further five seconds of triumphant hush she left between the line and the anticipated laughter.

'No, it was Marie Lloyd as you've reminded us so prettily, my dear. I knew it all along.'

Miss Bayliss neatly killed the laugh with a look of deadpan boredom on her face. 'The most risqué piece that Florrie Ford could lay claim to was "Has Anybody Here Seen Kelly".'

WHOA! (Or even *CRIKEY!*)

Miss Compton's own face remained as blankly beautiful as Grandpa's mask, when you weren't close enough to see the cracks.

'Wonderful everybody! Glorious everyone!' Either by chance or intuition, the show's producer-cum-director, Martin, chose that moment to burst through the wings on to the set. 'Sadie, lovely lady! They all adored you, naturally my darling!' he cried flourishing his clipboard. 'Freddie, just the ticket! Perfect Enid – the bit with the ferret went over like a dream. Lovely, all the rest of you! First class! Super!'

The cast smiled modestly, while Martin, lanky, bespectacled and uncoordinated in a red polo neck and corduroys, bounded across the stage and fell head-first over a footstool.

'Settle down now everyone, settle down!' Martin scrambled to his feet and hooked his glasses back in place. The cast looked every-which-way, suppressing smiles.

'But look here.' He forced his face into a stern expression. 'There have been one or two problems that you may have, er, noticed...' (And I was suddenly reminded of an excruciating facts-of-life talk at St Edgar's beginning with: 'Now boys, you may have noticed between your legs...')

'... you may have, er, noticed with the props since Oxford,' Martin pressed on awkwardly. 'I'd call them funny business, but they aren't. Funny that is, not at all!' Without looking at anyone in particular he went on to enumerate the green filter, the missing wig and broken beads in Bournemouth, the telephone flex and collapsing bed.

And it was then – partly to distract myself from unwholesome images of Cordelia without the dark blue pinafore that she was wearing, imagined from the viewpoint of what I'd noticed all too frequently between my legs since leaving school, and partly because I thought it would be fun... yes, it was then that I decided to cast myself as a sort of classic Christie private eye along the lines of Hercule Poirot (let's make him Corsican and call him Gaston), to review the suspects and bring the phantom saboteur to justice.

'*Eh bien*,' exclaimed the dapper little Corsican, snapping off the waxed point of his moustache in his excitement. 'The culprit, he will expose himself to Gaston *très bientôt, n'est pas, mes enfants*.'

We had the crimes, we had the victim in the glamorous person of Miss Compton; and as I saw them *tout ensemble*, grouped onstage as artificially as any super-sleuth could hope for, we had the suspects – all looking as if butter wouldn't melt, all pure as driven snow.

There were twenty-one of them if you exclude the victim; too many on the face of it for a vintage Christie or Dorothy L Sayers. But we could discount Martin, whose success as the producer of her comeback was so obviously dependent on his star, and dispense with all the bit-part players, I decided: a maid, a butler and a number of hotel guests. Then do what's done in all the best detective stories and scratch out the rest of the extraneous characters (in this case the stage staff and management, the lighting and effects bods, the dressers and the understudies) at a single stroke.

'They gave each other alibis, so we just took statements and let them go,' is how they're usually dealt with on such occasions. Which brought my list of suspects down to seven – and yes I do know how arbitrary that sounds, but bear with me, will you?

'What fun! Let's see if we can identify all the ship's/train's/ aircraft's passengers, stranded house/dinner guests, casts of offstage actors, shall we?' Isn't that the sort of statement a Queen of Crime is apt to put into the mouth of some minor character who clearly isn't in the frame, to help her readers to keep tabs on the suspects in *The Case of the Persecuted Star*?

I know it's difficult to begin with to fit names to characters, especially when they march around in gangs. But having watched the whole performance through the previous night and matched the actors to the prop room cast list, I was in a fair position to record my first impressions of them all.

So if you're up for it, I'll use the next scene to describe the seven suspects as I saw them on the stage that morning, allowing for the fact that as a lowly ASM I only saw as much of them as they were ready to reveal. I've also more or less tied labels to their collars in the Dramatis Personae list of performers at the front of this book.

So feel free if you like to use that as a handy crib for future reference.

Scene 8

The suspects are assembled.

SUSPECT ONE was Crispin Blake, the actor who played Sadie's third husband Freddie in 'Autumn in Antibes', and was just then failing to look boyish, sprawled on the carpet beside the St James's sofa within kicking-distance of his leading lady's slim right foot. Dark and fleshy, you might call him handsome I suppose in the way Jane Austen or a Brontë might, with thick red lips, unfeasibly white teeth and curly hair which looked like dark brown cauliflower. More hair sprouted from the open collar of his fitted Toplin shirt, with (revoltingly) a gold chain threaded through it. If the 1960s hadn't been too early for medallions, he'd doubtless have worn one of those as well. Trust me, he was that kind of creep.

In the prop room copy of the Spotlight casting directory, Crispin Blake was listed as a 'Juvenile Lead', despite being the wrong side of thirty with just the one lead to his credit (as a stand-in for the London run of *Counsel for the Defence* after the lead, Ronald Bloom, was arrested for loitering with intent). According to Cordelia, Blake hadn't even managed to retain his role as her mother's onetime live-in lover. On our walk back from the Cosmopol the previous night she told me that he'd changed his Christian name from plain old Christopher to poncey Crispin – which prompted her mother to name him 'Crispy', while behind his back the stage staff called him 'Crispy Flake' to match his flaky personality.

It was obvious that Blake didn't listen much or ever had, he so often got his words wrong – said *impassive* for *impressive* and misquoted lines from movies: 'Frankly my dear, I don't give a shit.' That kind of thing. His comic timing was way off as well I thought, although he'd coped with the collapsing bed as if he had rehearsed it – which rather made me wonder if he had; with rejection by Miss Compton a motive for revenge?

* * *

SUSPECT TWO was Barbara Bayliss, the actress you've already met in the leaky Marie Lloyd debacle – cast in the Antibes play as Blake/Freddie's ex-mistress, the Contessa Claudia di Castioni, and understudying Miss Compton in the lead (unsuitably, one would have thought, considering how plain she was). As Neil Craven might have put it, nature had shown unnecessary restraint as far as Miss Bayliss was concerned, in giving her a flat peasant face with scarcely any neck, and features which looked and largely had been painted on. Without being too unkind, her figure might best be described as cylindrical, with short legs like mine which the high heels she wore made look a little like pig's trotters.

If you were auditioning for a Mrs Danvers say, or a Lady Bracknell, Barbara Bayliss might well be on your shortlist; and the real mystery considering her lack of sex-appeal was why she had been booked to understudy anyone as beautiful as Abi Compton. For her talent as a comic actress? Because she'd worked with Martin in the past? Or, if we're talking motives, for something more sinister, like bribery or blackmail?

Then there was the knitting. I'd watched Miss Bayliss in the wings the night before, waiting for her entrance – knitting while she chatted to the effects man, Paul, not only up to, but right *over* her cue line of: ... *to see you dear, don't be obtuse, and then skin you alive...* before she thrust at Paul the ball of wool, the needles and her knitting, swept up her handbag from the floor and dashed onstage to pull a pistol from it, screaming: *I've got a gun, you nasty little swine, and now I'm going to shoot you!* – before calmly retrieving the bundle on her exit seven minutes later, to resume both knitting and conversation as if she'd never been interrupted. The knitting (long, grey-greenish in 4-ply) was in itself a mystery, as the woman seemed to have no chums or relatives of any kind. A weapon in the making? A scarf for throttling the leading lady, to clear her own way to the West End and who'd-have-thought-it stardom? Or is that too absurd?

***

SUSPECT THREE was Nigel Hughes-Milton; the young man standing just behind and to the right of Barbara Bayliss on the sofa, with one hand in the pocket of his cavalry twills and the other smoothing his already very smooth hair. Engaged to open the Singapore play clamped to Miss Compton's perfectly moulded bosom as her first husband Max, he was typecast as an actor used to playing well-bred types in white ties, or in blazers with cricket bats or tennis racquets in hand. Fairish, cleanish-cut ('well-knit', as Barbara Bayliss might have put it), he had a good physique, a face perhaps a shade too vacant to be dashing, and was the kind of chap who would have an old school tie with blue stripes on it in his wardrobe. No one said, but you could well imagine that he'd gone to Eton then to RADA. His voice went with his schooling. He hit his marks onstage and might well have made a favourable impression – if Miss Compton hadn't ruthlessly upstaged, outshone, outclassed and eclipsed him.

Another thing – H-M reminded me quite strongly of someone else I'd known; although at the time I couldn't for the life of me think who. Or why for that matter he would want to jeopardise Miss Compton's comeback. Unless he'd had enough of being upstaged, outshone, outclassed and eclipsed in every scene they shared?

But to catch up with what was going onstage while I was studying the form as a pseudo private eye...

'I'm telling you that I won't have it folks,' Martin was insisting, trying hard to sound authoritative, but tending to look woebegone. 'If anyone knows who is responsible, I'd like to hear it now please.'

Silence.

'Now,' repeated Martin with eyes firmly on his clipboard. 'Has anyone anything they'd like to tell us?'

More silence, longer this time.

'Well anyway, next time it happens...' Martin cleared his throat. 'If there is any recurrence of these silly tricks, I'm giving you fair warning, I'll call in the police.'

Sensing a background crowd scene, the assembled actors began to mumble incoherently while waiting for the principal to speak (not actually with *rhubarb, rhubarb*, but along those lines).

'Yes, Martin dear, we hear and understand.' Miss Compton awarded her producer a fraction of the famous smile. 'But there again, there's only so much wild excitement we poor thespians can take – so if you've nothing more to add, could we just have the notes my poppet, before we all go raving mad?'

'Yes well, we'll leave it there, folks, provided you all understand?' Martin had come to rest by then down centre, and someone brought him out a chair.

'Let's see then... Hubert, Lummy dear, when you make your exit from the veranda – just a tiny hint, but *do try* to use the door. Enid dear, perhaps you'd steer him? The audience can't read the gap when you step through the flats, you see old love, and from the front it looks as if you've just strolled through an outside wall.'

***

SUSPECT FOUR, now that we've come to him, was Lumsdon (Lummy) Gould; the veteran actor cast as Colonel Hubert Westgate in the Singapore play, who in his time had played just about every king in the Stratford repertoire, as well as Prospero and Shylock at the Old Vic. He had an obvious paunch, an overripe complexion, untidy eyebrows and bulgingly short-sighted eyes. Offstage he wore a wig that looked exactly like one (why *do* they have to dye them that unlikely shade of chestnut brown?), spoke like Gielgud through a megaphone, spewed undigested chunks of Shakespeare in a voice that trembled slightly at full pitch and called everyone 'old chum' or 'my dear fellow'. As an unacknowledged 'queer' (to be gay in those days was to laugh a lot and skip about), he dressed the part in velvet smoking jackets with cravats worn high to brace one chin and hide a couple more.

Then as we've heard, old Lummy had developed in his autumn years a seriously alarming habit of exiting through walls – because, without his glasses, which he wouldn't wear onstage, he was myopic to the point of blindness. 'He played his Shylock once al fresco at St Mark's in Venice,' Primmie Allan told me later up at Mag's. 'They had to drag the poor dear out of the Grand Canal with boat-hooks I believe, and then fish for the hairpiece.'

More to the point, she'd added that Miss Compton,

67

playing Portia at the time, had laughed until she cried. Which you could say made Lumsden Gould another candidate for revenge, with the stolen wig in Birmingham a telltale clue?

**

SUSPECT FIVE was Yvonne Hayes (although I'm not sure that was her real name, you never are with actors), who played Enid in the Singapore play; Lumsden/Hubert's unloveably acidic wife. Like Barbara Bayliss, she'd been cast in character roles for most of her performing life – which came of a large nose and 'schoolgirl figure'; i.e. no bust and stick-like legs. Known for playing posh, by late middle age Miss Hayes was still sufficiently well preserved to work regularly on TV, advertising twinsets and denture cleaners. Wherever it began, her voice had long been resident in Knightsbridge. Her clothes were elegant, with scarves and beads to camouflage a stringy neck. But the thing that struck you first and last about the lady, had to be her hair – which, after being flattened beneath the plain grey wig she had to wear as Enid, she somehow managed to re-inflate into what looked like a large, pale blue meringue. No really.

What else is there about Miss Hayes that I can tell you? She had an adult son abroad somewhere apparently. We gathered that she'd travelled First Class on the train from London – and Mag, who'd had to deal with the blue hair at Antoine's on the Monday, heard she trained at the Central School of Speech and Drama with Miss Compton when they were bright young things together, and went on to share digs together on a tour of *Lady Windermere's Fan* – circumstances which, considering the contrast in their fortunes since, might well suggest that underneath the blue meringue there lurked things greener. Like envy and resentment.

Which brings us to the last two suspects in the cast, handily a married couple.

***

SUSPECT SIX was Primrose call-me-Primmie-dear Allan; someone you'd find it next thing to impossible to picture in the role of phantom saboteur – that is, if you hadn't seen her acting. Offstage, Mrs Allan twittered cosily, was hopelessly attached to her large husband and small dog, rushed to read her horoscope in the *Daily Mail* each morning, and claimed to think that everything depended on the stars. Onstage as Primrose Malory the actress she was something else entirely. To see her in the 'Summer in St James's' piece as Sadie's friend, Gaye Gaynor, striding across the stage good-lording and hells-belling in the hearty manner of a Roedean games-mistress, was a revelation. As with the Misses Hayes and Bayliss, she was a veteran of the provincial circuit – and if Mrs Allan could play anyone from Mrs Mop to Lady Muck, what was there to say she couldn't act the cosy little wife and dog-mother, while plotting to bring down another shallow *Gemini* to her own repertory level? Least likely of all the suspects, in any self-respecting whodunnit she'd be up there for the lead.

***

SUSPECT SEVEN – Primmie's husband Tom had based his whole career on the burly character he played in every role, which clearly was his own. He looked as if someone had carved him out of something hard with something rather blunt. You know the type: fortyish and solid with it – the sort of man who'd camp in Greenland given half a chance. As an actor he'd been regularly cast as doctors and police inspectors. I'd noticed that his Spotlight entry described Tom Allan twice as 'stalwart', and when he first arrived at Mag's, had recognised him straight away from *Doctor in the House* and several episodes of *Z Cars*. Tanned and healthy-looking even without make-up, he smoked a pipe, was comfortable in tweed and fairisle, sported a moustache that was bigger than a toothbrush but smaller than a walrus, spoke in a hearty baritone, was prone to taking charge and striking manly poses – oh, and played the piano rather well in the St James's piece as Miss Compton's second husband Vincent.

These days according to his wife he was also a dab hand at directing, but took acting roles to keep her company on tour. 'Tom's a *Leo* dear,' she told me proudly. 'Dependable you see, and loving.'

* * *

And there you have it – seven suspects, seven ducks all in a row for you to pot at; and maybe I should add that none of them were very tall, not even Crispy or Tom Allan, whose bulk was more in width than height. Or is that beside the point? I'm fairly short myself and don't do bad things to be noticed. Not often, anyway.

So, any thoughts yet of your own?

If not, or maybe just to give your little grey cells time to process all the information, might this be a good time for a break? To make yourself a cup of tea or something?

FIRST INTERVAL

ACT II

Scene 1

I wouldn't think the meeting on the stage that morning lasted for more than at most half an hour, before Martin wrapped it up with: 'That will be all then, dears, and bless you,' and dashed off to talk to Len about Miss Compton's follow spot.

As the others started to drift towards the stage door corridor, Cordelia caught my eye and then my arm. 'I've told Abi all about you, Sam, and she wants you to come with us for a drink at the hotel if you could bear to? Crispin will take us in his sports car.'

'Really?'

I wasn't needed at the theatre until mid-afternoon. So when Cordelia backed the invitation with a friendly squeeze, I reckoned I could bear to – just about!

'Hello darlings,' Miss Compton cooed when we came up to join her; then on an exit line of: 'So long troupers; we're off in Crispy's batmobile to terrify the locals – toodle-oo!' she set course for the stage door with Crispin and Cordelia, and me in a lingering cloud of *JOY* by Jean Patou astern, feeling like a farm dog on a lead.

Blake's batmobile was parked across the road from the Meads Theatre; an old Triumph Roadster that was obviously his pride and joy, despite a large dent in one mudguard and sunshine yellow paintwork that had clouded over here and there. Miss Compton produced sunglasses and a headscarf from her handbag; and having donned a loudly-checked flat cap, Blake made a big performance of lowering the Roadster's canvas hood. I helped Cordelia to unfold a pair of dickey seats behind, and then to stack ourselves like luggage in them for a terrifying 80 mph scorch up the Grand Parade, burning rubber all the way.

Even viewed from a supine posture flattened in the Roadster's boot, the Excelsior Hotel succeeded in excelling in every way a five-star hotel could excel. Rising from gardens with enough palm trees in them for a Bounty commercial, it looked like a whopping great wedding cake with too much sugar icing piped around the top; the sort of establishment where haughty doormen dressed as admirals examined you for defects – where columns painted to look like streaky bacon stood around supporting nothing in a vestibule the size of a cathedral – where rolling acres of deep pile carpet and everything above it reeked of excess. A home-from-home for minor royalty, retail millionaires and stars of stage and screen.

Ours drew the doorman's fire by awarding him her most bewitching smile while sweeping off her headscarf to reveal the gleaming glory of her hair. There wasn't any kind of door out of the vestibule to serve her as an entrance to the Starlight Bar. But she made one anyway.

'Just ignore me everyone,' Miss Compton cried in ringing tones, immediately turning every head. 'I've been in *the most frightful* open car, am simply battered out of recognition – *totally repellent!*' Unnaturalness came naturally to Abi Compton. Cast as THE FAMOUS STAR, she played it to the hilt, enlarging every movement, acknowledging allegiance to right and left, bringing Hollywood to Eastbourne and creating a sensation.

'A pint of best Campari please, darling.' She harpooned the bartender with another open-ended smile and reeled him in. 'Everything in moderation I say,' she proclaimed, 'including moderation.' Cocking a hip, she hopped on to a barstool and crossed her shapely legs. 'On second thoughts let's make that a small brandy. I'm back onstage at seven-thirty, and there's nothing more *disheartening* I always think than a pissed leading lady. But what will you have Mouse? It's on me, my children,' she projected to the furthest tables. 'What for our young friend here with the *indecently* tight jeans? And can I get you something, Crispy dear?' she put in as an afterthought. 'You must be gasping darling after all that *gruesomely* suggestive business with the gearstick.'

Miss Compton's laugh when she unleashed it was a silvery cascade, as faultlessly delivered as her diction. A group of women at a table just behind us joined in with the giggles, and Cordelia and I exchanged embarrassed grins behind her mother's back. I wasn't sure where I should sit, until Blake commandeered the stool beside Miss Compton's and Cordelia patted one beyond it next to hers. She ordered Babycham, so I did too. It was lukewarm and tasted like diluted glue.

'Here's laughin' at you, pal.' Blake raised his glass, then slumped morosely in the role of a fleshy Hamlet on the receiving end of slings and arrows of misfortune, who wasn't sure if 'twould be nobler to suffer them, or not? He tried to thrust his fingers through his curly hair and failed. 'I'm bloody knackered; next thing to a stretcher-case,' was how he chose to put it.

'And look it, Crispy,' confirmed Miss Compton. 'I hope it isn't catching, dear. But aren't you too fabulous,' she added sotto voce sipping at her brandy. 'I totally adore you!'

'Is that you talking, Abi, or the brandy?' Blake asked her, brightening somewhat.

'Me darling, don't be silly; me talking TO the brandy.' She made a little business of brushing an unwanted speck of something from her turquoise trousers. 'The Mouse tells me, my lovely, that you're pining to perform?'

I realised with a shock that she was looking straight at me. But Blake hadn't finished, not by any means. 'D'ye know what I think, Abi?' Pitching as for the back of the Glasgow Empire, he made it clear to everyone that they were about to play a scene.

Scene 2

The Starlight Bar of the Excelsior Hotel in Eastbourne on an early afternoon in June.

CRISPIN BLAKE: *D'ye know what I think, Abi?*

MISS COMPTON (taking the cue): *If I don't my pet, I'm sure you're going to tell me.*

CRISPY/CRISPIN (loudly): *No doubt I'm speaking out of turn, but to me your heartlessness is one of the things that makes you so devilishly attractive, Abi; the reason why I graduated to you in the first place.*

MISS COMPTON: *Now Crispy don't be tiresome – and you mean 'gravitated' my poor lumpington; do try to get the line right.'*

CRISPIN (at his flakiest): *But to think I thought you loved me!*

MISS COMPTON: *Yes dear. But 'I thought you loved me,' is all the line requires.*

CRISPIN (repeating it with increased intensity): *But I thought you loved me, Abi!*

MISS COMPTON (with a wistful smile): *Lechery; the cheap substitute without the bitter aftertaste. That's all there was to it, my dear.*

CRISPIN (contriving a short laugh and staring up at the ceiling of the Starlight Bar, which is dark blue and covered in tiny lights in imitation of a starlit sky): *I don't suppose that you can help being what you are, any more than I can. The fault lies in the stars – isn't that what they say?*

MISS COMPTON (as Eliza in *Pygmalion*): *Lor' love us, 'ardly hever duckie as I've found.*

CRISPIN: *You can be incredulously hurtful sometimes. Do you know that, Abi?*

MISS COMPTON (serenely and with her own eyes starwards): *Only when it's for the best, dear heart.*

CRISPIN: *To hell with that! What's best for you is what you mean.*

MISS COMPTON: *Precisely lamb, I knew you'd understand.*

CRISPIN (tossing back his cocktail and sliding off his stool with a look of affronted dignity that was so unlike him I guessed he'd practised it in a mirror): *But I don't, DON'T understand you! Abi, you're imspicable!*

MISS COMPTON: *Despicable?*

CRISPY: *Impossible, that's all I have to say!*

It was too. Exit Crispy Flake. His walk across the vestibule takes far too long and nobody applauds.

'I really don't think Crispy could do justice to an exit if it was handed to him on a plate with pickles on the side,' Miss Compton reflected, regarding her ex-lover's backview with disfavour – but then, remembering her audience: *What imbeciles we were to spoil it; what hopeless fools to think our love would last!*

'That was a line from *The Lost Cause,* and even if I says as shouldn't, I was sensational as Isabella. So darling, do tell me why you want to act—' (to me again across Cordelia) 'the *motivation,* sweetie-pie?'

She had this thing; a kind of rapt attentive look that made it easy to believe Miss Compton was fascinated by you as a person.

I assumed it was a knack, because I couldn't think she was.

'I, well I acted quite a bit at college,' I confessed, hoping that it didn't sound too foolish to Cordelia, whose eyes were fixed on me as well. 'I don't suppose that I was all that good. In fact I'm sure I wasn't.' Under their double scrutiny I felt my throat constrict to make my voice sound chalky. 'But maybe I could learn?' I finished huskily, and in a vain attempt to cover my discomfort crossed my legs. (Shyness makes you awkward, don't you find? Then awkwardness makes you shyer still. It's all a vicious circle.)

'*Adorable!*' Miss Compton still seemed rapt. 'Although if you really want to learn, my pet, the best advice that I can offer... Oh but *look* at you, my poppet!' Her lashes and plucked eyebrows parted company as her gaze settled on the place where, in taking up the slack, my Oxfam jeans had momentarily produced a James-Dean-poster-bulge-effect beneath their zip-up fly – to make a mountain out of, well let's not say a molehill, but you take the point?

81

The arches of Miss Compton's brows arched higher; the startlingly blue eyes became more startling, and the perfect lipline contracted into an appraising moue. 'My precious boy, have you a licence for that thing?' she demanded, while I hurriedly uncrossed my legs and squirmed about until things found some kind of natural and less obvious level. 'It's a wonder honey-child you haven't been arrested. Do you know, I think I'm going to have to call you "BUBO" just between ourselves, and recommend you for the *very largest part* in Martin's next production!'

For me it was the worst, the ultimate embarrassment – one of those moments when you'd like to halt the action and beg to play the whole thing differently and better. There's no way to conceal a blush when both your ears are flashing like Belisha beacons; and to make things worse, the Starlight Bar was mirror-topped to give me an unnerving view of Cordelia's disapproving frown and my pulsating face. Miss Compton put her glass down to reach into her handbag for a cigarette. I expected her to laugh at my expense, but she didn't.

'Ignite me darling, would you?' she asked the bartender, who leaped forward to light her Rothmans King Size (they were allowed in bars back then). 'You know you mustn't mind me, darling. I am the *most* appalling show-off. Ask the Mouse.' Cordelia looked down, refusing to be drawn. 'A ghastly old hag with a pathetic need to upstage everyone in sight.'

The smile when it came was not the Famous One but something more disarming. Reversing the technique she used for stage work, Miss Compton turned the volume down to *natural* and took a long drag on her Rothmans. 'To return to the last conversation but two, as someone said, I'm here to tell you darling that most actors are unreliable beyond belief, deplorably and deeply shallow with the moral standards of guttersnipes.'

Exhaling a thin stream of blue smoke, she subjected my lumpy jeans to another long appraising stare. 'Try not to take against us for it, darling. You'll understand it when you know us better; and when you do I have this feeling, Bubo sweetie-pie, that you and I are going to be the *very best* of pals.'

~~Yes?~~

NO, not in *that* sense, not the way I felt about her daughter – not an option. Definitely couldn't happen.

Could it?

* * *

Anyway… I left them with the fleshpots of the Excelsior to eat their lunch and take a nap before the evening show, and with ears still pulsing faintly walked back through the Meads to make myself a sandwich in Mag's kitchen.

An hour later, finding the stage door of the theatre locked, I went in through the front of house to start early on the props for the evening performance. The auditorium was still unlit, but the green exit sign was on above the pass door with a working light switch on the other side – and if you've never been backstage in a completely empty theatre, believe me when I say there are few things spookier. Dim working lights throw eerie shadows up into the grid. An unlit set looks shabby and unreal, with stale air that smells of dust and glue-size; and there are noises.

I'm not and never have been insensitive to atmosphere. I'd heard the stories superstitious actors love to tell of hauntings, jinxes and theatre curses, and don't mind admitting that I felt jumpy as I stumbled through the wings that afternoon. The borders creaked above me, and something scuttled at the rear of the revolving stage. The prop room with its shiny yellow walls and familiar pong of fags and instant coffee was more comfortable and reassuring. But I was there to do a job and only lingered long enough to snatch the prop list from its hook beside the phone, before I winched up the safety curtain and turned on the footlights.

The Antibes bedroom set was much as it had been left the night before, with curtains closed, a single chair downstage right and the brass bed dead centre where it ought to be. The main difference being that a body sprawled across it.

I was still a lot too young then to have ever seen a corpse, and Blake's wasn't looking pretty. His face beneath its mop of dark brown cauliflower was putty-coloured with its mouth agape.

'*Mon Dieu!*' Gaston ejaculated violently. '*The blow has fallen, n'est pas? Our worst fears, mes enfants, they have come to roast!*'

In the short time I'd known him there was more than one occasion when I'd rather hoped that Crispin would drop dead; and now it seemed he had. Of course I should have left the body well alone. 'Don't touch anything,' is the general rule of thumb for murder mysteries, isn't it. Yet perversely when you consider my heart was leaping about inside my ribcage like a trapped frog in a bucket, I went on creeping silently towards it with a hand outstretched.

The corpse was still warm when I touched it; heavier than I'd supposed and closer to the edge. I knew, because without quite meaning to I rolled it off the bed. It fell on to the floor with a decided thud – a loud one, followed by an even louder oath. Or actually a string of them. 'You lumbering halfwit fucking bloody *squit!* You must be round the twist,' were some of the less offensive insults Blake hurled at me as soon as he found his voice – and when his head appeared above the counterpane, still putty-coloured but quite obviously by then

84

in working order, I have to say it crossed my mind that he looked better dead.

'Well you must admit it's a funny place to choose for a nap, Mr Blake,' I told him with as much dignity as I could muster, 'and you really did look like a corpse you know.' (Still do, I thought.)

By then he'd clambered back on to the bed, to sit staring at me like a baleful Buddha, muttering obscenities and massaging his neck. His dark eyes gleamed unpleasantly; and I caught something about pipsqueak amateurs and moronic public schoolboys before he went on to recommend I take a trip to Beachy Head, starting at the top and ending in the sea – and then flopped back across the bed again, exhausted by the effort.

Are you totally convinced though that he *was* asleep? Or could you see him in the role of the rejected lover sneaking back to tinker with the props? In any event, you may be sure that after that I went through them with a toothcomb. The furniture as well, sitting heavily on all the chairs, and even climbing up into the flies again to satisfy myself that no one was about to drop a lethal weight on to the stage, or release a pair of comic bloomers.

***

By five-thirty the theatre had come back to life, with the stage crew racketing about and Len glumly moving lights and changing coloured filters. On the revolving stage I watched the Antibes bedroom set, complete with Crispin on his deathbed, swing off into the shadows, and heard the stage door clang repeatedly as the First Act players for 'Spring in Singapore' trudged in to get made up. Andrea made tea soon after six and I helped take it round, starting with the top-floor dressing rooms allotted to the bit-part players and the stuffy little wardrobe room the Allans shared with Nanki-Poo.

Actors backstage tend to look like distressed gentlefolk forced by circumstance to live in squalor – and coming on them in their rows of little hutches, sipping tea and working in the Leichner 5 and 9, you couldn't help admiring their forbearance. Each night they stepped out from a grimy backstage world of flex and canvas, cleats and braces on to a set which only from out front seemed real. Each night they sat in windowless and airless dressing rooms, to pull on wigs and paint their faces, and then emerge onstage as vivid characters with fine complexions and beautifully managed hair. Lines were learned, moves executed on one side of the proscenium, to enthral rows of punters comfortably seated on the other – with both sides conspiring to pull off the magic trick of a performance.

I could hear the cricket commentary on Nigel Hughes-Milton's portable Bush radio before we reached his door, and found him when I knocked and entered, fully dressed and made-up, glued to the Second Test at Lords and looking quite unusually intent. 'First ball of the over, Sobers facing Trueman...' Brian Johnstone's plummy voice intoned as I slid the tea on to the dressing shelf beside Hughes-Milton's elbow, but then began to scream into his microphone like a demented schoolboy. 'He's lofted it to leg! It's up, up... Parks has it – has it, yes... *yes, by God*,' shrieked Johnners. 'He's CAUGHT! Sobers caught off Trueman for just eight! Just eight, I can't believe it!'

Nor could Hughes-Milton, who punched the air and shouted, 'YES!' as if he'd done the deed himself. And in the moment that I met his triumphant grin, I suddenly knew who he'd reminded me of – of *Romeo*; the boy who looked the part at the college Senior Drama Soc stab at the Star Cross'd lovers, and who couldn't act for toffee. (Both cricket-mad and less than sharp above the collar line, you see.)

Yvonne Hayes shared a dressing room with Barbara Bayliss, who was yet to come; and sitting at her mirror when we knocked, looked old and tired without the benefit of make-up. Crispy Flake's room the next floor down was empty still. But Lumsdon Gould next door was there all right and in the flesh – so much of it, that at first sight I thought we'd caught him starkers, before a glimpse of grubby white elastic in the shadow of his belly showed that he wasn't, quite.

A trained voice projecting: 'Come,' at declamatory pitch, followed by a: 'Thank you my dear fellow. Just put it there,' was the sort of thing that one expected from male thesps when delivering their tea. But, 'Step forth ye whoreson valiant villain! Be bold and play the saucy cuttle for us, pray,' was what old Lummy bellowed at me that night through a pervasive atmosphere of greasepaint and stale farts – and as I sidled past him, extended a puce hand to squeeze the pouched front of my jeans like someone testing supermarket fruit. These days we'd call the old queen a molester I suppose, and accuse him of it to his face. But all I could think of at the time was the mug of Brooke Bond which I mustn't spill, and that the fault was very likely mine for leaning in too close.

'About ten minutes to the half please, Mr Gould,' I managed from the safety of the door; and when I closed it heard his tremulous old baritone break into the 'I Could Be Happy With You!' song from *The Boy Friend*.

Miss Compton hadn't yet arrived. But Cordelia was in her dressing room, fidgeting with towels and bottles. Catching sight of me behind Andrea with the tea tray, she ran out at once to pull me in. 'I've got the jitters, Sammy!' Her eyes were anxious and disturbingly direct. 'Look, could you stay with me a moment? Have you time?'

Dressed all in brown; brown blouse, brown tights beneath a very short brown skirt, I thought that she looked wonderful and shut the door behind me. When I'd last seen it, the star dressing room just seemed a little larger than the others with furniture that wasn't quite so shabby. Now it looked and smelled like three floors of Swan & Edgar, with sheeted costumes and dressing robes, banks of flowers, framed photographs of famous actors, telegrams and fleets of greetings cards, three wigs on polystyrene stands and enough pots, jars and paint-sticks, cosmetics, lotions, powders and removers to stock an entire department.

Cordelia turned her mother's chair back from the dressing table and sat on it to face me. 'I've just been over all Abi's costumes and her wigs and make-up, and nothing's wrong or out of place,' she told me breathily. I said I'd checked the props as well, not once but twice.

'But don't you find that ominous? To check them twice and *still* find nothing?' she demanded. 'You see I have this premonition that something's going to happen. Tonight I mean. Don't ask me how but I can *sense* it, Sammy!'

I couldn't, not then – although it's clear with hindsight that I should have – and risked telling her a second time that we were making far too much of what I felt sure would turn out to be a series of bad jokes.

'Do you know what I'm afraid of?' Cordelia asked as if I hadn't spoken. I didn't have a clue and said so. 'I'm terrified that whoever's doing this is trying to force Abi off the stage, to make her give up acting and settle down like any normal woman of her age.'

I think I mentioned that I'd closed the door when I came in. So it wasn't until I caught the first pungent whiff of *JOY*, and looked up to see Cordelia's mother standing in the doorway in a stylish dark blue dress with a stand-up collar like the wicked queen in Snow White, that I knew I hadn't. Or if I had, the latch had failed to do its thing.

'My dear young imbeciles, what *is* all this about?' Miss Compton sounded just a tad annoyed. 'You know as well as I do, Mouse, that in my time I've been in more tight corners than a feather duster, and have never had the faintest problem getting out of them.'

Crossing the room to spread the *JOY* about a bit, she took the chair her daughter had vacated and automatically smoothed back her golden hair for the muslin scarf Cordelia already held to tie around it. 'As for what I *should* be doing at my age...' Carefully and one at a time Miss Compton removed her rings and dropped them into a glass jar. 'I may not be in the first dewy flush of youth, my dears, but I wouldn't say I'm altogether ready for the scrapheap.

'And now young man, if you would run along and do whatever ASMs are meant to do between the half and curtain up?' She nodded at me in the mirror through ringless and already busy fingers. 'The Mouse and I will do our best to prove that statement true.'

'Oh right,' I said. 'Right, *super!*' (A word we used a lot back then, but only Jilly Cooper does these days.) While Andrea announced the half-hour through the tannoy speaker above the door, I shuffled out into the corridor on two left feet.

Scene 3

Andrea was prompting as she had the night before. I was on the OP side again shadowing the effects man Paul, whose table had been set up behind a floodlight near the back of the Raffles Hotel veranda. Hughes-Milton was already waiting for his entrance; and when I saw Miss Compton stroll up to join him, I stepped back into the shadows.

'No need to hide, no need to skulk, I wouldn't eat a boy like you,' she sang softly as she passed me to the tune of 'Our Language of Love' from *Irma La Douce*. 'Not tonight in any case,' she added in an aside – then on the next breath: 'Sparkle, sparkle darling!' and with one hand on his shoulder, spun H-M out on to the stage to the anticipated round of deafening applause.

I had my own copy of the effects script, and stood behind Paul to watch him take the cues for MUSIC OFF, APPLAUDING DANCERS and NATIVE HADRAH DRUMS.

If only music lasted, Miss Compton sighed onstage as Paul depressed the button of the tape to stop the MUSIC OFF.

And one could rely on moonlight, said Hughes-Milton, doing everything short of indecent exposure to catch the audience's attention.

The sad thing is one can't. Miss Compton struck a downstage pose to ensure he didn't, while Paul's tape broadcast the effect of APPLAUDING DANCERS from the ballroom.

He timed it for ten seconds then depressed the button. That's how Scene 1 began.

I was back in more or less the same position after the first interval, when I was passed by Primmie Allan in a brassy wig as Sadie's friend, Gaye Gaynor. 'Good luck,' I whispered.

She jumped at least a foot into the air. 'Never say that Sammy, NEVER! You must know that it's *fatal* to wish anyone good luck,' she told me looking horror-struck. 'Now run out into the alley. Turn round twice, spit, swear – any foul obscenity will do, then knock for Terry-on-the-stage-door to let you in again.'

'You mean Trevor.'

'Trevor-on-the-stage-door then – and make sure to shout: *ANGELS AND MINISTERS OF GRACE DEFEND US*, to break the thread of the bad luck you see.' By way of encouragement she gave me a little shove. 'Next thing you will be quoting from Macbeth, you silly boy,' she added. Then, 'OH NO, that's even *worse* bad luck! I should have said, *The Tartans* or *The Scottish Play*. So now I'll have to come out too. Hurry up then dear, chop-chop. We'll just have time before my entrance if we're quick!' And we'd been in such a rush to tear out into the street, perform the superstitious rigmarole and hustle Mrs Allan back in time for Paul's doorbell effect to cue her entrance, that I hadn't thought to tell her about Miss Compton's blatant extract from *The Scottish Play* when she'd first arrived that Monday. Or ask her if she thought that kind of bad luck could be deferred, to strike when least expected?

Phone cues are tricky at the best of times. There's no surer way to make an actor look ridiculous than by forcing him or her to juggle with a telephone that's off the hook but won't stop ringing anyway. Then Martin had complicated all the cues in the St James's play by insisting on another little ping five seconds after the receiver was replaced (all telephones being liable to reflex pinging in the sixties) – involving Paul in seven ON cues, seven OFF cues and nine extra pings, not counting all the cues for the front doorbell on a separate board.

Well the next few minutes of the thing went off all right. Onstage, the actor playing the butler, Trenton, answered the first ring in the effects script and rang off. Paul did the after-ping. Miss Compton dialled out and rang off; Paul pinged. Paul rang, Miss Compton answered: *Who? I've never heard of you, please hang up at once!* rang off and made her exit for the first quick change – leaving Paul to ping again and ring the doorbell. Then Primmie Allan made her entrance as Gaye Gaynor. Paul rang the phone again, and while she answered, turned to tell me he was desperate for a pee. 'Are you OK to hold the fort, Sam, while I shake hands with Percy? It's only bells from now until the curtain,' he assured me.

'Sure,' I told him casually, immediately starting to sweat. Primmie was on the phone still, saying: *Would you believe it Maudie, they were on the sofa in full evening dress. No totally horizontal dear, and in broad daylight...*

Waiting for my cue line of *Good-bye then, love*, before counting five seconds for the after-ping, I was concentrating hard on the effects script, when Nanki-Poo pranced past me in the wings. I heard the audience's 'Ahhhh!' (lord knows how anyone could *ahhhh* at Nanki-Poo!), before I fully realised what was happening; then saw him bouncing out across the St James's carpet in the direction of his mistress, in the way that cheerful pekineses bounce with tails curled across their backs and all their trouser-feathers flying. Primmie must have caught sight of him in the middle of her third line: *Yes of course they're married, but there is a limit...* and having obviously decided to play the little beast for laughs, leaned down to pat the sofa as she said it.

You can't train pekes. But Nanki-Poo bounced up on to the

cushions just as if he had been, and the audience indulgently obliged. Primmie delivered her *Good-bye* cue line and rang off. I counted for five seconds and pinged – which was when I heard Miss Compton, changed and ready at the door, say 'Fuck it!' quietly as she launched herself on to the stage.

Gaye my dear, how too divine of you to come, and with your gorgeous little pooch! I'd keep a dog myself if I didn't have a man to lollop about the place and slobber over me. That charming couple we met at Evelyn's had packs of poodles, she went on, improvising madly, before jumping a whole page in the prompt script to the next line which seemed to fit, but happened to be in the middle of a phone call that she'd yet to make. *Do you remember darling? I asked them if they lived near the gloomy house in Fulham that someone had completely ruined with ghastly stained-glass in all sorts of lurid colours, and they said 'IN IT'. So unfortunate, and all I could do was hoot!*

She waited for the laugh, then turned to beam directly at poor Andrea in the prompt corner to show her that she'd dried.

I really can't think why I chose that moment to ring the phone again. Blind panic I suppose. Nor can I think what would have happened if Miss Compton hadn't seized the chance to make a dive for the receiver. *Hello? Algy, angel, what was the meaning of that intriguing message that you left with Trenton?* To reveal that she'd only gone and jumped two more pages in the script, to set the St James's piece on course for the shortest one act play in history!

Or she might have, if Nanki-Poo hadn't chosen to see her as a threat to Primmie, springing to his mistress's defence with both ears flapping and jaws so wide apart it looked as if he'd turned his whole head inside out. The acoustics of the Meads were plenty good enough I should have thought for evening promenaders to have heard that dog's first piercing yelp down on the seafront, even with the bandstand playing. Nanki followed it with an ear-splitting fusillade of yaps that had the audience in tears of laughter – while offstage, our long-suffering stage manager, Stan Wilson, began to strike his forehead rhythmically against the prop room wall.

Onstage, Miss Compton turned her voice up several notches. *Can you speak up duckie? Gaye's loathsome dog is savaging me. All hell has broken loose and I'm in shreds. I promise you, it's Armageddon!*

Tom Allan's cue, it had to be, and he rose magnificently to the occasion. *Gaye, let me park the little blighter in your car to save it being pinched,* he cried, striding on to seize Nanki by the collar in mid-yap and stride off again OP side with a bland: *Back in a tick then folks,* delivered over one broad shoulder.

GIVE THE MAN A CIGAR! was what I'm sure we all thought. I did anyway.

Meanwhile... *Thank heavens for dear Vincent,* Miss Compton spoke into the phone. *Did I tell you how much we all adore his new production? No, not seduction dear; after two years of wedded bliss you may be sure he's nothing new to offer in that line* – miraculously conjuring the cue for Tom's real entrance from what appeared to be thin air. *And now here he is himself, the little love, to tell you all about it.*

I thought it brilliant of her not to sound relieved, as with elaborate nonchalance she waved the telephone at her stage husband. To bring the whole scene back on to the rails in time for Paul's return to his effects board and ping his final ping.

In retrospect, I can't imagine how Tom Allan managed to dispose of Nanki-Poo in less than half a minute, or where. But however he achieved it, we didn't hear another yip out of the little beast for the rest of the performance. Shorter by a good ten minutes, the St James's play still received by far the longest, loudest and most heartfelt applause of the triple-bill. The cast took five curtain calls, and Miss Compton three more on her own before the Anthem, followed by a lot of noisy hugging and hand-kissing on our side of the curtain when it finally came to rest. So there you are.

***

All through the rest of the show I'd been hoping for a chance to catch Cordelia and ask her what she made of Nanki's great escape. But she was holed up with her mother in the star dressing room for both the intervals. Beyond acknowledging the tea that I helped Andrea to deliver, they'd neither of them spoken – and it was not until we'd cleared the Antibes set, and were sorting out the rumpled bed, that Cordelia appeared backstage. 'Abi's almost finished her street make-up, so I haven't time to talk,' she told me, 'but I need to see you, Sam.'

'I know.' I glanced across the bed at Andrea, who went on plumping up the pillows and pretending not to notice. 'How about a walk then, in the morning on the seafront? I mean the two of us,' I added firmly, as Andrea looked up and cleared her throat.

'Right you are then.'

'Seriously? You mean you'll come? You'll meet me for a walk?'

'Of course I will, you only had to ask, Sam. I'll meet you on the green beside the Wish Tower at eleven if you like.' And without waiting for an answer she turned to run.

'Great, that's great, I'll see you there then,' I called after her retreating figure. 'At eleven, super! Really super!' (Too much, I know. But I was still in my teens remember, and eager as the eagerest of beavers.)

***

95

The next morning... I'm pretty sure it must have been the Wednesday morning, when Primmie Allan told us all about her dream. We'd just heard on the eight o'clock news that the female astronaut, Valentina Tereshkova, had reappeared from space – and Mag had pointed out that it was probably the only way the poor cow could escape from Russia, when apropos of nothing, Primmie launched into her scene.

Scene 4

The breakfast table in Mag Goodworth's kitchen the following morning; a Wednesday.

Primmie Allan (buttering her toast): 'I dreamed of Marilyn last night, I can't imagine why.'

'Marilyn? Monroe?' I asked her, thinking of the tragic little star who'd died the previous August.

'I was in *The Prince and the Showgirl* at Pinewood playing one of darling Sybil Thorndike's ladies in waiting. The thin one, dears, which meant I had to diet *crazily* – just rabbit food for weeks!'

'What was she like?' I meant Monroe of course.

'Marilyn? I'd call her scatter-brained if I thought she had anything to scatter. A grubby little thing when she wasn't coated with Vaseline and lit like a stadium. If you ask me dear, that girl's main talent was for facing a thousand-watt bulb without squinting. She was a bottle blonde you know.'

We knew. 'But she was gorgeous, surely?' (Mag.)

'Big teeth, dear, tombstones, and all the worst faults of a *Gemini* – shambolic, shallow as a puddle, *hours* late on set. She drove poor Sir Larry round the twist.'

'But you said you dreamed of her?' (Me.)

'Well yes I did, and I can tell you dear it came as *quite* a surprise. She knocked on the front door – that door out there.'

She gestured vaguely with a marmaladey spoon. 'I went to answer it... I hope you don't mind, Miss Goodworth dear, but you weren't in the dream you see.'

'You're welcome, Mrs Allan. It couldn't matter less,' Mag assured her with a precarious straight face.

'How *sweet* of you! But do call me Primmie, dear. Everybody else does... So there she was, just there outside the door, in the old mac she wore in the last scene of the movie to hide that vulgar little dress they had to sew her into... But I wonder where Tom's got to?' Primmie cocked her fluffy head to listen for the stairs. 'He'll have to get a move on won't he if he wants to catch the train.'

'So what happened then,' Mag asked.

'What dear?'

'What did she do next?'

'Marilyn,' I prompted, 'in your dream.'

'Well not a lot dear really. Just stood there looking daft and lost for words – she always was you know unless that dreadful Strasberg woman from the Actors Studio was there to feed her lines.

"So Marilyn," I said, "I thought that you were... " '

'Just wonderful as Elsie Marina?' Mag suggested.

'No dear, *dead* dear. I said I thought that she was dead.' Primmie took a bite of toast and marmalade and chewed it meditatively.

'And then?'

'She did that breathy, giggly thing that always made you want to hit her hard with something solid, like a brick dear. "No sugar, I'm not dead," she said.

'"Then who *the fuck* dear was it that they buried in Los Angeles last year?"' related Primmie, poker-faced.

That's when Mag performed the nose trick with her tea; and it was only after she had mopped the table and sponged the various parts of us she'd sprayed, that we heard what Marilyn did next in Mrs Allan's dream. 'Well if you must know dears, I believe she tried to sell me something. You wouldn't put it past her, would you – in the mackintosh you see. All the salesmen wear them, don't they? So naturally I shut the door.'

'You shut out Marilyn Monroe?'

'We all knew she wasn't famous for her brains of course – but really dears, she can't have thought I'd buy a *carpet sweeper* from her,' Primmie said with what for her passed as a frown, 'and hardly on *the doorstep!*'

And if you're wondering what's relevant about that scene, I've put it in as an example of the way that Primmie Allan (SUSPECT SIX) tended to act offstage. *Obliquely* is perhaps the kindest way of putting it – but back to that Wednesday morning...

After breakfast, Mag dropped Tom Allan at the station on her way to work, for a meeting with his agent up in London so he told us; leaving Primmie in the kitchen with Mag's twin-tub and a morning's worth of laundry.

For my own part (and without dwelling on the fact, I'll just mention that I'd woken early with the engine revving), I made great efforts after breakfast with the quiff, the T-shirt and the Old Spice aftershave for my assignation with Cordelia.

'You're not planning to go out dear, are you?' Primmie popped out from the kitchen when she heard me bounding down the stairs. 'Because if you are dear, I'd be so grateful if you would take Nanki with you. He has to have his walkies, the poor darling, and I can't move a step until I'm free of all of this.' Opening her softly shining de Havilland brown eyes as wide as they would go, she pointed at the heaps of pants and shirts and socks she'd dumped around the wildly shaking twin-tub in the middle of the kitchen floor.

But when I told her I'd arranged to meet Cordelia, 'actually, Mrs Allan' – hoping she would take the hint, all she said was: '*Lovely* dear, he'll be no trouble. But *do* call me Primmie, dear. I *loathe* it when you don't – and who's the lucky boy then going for a gorgeous walkies?'

I wasn't quite sure to be honest if she was talking to me then or the pekinese, who'd just emerged from underneath a shirt. 'I do so wish that Tommy wouldn't do this though on a performance day. Imagine if he missed the train!' And smiling back into her anxiously perspiring face, it crossed my mind (or rather Gaston's) that once Mag dropped him at the station, Tom Allan might have gone anywhere, done anything – even sneaked back to the empty theatre for all that anyone would know.

'You will make sure that Nanki does his poo-poo, won't you, Sammy dear? I always get so worried when he doesn't. It's just the same with Tommy,' Primmie trilled, unnecessarily I thought. 'Then when you're back, we'll see if we can find you a nice chewy chew-stick, shall we? Ah, *here's* the lead; I knew I'd left it somewhere!' She disinterred it from a heap of underpants and clipped it on to Nanki's jewel-studded collar. 'Now don't you be a naughty boy and jump up on Cordelia!' (The dog or me? Still wasn't sure.) 'And Sammy dear, in today's horoscope Katrina says that Virgos, no I mean Pisces, are in for a surprise.'

A pleasant one or otherwise? Katrina didn't say.

***

'Why did you have to bring that beastly little thing with you?' was the first thing that Cordelia said, shouting to be heard above the seagulls. We'd met as she'd suggested beside the old Napoleonic fort on Wish Tower Green; and after I'd explained about wash day and the impossibility of refusing Primmie as Melanie Wilkes, and Cordelia told me I was too nice for my own good, she let me kiss her – not for long enough to make a deep impression, but on the lips at least.

Without make-up, with her hair pulled back into a ponytail like Brigitte Bardot in *Doctor at Sea*, she looked about thirteen – from the neck up. From the neck down, she looked like Bardot at San Tropez, in a jungle-pattern shirt with a red orchid splashed across one very perky boob and a delighted monkey swinging from the other. She also wore the tightest, whitest slacks I thought I'd ever seen (if one could seriously think of anything that clung so avidly to all her ins and outs as *slacks*) – with under those a pair of cork-soled platform sandals that promoted her from short to medium height.

'So who do you think let *that thing* out last night?' she asked me, pointing to the business end of Nanki's lead. 'Because I'm certain it was done on purpose, aren't you?'

'Well even if it was,' I said with both eyes on the open neckline of her shirt (and just then feeling less keen on being Gaston super-sleuth than Errol in-like-Flynn). 'Even if it was, I still can't see it as anything much worse than a rotten joke.'

By then we'd left Wish Tower Green, holding hands self-consciously for the first stretch of the promenade, until our palms began to stick together and I used Nanki and the way that he kept darting off to pee as an excuse for letting go.

And if you'll forgive me for digressing from the plot again here briefly, I should like to add that pekineses as a breed do offer quite a bit of scope for anatomical improvement. In much the way that one would like to move a rhino's eyes from halfway down its nose to where they ought to be beneath its ears, or stick shoulders on a penguin, if it was up to me I would pull out a pekinese's squashed nose to stop it wheezing,

101

push in its bulging eyes to stop them running, and shave all the feathers off its bum to clear a non-stick route for passing turds. Then jack the whole thing up by something like eight inches, to let its pee go where it's aimed instead of drenching the poor wretch's inside leg.

What's more, the way Nanki produced the poo that so preoccupied his mistress, was if anything still less attractive. That morning as a case in point, when halfway down the promenade I'd felt a sharp jerk on the lead, I looked back to see Nanki crouched into a feathery hoop slap in the middle of the footpath, squeezing out a stinking yellow spiral of excrement from beneath a violently pluming tail, reminding one in quite the worst way of a Mister Softee caramel ice cream. Which I suppose is why I capped it with an upturned ice cream tub from a passing waste bin.

Naughty of me really, but at least it made Cordelia laugh.

* * *

Well the day was hot, we all were hot, the sun bounced up from the pavement to assault us from all angles, and by the time we'd reached the pier and crossed the Grand Parade into the town, Nanki-Poo was chuffing like a steam train. To make the point, in case I hadn't realised, that I would have to carry him back up the hill – if I planned to get him home alive that is. 'Sorry Call-me-Primmie, I'm afraid your dog is dead; the heat you know, he must have had a heart attack.'

Not likely to go over well one would have thought, on washing day or any other.

'I could accept all this as... how did you put it Sammy, as not much more than a rotten kind of joke?' Cordelia was saying while we waited at a junction. 'I could accept that if I didn't know and wasn't *absolutely sure* that someone's doing every bloody thing they can to ruin things for Abi. But look, isn't that Miss Bayliss over there?' She pointed at a woman trotting along the opposite pavement, wearing a moss green Robin Hood hat, but looking more like Friar Tuck – and she was right, it was; although in the moment I agreed, Miss Bayliss vanished through a door with EASTBOURNE GAZETTE & HERALD printed in large capitals above it.

We'd both wondered at the time what she was up to; and when I mentioned it to her afterwards, Mag thought that ten to one the silly moo was advertising for a toy-boy.

All that before we knew the truth.

Ten minutes later, Nanki-Poo and I were standing on the pavement outside WH Smith. At least I was standing, he was lying flat, when Cordelia emerged with a roll of wrapping paper and a bunch of greetings cards. 'I've bought one for you, Sam,' she announced, handing me a pink card with the pink words *Happy Birthday* on it, garlanded with bright pink roses. 'It's for Abi's birthday bash on Sunday.'

'Ah – oh thanks Cordelia.' (For choice I would have gone for something 99.9% less pink.)

'There's going to be a cricket match and birthday picnic for her out at Hadderton, and you're invited, Sammy,' she assured me. 'It's to celebrate her fiftieth, but of course no one's meant to know that.' (And back then, *you* need to know that fifty was the new sixty-five. It worked the other way around.) She'd have to leave me then in any case to see what Abi wanted for her lunch, Cordelia added. 'But I'll be in the theatre from about three onwards, pressing her costumes up in the wardrobe. If you would like to come and find me there, Sam?'

Again the small hand on my arm. But this time an unmistakable invitation in the khaki eyes. Cordelia took a deep breath to animate the monkey on her left breast, inflate the orchid on her right – and activate a stealthy movement in my jeans.

'Right, right you are then!' Having tried and failed to channel floppiness – yeasty, verging on the beastly and standing partially to attention, I stooped to grab a startled Nanki and apply him to the problem like a panting poultice. 'See you there then – bye!'

Resisting the temptation to break into a run, I marched away bow-legged, with Nanki looking by then less like a poultice probably than some sort of steaming sporran.

Scene 5

In the eaves of the Meads Theatre the wardrobe room is windowless, which makes its distinctive odour of wax-crayony greasepaint and musty fabric all the more intense. Between a sink at one end and a walk-in closet at the other, a mirrored shelf along one wall provides for both the Allans' make-up, Primmie's wig, Tom's spare tobacco pouch, a tray of bottles with a soda siphon and two glasses, and a large box of 'small dog mixer' biscuits. Tucked underneath it is a dog bed covered in blue and red MacDonald tartan. Forgotten costumes from forgotten plays overflow from wicker skips, or lie in heaps inside the open closet. An old-fashioned Singer sewing machine sits in a corner with bunches of assorted safety pins strewn around it. A stack of plastic armour, chain mail made of silver-painted string and three wooden shields lie in another. In the centre of the room an ironing board has been erected.

Still in her jungle shirt and unconvincingly-named slacks, although without her sandals, Cordelia was already busy pressing her mother's Singapore gown through a damp linen cloth. She looked up when I came in to say hello; and when I said how nice she looked, remarked that I did too. (I'd changed into a shirt and re-gelled my hair into a pale approximation of James Dean's.) At her suggestion, I pulled Tom Allan's chair out from the shelf to sit and watch Cordelia working while we talked.

My mother had always been too busy with her painting at The Bury to waste time on ironing. But old Sim loved to do it when she could. She found the action soothing to the nerves, she said; and watching the steam iron move back and forth, smelling the Mrs Tiggy-Winkle smell it made and listening to the creaking of the board, I was reminded of how safe and cosy it always felt to be with Sim when she was ironing – a memory from childhood which almost, very nearly drove from my mind all thought of pushing Cordelia roughly back against the dressing shelf, kissing every part of her the jungle shirt exposed and fondling what it didn't (I did say *nearly*).

I suppose we might have sat together in what civilised people call 'companionable silence'. If I could endure a silence, which I can't and never will. Instead I steeled myself to pose the question I'd been wrestling with all morning and hadn't found the time or courage yet to ask. 'Erm, I've been wondering, Cordelia...'

'Yes?'

'I've been wondering if you like me well enough you know... er, to be my sort of girlfriend?' And there it was, I'd made my move but was so busy studying my shoelaces while I did it that I couldn't tell at first how she'd reacted. She must have been a fan as it turned out of Thomas Hardy, as: 'You're likely to go on wondering then,' was what she said eventually. 'You'll never know Sam, because you never ask.'

I looked up then all right, to see her slip a padded hanger through her mother's ball gown and hang it on a hook behind the door. 'The answer anyway is yes.' She plucked Miss Compton's green pyjama top from a basket on the floor, then dropped it back again. 'You can have me now,' she added quietly. 'In there if you like?'

FRONT PAGE NEWS IN ALL THE EVENING PAPERS! While I was staring at her still and wondering if I'd heard right, Cordelia demonstrated how walk-in closets work, by calmly walking into one and lying down.

It's curious the things you can remember through the years and those you can't. Under the circumstances, the gentlemanly thing for me to have done would be to ask if she was sure. But all I actually remember of that moment was a childish impulse to shout: 'Coming, ready or not!'

After that, to say I did what was expected of me would be to put it far too simply – and amongst the many other things I can't remember is the look on Cordelia's face while she lay half-submerged in costumes, waiting for me in the closet. Was she smiling that sexy little Mona Lisa smile? Or was she gravely serious, looking anxious even – what? Maybe the James Dean quiff had drooped by then to block the view. I can't even say with any certainty what I did next. Jump up from my chair with an incoherent cry; eyes and trousers widening, hairs sprouting from my manly chest, to take a flying leap into the closet? Or did I just creep into it politely with a mild expression of enquiry?

However hard I try, I'm sorry but I simply can't remember.

If the quiff *had* flopped, you can be sure that something else had risen to report for duty. Because by then I wanted her, or IT, quite badly. That I do remember. And sad to say, *quite badly* was the way I went about it – fumbling blindly for the Durex Pack of Three (we never called them condoms in those days), and fumbling again to lift the flap and prise the trio of foil-covered lozenges apart. Unable to decide if I should rip the one I'd chosen open before or after I unzipped, I attempted both, failed twice, then had a struggle to persuade the zip to move at all against a good deal of unhelpful pressure from within.

But now we're into details, I've had a sudden flash of how Cordelia did look – and can tell you that the expression on her face just then could best be described as one of disbelief. Down finally to the more unhelpful aspects of y-fronting (and can we agree that men and underpants have never got on well), I faced the fact that foreplay of any kind was definitely out. With the main acting part released from its moorings and red blood coursing where it ought, I rolled the Durex on... I thought effectively enough, until I found I'd rolled it lubricated side *in* and chalked side *out*, resulting in more intimate manoeuvres and a sharp yelp of pain. Stoically, I braced myself to try again (I say stoically, but was shaking like a leaf), and managed at the third attempt.

That got me roughly halfway there. Next I started working more or less at random amongst the costumes to undo every zip and button I could reach, hoping some of them at least might be Cordelia's. Having at last gained access to a patch of humid female flesh somewhere beneath the jungle-shirt monkey's tail, with my right hand I began to fumble southwards, with the impression that my other hand was wedged somewhere between our bodies. That is until it dawned on me that something (possibly a third hand?) was still unbuttoning away for all that it was worth. Cordelia decided things at that point by grabbing one of mine in her own hand (left or right, I couldn't say) to thrust it briskly through the opening of her now-slackened slacks... and look, I'm sorry if this is beginning to sound like a manual handling training session, but in many ways that's how it felt. I so wanted to be gentle; to be loving, to be tender – just hadn't reckoned with the technicalities involved. But then, and operating on some kind of automatic pilot, my hand (I think it must have been the right one) slid up Cordelia's thigh as far as possible, to seize my opportunity if I can put it that way?

Making the sort of *uurghh!* sound tennis champions make when serving, and not to beat about the bush (which let's face it is rather what I had been doing), I prepared to plunge into the possible; now rapidly becoming probable and gloriously exposed.

'I suppose you realise, my poor nincompoops, that you've set the ironing board alight?' announced Miss Compton, making a dramatic entrance with her usual flair. 'And darlings, much as one adores fire fighters, I'm not sure this is *quite* the time or place for them to bring their little hoses into play.'

Classic.

If Mag had been there she'd have laughed her socks off. But you won't be too surprised to hear I didn't. An all too familiar sinking feeling (the word *wilt* springs, or rather doesn't spring, to mind) did nothing when it came to it to stop the rest of me from leaping into action. Yes, finally!

Still panting heavily and with someone's self-adhesive stockings clinging to my jeans, I pulled up, pulled down, re-zipped and belted in almost less time than it takes to tell. The soda siphon from the shelf was all I needed to put out the fire. I mopped up later with a towel. But, BUGGER! BUGGER! BUGGER! BUGGER! BUGGER TO INFINITY!

I was stuffed, and not to put too fine a point on it, Cordelia still wasn't.

***

'Come Bubo, *en avant!*' Abandoning her daughter to finish what she'd started in the smoky wardrobe (with the ironing I mean, not the other thing), Miss Compton led the way down two flights of concrete stairs. I turned back once before we left – partly I'll admit to cast off extra bits of clothing from the wardrobe, but mostly hoping for some sign from Cordelia of how she felt. But by then she'd found more cloths to cover the singed ironing board, and was working steadily with all her buttons buttoned, refusing to look up.

'Let's make a bargain shall we, Bubo,' her mother offered halfway down the stairs. 'I'm happy to forget that little bedroom farce back there, if you would grant me just two teeny-tiny favours?' She turned to face me at the bottom with a bewitching smile. (And the other thing that made Miss Compton's lip-parted smile bewitching, I've since decided, was that it made her look as if she was just faintly panting with desire.)

'For one thing, darling,' she was saying, 'I'm rather *clinging* to the hope that you'll agree to join us for my birthday treat on Sunday.'

'Your birthday?' I pretended not to know.

'A particularly vile one. Martin's had this totally bizarre idea of celebrating it, well at a *cricket match* of all things that dear Nigel's organised. They've laid all their plots and plans for a picnic. On the "touchline", if that's the word – with bubbly and a birthday cake and God knows *what* besides. Do say you'll come to keep my poor Mouse company and save us from insanity. Shall we clap hands and make a bargain, darling?' I think the last bit must have been a quote from something, because she didn't try to do it.

But I ask you, how could anyone who'd just been caught as I was (*actually* with pants down) possibly refuse? Besides, the picnic and the cricket match both sounded fun. So I agreed. Although would you think me hypocritical if I confessed to being just a little shocked by Miss Compton's casual attitude to what she'd witnessed in the wardrobe? As a mother I mean.

From the level of the lower dressing-room corridor,

meanwhile, she ran up the steps into the wings to flick on a couple of light battens and illuminate the stage. 'Which brings me to my second teeny favour, Bubo darling,' she said briskly. 'I'd like to try out some new business for that last scene in the Singapore piece, if as your next good deed you'd be a perfect angel and walk it through with me?'

'You want me to rehearse with you?' I felt a thrill, astonishment, I don't know what!

'In a nutshell, darling. It won't take long.' She snatched the prompt script from its table and threw it at me. Literally.

Scene 6

As the curtain rises, Sadie is discovered leaning over the Raffles Hotel balustrade, stage left, staring at the moonlit ocean. (In this case having to make do with the windowsill of the Antibes set, which was still in place). Max is sitting at a table with a plate of sandwiches beside him. He is in shirt sleeves and without a tie; her hair is loose about her shoulders.

Miss Compton/Sadie (instantly a different and much younger woman): *I feel utterly deflated.* I'd caught the script, rifled through it for the scene, and found it while she waited to repeat the line.

Miss Compton/Sadie (staring with unfocused eyes into the gloom): *I feel utterly deflated.*

Max/Me: *But you know I love you!* Our voices sounded hollow on the empty stage. But seated by then on the big brass bed, I found that I was warming to the task.

I know you think you do. She crossed back to the imaginary table, picked up an imaginary sandwich and beckoned with it for me to join her in a dance. (Yes really! *Me* waltzing with Abigail Compton! The lessons in the village hall that Grannie forced us to attend had finally paid off!)

112

I'd like to kiss you, may I? It came out badly while I was concentrating on not stepping on her toes.

Well then... She turned her face to mine. But then just when I really thought she'd do it, introduced this new business, with the invisible remains of the invisible cheese sandwich she was holding becoming trapped between our lips. If it had been a real one, she would have had it halfway up my nose! Well it fazed me, and before I could recover she seized a handful of my shirt and moved in for the kill – or actually the kiss. Her mouth tasted of nicotine and brandy. Not unpleasant. But that wasn't it. The thing was that she deployed her tongue, and I could swear that it was THREE FOOT LONG!

Eventually I broke away; trembling, snorting like a spooked horse.

They've spoiled it – ruined it you see with their incessant bickering, Miss Compton told me sadly.

I'd lost my place; my nerves were shredded beyond shreds. *They can't have spoilt it, I won't let them!* I gabbled from the script

Won't you, dearest boy? Can you say honestly that you still want me in that way?

I do, of course I do! I said, and meant it – because it was then I realised for an obvious reason, and with what one might describe as a constricted feeling, that I still had the Durex on.

We'll put in a bookmark then, shall we darling, and leave it there for now? The question in those bluest of blue eyes

113

was from another situation in another scene, and she wasn't speaking from the script.

* * *

That night, and long after I'd disposed of the redundant item down the backstage toilet (the one you had to pump to make it flush), I watched Miss Compton do the same scene with Nigel Hughes-Milton; and watched her play it as she always had, quite straight without a hint of the new business and a chaste kiss to finish.

BLACKOUT

* * *

I love it when the sun comes up, especially in summer. On the whole I need less sleep these days, which makes getting up less of a chore. Although the morning after my adventures in the wardrobe with Cordelia, and onstage later with her mother, I must admit it took me a while to shake off drowsiness and tell myself how good it was to be alive.

I'd like to say that I sprang lightly to the floor with a glad cry, and could well have done with someone else's legs – but was glad anyway to hear a bantam cock crow from his coop in the allotments, and to watch the sun disperse the sea fret from the cottage roofs when I drew back the curtains in my attic bedroom. It looked like that effect they used in panto for the Transformation Scene, with the diffused spires of Dick Whittington's London town slowly taking substance through the gauze.

The downstairs hall still smelled of Mag's last fry-up. But outside the air was fresh and salty. With swimming trunks on underneath my tracksuit, I squeezed into my running shoes

114

(we called them that back then, not trainers), and thwacked on down the hill towards the theatre. Built in the English-cosy-classical style old theatres favour, with pilasters and urns and a majestic statue of the dramatic muse Melpomene, its terracotta mouldings glowed like Petra in the morning sun. On either side of its engraved glass doors, Abi Compton's celebrated smile and starry eyes beamed through the air-brushed mistiness of two enormous portrait photos, three times as large as life – images of stardom which for me were hard to reconcile with the real woman, or her prehensile tongue.

Between them in the past few hours Miss Compton and her daughter had managed to confuse me as totally as I was capable of being confused. That I was stimulated, flattered and astonished by their interest in me as a male could hardly be in question. I was in love, I knew I was. The question was with which?

I swam that morning where I always swam, from a spur of crumpled chalk known as 'the pinnacle', projecting like a mini-Matterhorn from the white cliffs beyond the village. A narrow path wound round it to the beach below, cut into steps where it was steepest, and fringed with strawberry pink valerian flowers. Later in the season there'd be butterflies and daytime moths; hundreds of them – tiny dancing Chalkhill Blues, Small Heaths and crimson Cinnabars.

I loved that path as well. It was like a picture in a book Sim used to read us of the dragon's castle in *Where the Rainbow Ends*. From the wooden stairway at the bottom you could see the whole sweep of the Eastbourne seafront from the chalk cliffs to the pier, with all the wooden groins between. The sea was blue-green when I reached it and dead calm. The tide was out and the beach smelled of seaweed. I had to wade across the lagoon that formed at low tide between the shoreline and greensand reef, and dived from that, counting to three,

three times as always to summon up the nerve. Even so, the water was still colder than expected; and after the first frantic burst of racing crawl to get acclimatised, I swam sidestroke to watch its dimpled surface spangling with gold and silver lights. So clear and pale it would have felt like swimming in the sky – if it hadn't been so bleeding freezing!

***

The first thing that I saw when I got back to Meads Village was a broad expanse of tulip-spattered rump, up-ended in my cousin's square of the allotments. The second thing I didn't see, was Auntie Bill's Harley-Davidson – reminding me that it was Tuesday, the morning she reported early at the station. Mag straightened in her quilted dressing-gown as I crunched up the gravel to the cottage. Her eyes were slits, her head a jangling battleground of multicoloured rollers, and if she'd had a tail beneath the tulips I reckon she'd have lashed it. 'That pitiful excuse for a pooch only went and woke half the neighbourhood when you waltzed out and slammed the bloody door,' she said accusingly. 'And now the sodding slugs have had my carrots. Not that you would care,' she added bleakly, 'swanning in like love's young dream with sunshine blasting from your backside!'

Mag never was much good first thing, not even when the sun shone; and as things stood I judged it wise to snatch an early breakfast and lie low until she left for Antoine's. By which time I was desperate to hear Cordelia's take on the fiasco in the wardrobe – to hear if she blamed me for what had happened; to tell her I was sorry and put things right between us if I could. Then after that, less worthily perhaps, to ask her if she might consider any sort of replay?

Mag's telephone was an excitingly bright red affair in

Bakelite, the latest thing. Even if you'd wanted to you couldn't miss it in her hall. As a rule she only ever let me use it after six on Sundays, provided that I left threepence on the table and she and Auntie Bill could eavesdrop from the lounge. But that Thursday morning, feeling reckless and with a threepenny bit to hand, I cast caution to the winds and dialled.

'Is that the Excelsior? Yes, could you transfer me to Miss Compton's line please in the Mayfair Suite.' I waited while it rang with fingers crossed, knowing that although she slept in an adjoining bedroom in the suite, Cordelia would be likely to pick up.

'Cordelia? I'm glad it's you, because...'

'Sammy, is that you? I can't speak now,' she whispered. 'Abi's being interviewed by some awful woman from a ghastly magazine. I'll come and find you later at the theatre, in the first interval if I can get away, OK?' She hung up before I could reply, but hadn't sounded cross, which was *something*, I decided. In fact it's likely that I would have spent the first act of the triple-bill that night in a state of pleasurable anticipation – if another and far worse something hadn't intervened.

Scene 7

As the curtain rises the orchestra is playing the 'Moonlight in Mayo' waltz. The stage is empty for a moment, then Sadie Swanson dances out on to the moonlit veranda of Raffles Hotel in Singapore, etc.

As usual there was applause for the set that swelled to something more substantial as Miss Compton and Hughes-Milton waltzed into view. I remember thinking how beautiful, how glamorous she looked – and wondering for the hundredth time what made her kiss me – when an unfamiliar rustling, scratching sound made me look down from where I stood with Paul on effects, to see a lighting cable snake across the stage entirely of its own accord.

I stared at it stupidly, until it tautened and the floodlight nearest to me toppled over, beaming ballroom lighting through the wings.

Unscripted stage direction: the set starts to revolve, anti-clockwise silently and smoothly.

The dancers had just completed their first circuit of the veranda and were level with Miss Hayes and Lummy Gould crossing the Raffles ballroom for their entrance, when Miss Compton signalled to me over H-M's shoulder. From where I stood rooted to the lino her voice was clearly audible through

118

'Moonlight in Mayo'. 'Keep it going, Bubo – all the way, dear. Keep it *going round!*'

I think I've mentioned haven't I that at St Edgar's we were taught to act decisively in any sort of crisis? So by dashing like a mad thing through the wings to the controls for the revolve on the back wall, I'd been in time to save the dancers from the head-on crash into the scenery which halting Singapore would have precipitated. The dash in both directions, with a gabbled explanation to the stage staff in between, can't have taken me more than thirty seconds at the most. By which time the balustrade that blocked the end of the hotel veranda had reached roughly centre stage. Beyond it were three painted canvas flats supported from behind by cleats and braces, with just a narrow gap between them and the St James's set, now steadily approaching.

Miss Compton and Hughes-Milton were still dancing beautifully despite their youth in the small segment of veranda that remained. She whispered something in his ear as the balustrade swung up towards them, and on a fortuitous crescendo of the music they twirled each other over – Fred and Ginger, absolutely! Quite how they managed to squeeze through the gap I couldn't tell you; one moment they were caught between the flats, the next had broken free into St James's. The audience by then were whooping like Comanches round a waggon train, which I took to be a good sign. Then with a crinkling sound, the piece of paper which had marked the last few bars of 'Moonlight in Mayo' on Paul's tape, fluttered to the floor.

Then silence; the sort of silence that drips from the stage to seep up through the stalls, the boxes and the circles, row by row, to freeze the punters in their seats.

Paul stared at me in panic across the tape recorder with its still revolving spools, while in the shadowed part of the

119

St James's set, Stan and Andrea worked frantically to clear furniture and carpets – anything that might impede the dancers.

Disaster loomed!

In retrospect, there were a number of things I might have done while Paul wound back the tape. In retrospect, the best thing undoubtedly would have been to do nothing (and I'll repeat that, *nothing*). But as ill luck would have it, that was the moment when the motto they'd brainwashed into us all at St Edgar's, *Per actionis vinco*, propelled me into action. At the basest of basic levels you would have thought I'd see it as the worst idea since Adam said he'd like to try an apple for a change. But it seems I didn't, because that was the moment that I chose, as loudly and decisively as I could manage, to break into the old party piece my sister Caro and I had learned from Sim when we were children:

By the light of the silvery moon,
I want to spoon, to my honey I'll croon love's tune;

I was already sweating buckets, but there was no way back.

Honeymoon, keep a-shining in June;
Your silvery beams will bring love dreams, we'll be cuddling soon
By the silvery moon!

It's said that after you're involved in a traumatic accident, your brain mercifully blanks out the details, as I'd love to say it did that evening. But tragically the recollection's all too clear. I still have a picture in my mind, for instance, of Yvonne Hayes and Lummy Gould, standing waiting for their entrance with both their mouths wide open; totally appalled. Onstage, I have an image of Miss Compton smiling radiantly as she leaped on to a passing sofa to perform a graceful arabesque. Nigel H-M was smiling too as I recall, but with eyes starting like a rabbit's in a football crowd; and as they moved back into hold, I saw that he was frothing slightly at the mouth. I pressed on grimly anyway, in what I hoped was a light tenor but probably was shriller, groping for the notes.

> *By the light – by the light – by the light*
> *Of the silvery moon – the silvery moon,*
> *I want to spoon – want to spoon – want to spoon*
> *To my honey I'll croon love's tune...*

Crossing from St James's to Antibes through what was meant to be a bathroom door, Hughes-Milton left a trail of nervous spittle on the stage-cloth. But yet again the audience applauded wildly, unaware of what was still to come. Between the Antibes bedroom and the inexorably returning hotel veranda there were, in order of appearance – a backless wardrobe, a brick-painted wall flat bristling with braces, a three-foot wedge of floor, and finally the looming OP side balustrade. The last fence, and in show-jumping terms certainly the worst; a triple-bar at very least. With the sweat running down the backs of both my ears, I filled my lungs for a deep breath:

> *Honeymoon – honeymoon – honeymoon,*
> *Keep on shining in June – keep on shining in June;*

Having just burst through the wardrobe, the dancers separated behind the wall. Miss Compton stepped between it and the balustrade to pirouette on to the apron, then back again to cast herself full length along the painted wooden coping of the balustrade in a gesture of eloquent surrender.

The wretched H-M plainly couldn't pirouette without

appearing spastic. But barely handicapped it seemed by the wire coat hanger from the Antibes wardrobe that had hooked itself into his coat-tails, he did manage some sort of a manly goose-step, before skirting round the balustrade to hand Miss Compton down the other side.

> *Your silvery beams will bring love dreams,*
> *We'll be cuddling soon,*
> *By the silvery moon...*
>
> *the moon, the moon, the moon...* (I couldn't stop!)
> *the moon, the moon...*

They ended centre stage, their arms around each other in an extended kiss – followed by the clatter of the dislodged hanger. Clear round for Abigail Compton on Mister Hughes-Milton! The audience awarded them a thoroughly deserved ovation.

> *... the moon, the moon, the moon...*

For me the wings were spinning in another plane entirely – upwards for a brief glimpse of the grid above me. Then down again to hit the floor, and bounce.

BLACKOUT

The first thing I heard when I came round was not applause, but a metallic clicking sound. From somewhere in the middle distance someone asked me if I was all right, dear? A pink blur fuzzily resolved itself into Primmie Allan's anxious face – and then Miss Bayliss came into focus knitting like a tricoteuse beside the guillotine, with Crispy Flake behind her about to hoist the blade. 'What the bleeding fuck do you think you're doing?' The question (rhetorical apparently) was delivered in a savage whisper. 'JESUS, what an unsufferable balls-up!'

'Insufferable balls-up,' said Primmie automatically. 'And Crispin, that's not fair,' she squeaked across me like an indignant field mouse. 'He might have sung a little flat, I'll grant you that. But the dear boy was only doing what he thought was best, and very bravely I consider.' She stooped to smooth my crumpled quiff. But it was long past help.

'A bloody menace, that's what he is,' sneered Blake – before becoming unpleasantly anatomical with the suggestion that I'd sung castrato with my balls retracted.

My cue, I think, was what I thought as soon as I'd assembled my scattered parts and could attempt to stand.

SWIFT EXIT SAM WITH NO APPLAUSE

SECOND INTERVAL

ACT III

Scene 1

The illuminated and empty auditorium still showed faint signs of life when Martin called us all back on to the St James's set for a debrief, and we pulled back the tabs. The used-up air still stirred with the warmth of all those bodies; with women's perfume and the fleshy odours that it masked. Then Len dimmed the house lights and it sank back into shadow.

The cast arranged themselves as usual with the smaller roles upstage; some in their costumes still, others in dressing-gowns of various shapes and colours. Miss Compton came on last with Cordelia in tow, and while we all waited, Martin leaped about the stage inconsequentially in preparation for the lecture I dreaded but knew was bound to come. Meanwhile, the actors looked down at the carpet, up into the flies or blank-faced out into the darkened stalls. Anywhere but at me.

'I'm sure you did it for the best of motives,' was what Martin finally came out with – to make me wonder if Primmie had already spoken up in my defence. 'But take my word dear, it's best to leave these things to the professionals.'

I couldn't have agreed more, and having mumbled an apology added that I'd panicked; then joined the others in their uneasy study of the carpet, my confidence in shreds.

'Well, well, just so you know,' said Martin kindly, taking off his glasses to rub them on his sweater. 'Let's leave it there then, shall we? Good lad – splendid; no need to beat the thing to death'; replacing the glasses just too late to save him from colliding with a chair.

If I could have folded up and dropped myself into the waste bin you can bet I would have. As things stood, I had already gone to earth in the prompt corner by the time Miss Compton swept on to the stage. Clad in a muslin headscarf and blue wrapper, she was carrying a mirror and an open tin of make-up remover. Cordelia followed with a box of Kleenex and a towel. The set's two-seater sofa had been left vacant for them, and seating herself dead centre to give it something of the status of a throne, Miss Compton draped the towel around her neck. Cordelia held the mirror, concentrating on the job in hand. Martin bounced over with a bin for the tissues, and the cast began to talk amongst themselves.

Thank God for that I thought, they've all forgotten me, and was immediately proved wrong. In the moment that Miss Compton turned her head to scan the prompt side shadows where I skulked, I began to fear the worst, and was immediately proved right. 'Bu-bo! Be-lov-ed!' she sang out on five clear notes in the act of slapping a dollop of verbena-scented make-up remover on her face. 'Wasn't he just *heavenly bliss*, everybody, and so professional!'

Enlarging her smile, she beckoned me across with greasy fingers. 'Come hither soul of my delight.' Crispin, on the other hand, was looking daggers at me.

The wider cast invented business with their clothing. Martin dropped his clipboard. I extracted hands from armpits to stroll on to the stage – although even when Miss Compton moved to let me in, there was scarcely room for the three of us on the two-seater. Clenching everything, I pressed my legs together to slot between them, feeling extremely foolish.

'Exhibit A: The Singing Clown.'

Then Miss Compton made it worse. 'I think I'm going

to kiss you darling,' she announced, and did so coolly on the cheek (with a retracted tongue). 'Martin, can't we keep him in, dear heart? I promise you that Neil will *just adore* the way he did it when I write to tell him!' I felt her seize my nearest knee, fondle it, move on up to stroke my thigh, and then forget somehow to reclaim her hand. It lay there negligently for all to see, while on the other side Cordelia moved her foot to give my ankle a sharp kick. The mirror wobbled, Miss Compton made a small sound of irritation, and I discovered that I still had sweat to sweat and plenty of it. That's when our producer gathered up his scattered notes to tell us he had taken action.

'What are you getting at, old chum?' asked Lumsdon Gould.

'I mean I've done exactly what I said I'd do. I've called in the police,' Martin announced defiantly, for the first time meeting Abi Compton's eyes.

'Then you will just have to call them out again, won't you my poppet.' Her voice assumed what's known in the profession as The Terrifying Tone; the one that fells giant redwoods and stops charging rhinos in their tracks. 'Because I'm here to tell you, dearest, that NOTHING ON THIS EARTH will induce me to play this as some sort of frightful murder mystery, with plate-footed coppers crying havoc and trampling the props!'

The blankness of Miss Compton's face without its make-up in no way deterred her from becoming grand, or from mauling my thigh with her long fingernails while she did so. 'There's no point in looking at me like that, Martin,' she warned him dangerously. 'In fact don't look at me at all until I've put my face on. I've said my last word on the topic. It's exhausted; fade to titles.' She gave us Garbo's Queen Christina sailing off into the sunset, with cheek bones gleaming to suggest a marble figurehead; as beautiful and as unyielding.

If there wasn't a great swell of music; if the end titles weren't already rolling they might as well have been, and Martin knew his star too well to spoil the end scene.

So that was that.

* * *

After they'd cleared the stage, and Martin had gone up front to stay the long arm of the law from Eric Benson's office telephone, I climbed the metal ladder to the hand-winch that released the safety curtain on a deadened auditorium. The cables made a whistling sound as it descended – and coincidentally so did I, as it dawned on me that three more of my suspects had sprouted alibis. Nigel H-M for one had been in full view on the Singapore set when the revolve began to turn, with old Lummy and Miss Hayes also plain to see while waiting for their entrance in the wings – to leave just four potential saboteurs; Miss Bayliss, Crispin and the Allans.

'*Enfin, the smoke, mes amis, it begins to clear!*' Yes, I was back as Gaston with a vengeance, and was about to subject my Big Four to a more detailed forensic study, when I heard the ladder I'd just climbed begin to creak, and realised that someone else was climbing stealthily up to the grid. The saboteur! It had to be, on their way to fray a rope or suspend a lethal missile above the stage. Without a pause for thought I started to creep back towards the open hatch; ready to surprise them and discover – who?

Not Barbara Bayliss on those tiny trotter feet?

Not sweet Primmie Allan, surely? I really couldn't picture anyone as nice as she was behaving quite so badly.

By process of elimination I'd come to the conclusion that it must be either husband Tom, or far more likely, Crispy Flake, when through the hatch Cordelia's brown head hove into view, to banish Gaston in a cloud of smoke for something more like... shall we say James Bond?

'Give us a leg up Sammy, would you?' she demanded – oddly, considering where her legs were. But of course I helped her anyway to scramble up into the dusty area beside the hand-winch. 'I heard the iron come down and had to come and find you,' she panted from the shadows which concealed her face. 'I came to tell you that I'm sorry, really sorry Sammy for what happened in the wardrobe.'

'Or as it happened, *didn't?*' (The sort of suave line I imagined James Bond might have used on Honey Rider in Jamaica, before they sank into the sand.)

'Yes, that's it, what didn't happen in the wardrobe. I'm so sorry it turned out the way it did.' She spoke hesitantly, and in the gaps between her words I heard a rope tap-tapping somewhere in the grid.

'But we'll be ready next time, won't we?' Cordelia moved into the square of light that shone up through the hatch, to show herself more clearly. Her long hair was cobwebbed from the climb, her smile apologetic. 'At the picnic for Abi's birthday, will you take me somewhere then, where we can be alone to try again?'

'You bet I will!' I grinned, forgetting to be suave. With something thrilling clutching at my insides, I felt around my outsides (in a way that I suspect Bond wouldn't have) for the square shape of the Durex Pack of Three in the back pocket of my jeans. 'If you're quite sure that's what you want, Cordelia?'

'I am Sam, cross my heart and hope to die – if only to thank you properly for what you did this evening.' She smiled again. We both did and my heart gave a great thump. 'How's your poor head, by the way? I forgot to ask.'

'My head?'

'Where you hit it on the floor.'

'Oh that, it's fine,' I said, and because I was embarrassed missed my chance to steal a kiss before she shinned back down the ladder. She looked up from the stage to give me one more tantalising smile, then hurried off to see if Trevor-on-the-stage-door had Miss Compton's taxi waiting.

* * *

Later, walking slowly up to Mag's, I thought about her offer, and then about her mother's indisputably French kiss; reran it as a scene from the life of someone who'd be likely to attract a major star – someone in the James Bond mould who wasn't me. The whole scenario was too fantastic to be real. Miss Compton had been playing with me for her own amusement, I decided, along the lines of cat and mouse; and I was old enough I thought to recognise the difference between an actual come-on and a playful tease. Because it's going to happen, Sam my lad, I told myself excitedly, and with Cordelia, not her mother.

And if that sounds to you a totally selfish view from someone randy, immature and verging on the beastly – what can I say? It's what I *was* that summer of 1963, before I broke my duck.

That night I dreamed that I was onstage (naked naturally) acting Crispy Flake's part while casually exposing mine. It's a dream I've dreamed with variations at least a hundred times since then; and when I woke up in the early hours of Friday morning, I can promise you the idea of prancing publicly around a stage with nothing on seemed harmless to the point of *sensible*, compared with what I'd really done.

* * *

There was nothing unexpected about the show on Friday. I barely saw Cordelia and we had no time to talk. Having discounted Primmie Allan – more I confess because I wanted to than for any better reason – to bring my suspects down to three, I watched them narrowly that evening: Tom Allan waiting for his entrance to the St James's drawing room; Crispin Blake arriving only just in time to join Miss Compton in the Antibes bedroom and being scolded by her for his lateness; Barbara Bayliss with her knitting distracting Paul from his effects. I studied them for unexpected movements, sly glances, any sort of break in their routines; which aside from Crispin's lateness didn't happen.

On first nights and on Fridays, the Three Seasons company had an unspoken agreement to convene after the final curtain in the nearest pub. Fridays were the nights the actors chose to let their hair down. But unfortunately the same applied to Mag and Auntie Bill – which had to mean that I'd be forced to introduce them to their Number One pin-up and favourite star in the saloon bar of the Ship Inn that Friday night.

With God knows what embarrassing results!

NEXT SCENE

Scene 2

The saloon bar of the Ship Inn, which frankly has seen better days, is long and narrow with a window seat along the back wall, assorted tables strewn with ashtrays and set around them a small forest of uncomfortable wheel-backed chairs. On another wall are four framed photos of Edwardian Eastbourne and a bilious print on laminated hardboard of Tretchikoff's green-faced Chinese girl. The bar facing it is carved from red mahogany with a row of brass-bound pumps. The shelves behind are lined with bottles, upright and inverted, packets of assorted crisps and salted peanuts, and mugs of dimpled glass on hooks. An archway leads through to the public bar beyond. Offstage one can hear the sound of traffic.

Cousin Mag, in a typically lurid outfit, surveys the action from a round table in the centre of the room, with Auntie Bill as large as life and twice as virile in bike leathers at her side. In the act of pulling up a wheel-back, young Samuel Ashby (me) stands above them with a pint of Harvey's bitter in one hand. The room is otherwise awash with actors, who've turned the place into a kind of pop-up theatre. Their voices have been trained, and if the pub door had been open might easily have carried round the block.

'It was the year dear Edith Evans opened at the Lyric in *The Way of the World*.' (Old Lumsdon talking, Nigel H-M listening politely with glazed eyes.)

'Do you mean the parrot in the Treasure Island movie?' (Miss Hayes to Martin at another table.)

'Talking of wardrobe malfunctions' (Tom Allan to his wife) 'there was that time in the seduction scene with Lady Anne, remember? When his Richard Crouchback hump slides down his back?'

'I'll remember Edith's Millamant until the day I die,' mused Lummy.

'In *The Way of the World* you say, by Congreve?'

'Good heavens my dear fellow, you surely can't expect me to recall the play?'

'They trained it to sit on Bobby Newton's shoulder,' Martin confided to Miss Hayes, 'and squawk "Pieces of eight! Pieces of eight!" each time the voice coach raised his hand.'

'Parrots are pigs to work with aren't they, absolutely bloody!'

'So where did the hump end up, my darling?' (Primmie to her husband.)

'Perched on his bum eventually to make him look like some sort of buttockly deformed baboon.'

'Alas, the only line the parrot learned dear, was: "TALK – why can't you fucking TALK, you witless fowl?"!'

That must have been when I looked up to see Cordelia backing through the glass street door of the saloon bar to hold it open for The Main Event.

'Darlings *what* a nightmare, simply ghastly!' Miss Compton's entrance suggested Joan of Arc or possibly Electra; and having passed her signing autographs for a jostling crowd of fans in the stage door alley, I wasn't too surprised. Tom Allan was on his feet by then, and on his way to meet them at the bar. But with a rare turn of speed for someone of my build, I got there first.

'So what will you both have to drink?' I offered, before

adding casually as Miss Compton had at the Excelsior: 'It's on me.' (In my case without the added *'darlings!'*).

'Darling, darling, *darling!*' Miss Compton made up for it in triplicate. 'But how too divine of you to offer. I'd simply worship a neat brandy if you're sure, my lovely? The Mouse will have a Babycham it's all she ever drinks.'

I paid out five silver coins and got two coppers in return. The brandy cost the best part of a ruinous 3 shillings; the Babycham was only 1/6.

'So tell me, sweetness, who are those two *very striking* ladies you were talking to when we came in?' Miss Compton asked with eyebrows fractionally raised. 'I'm wondering if the Mouse and I should be feeling just the teeniest bit jealous of them, darling?'

After I'd explained as best I could how Mag and Auntie Bill and I were all related one way or another (sort of), and become a little hot and shiny in the process, Miss Compton turned to Cordelia with a look I found it hard to fathom. 'Do you hear that Mouse? His landlady's in bed with the police – which has to be your chance to solve the Great Big Mystery for us, dear.' But then to me, 'Lead on MacBubo, and introduce us will you then my darling.'

If Cordelia's eyes were troubled by the Scottish quote, Primmie Allan's were as round as saucers. I half expected her to jump up from her table as we passed it – to rush Miss Compton out into the street, and spin her like a top before advising her to spit twice and swear like a navvy to avert the curse. But luckily her husband Tom restrained her.

We took our drinks across to the foam-padded window seat, after I had made the introductions, and Auntie Bill had planted bristly kisses on both sides of her idol's famous face, and then frustrated any hope I'd had of sitting with Cordelia by subsiding like a darted rhino in between us. 'Vanessa,' she began predictably as soon as we were settled, and was at once rewarded with the celebrated open smile.

'In my green and salad days,' Miss Compton murmured, lifting her chin a fraction to improve the line, 'I played it with Sir Oliver Barry – who said he must apologise if he became aroused in our big love scene, and then again, poor lamb, for every take in which he wasn't.'

'And was he?' (Trust Mag to ask.)

'Hard to tell with him dear, frankly.'

'I just loved the scene in that old movie, where you're standing on the hillside looking drop-dead gorgeous.' Auntie Bill, who'd had a few already, was spoiling for a weepy wallow in nostalgia with the darling of the silver screen. 'And you say "*Farewell!*" like that – except with so, *SO MUCH MORE* feeling; and the music's playing, and the tears are running down your face...' Bill stifled a bass sob. '... and we know the tears are real because the camera never leaves your face.'

'Do you know, I've always found the way to cry convincingly is to remember my first bad review; it never ever fails.' Miss Compton stared reflectively into her brandy. 'This detestable little man in Felixtowe, or somewhere equally dreary, wrote in his repulsive paper that I couldn't act – and what's worse, looked like Dietrich with a toothache when I tried. Can you imagine reading *that* when you're just starting in the business? *Torment, utter and complete!*' She tossed her drink back, laughing gaily. 'Even after all these years it's guaranteed to bring me out in floods.'

'TIME ladies and gentlemen, PLEASE!'

Auntie Bill was saved from comment by the barman flicking the saloon bar lights off – then on again and off twice more in swift succession, while he informed us that he'd lock up in a half a mo' and then take orders through to midnight. (Which is where I should explain for those too young to know, that back in the 1960s publicans were required to close at 10.30, but could stay within the law by taking payments in advance for alcohol served up to midnight – so long as their street doors were shut and locked between the two. It was laborious for them, but legal just about.)

That night, the flickering lights had been the cue for Abi Compton to remember that her taxi would be waiting for her in the street outside – for a rueful line or two involving beauty sleep, followed by a graceful exit, dispensing blessings as she went. Watching, hoping for a sign of some sort from her daughter; just when I'd decided that she wouldn't, Cordelia turned back with a smile (decoded optimistically by me as sexually implicit), which pressed her pink cheeks into dimples before she disappeared into the night. The barman locked the door, and following a scramble at the bar to refill glasses and pay for final rounds, the cast of 'The Three Seasons' settled down again to entertain each other and the late-night locals with more boozy tales of theatrical disasters.

Listening to them from the window seat with Mag and Bill, I asked myself again and for the umpteenth time which of my three remaining suspects could possibly have meddled with Miss Compton's props and costumes, flicked on the revolve switch or let the blasted dog out of the wardrobe?

Tom Allan, holding Primmie's hand across the table? Barbara Bayliss, knitting steadily and quite alone beneath a photograph of King George V and Queen Mary on the seafront? Crispy getting rat-arsed at the bar?

One of them, he practises these, how do you call them, grubby tricks, on Madame Compton. But which of them, we ask ourselves, mais qui? Or was it all of them together, with Tom Allan stepping out of character and the others into it, to scramble Gaston's grey cells with a *Murder on the Orient Express*-type conspiracy to bring Miss Compton down? *We look but we are blind, mes amis. We look but do not see...*

'It's the first night for *The School for Scandal* at The Queens. I forget the year.' Rolling his r's, his bleary eyes, and unintentionally the nut brown wig that all but covered his left ear, old Lummy was about to launch himself into his party piece for the assembled throng. 'The curtain rises, to reveal my dear old pal, Athene Seyler as Lady Sneerwell, being laced into a corset in her bedroom. Behind a screen lurks Mr Snake, played by young Alec Guinness fresh out of drama school and keen as the proverbial mustard.'

Rising unsteadily, the old ham hoisted in as much as possible of his anatomy to give us his Young Guinness as a Student Actor. 'Snake steps out from the screen for dear Athene's opening line: *The paragraphs you say, Mr Snake, were all inserted?* The boy has been for elocution lessons from Martita Hunt – knows his stuff, is fit and able to deliver: *They were Madam, and as I COPIED them myself in a feigned hand, there can be no suspicion whence they CAME.* Martita, bless her, was a stickler for hammering the verb, and Athene, dear old stick, is in tremendous voice.'

Lumsdon cleared his throat, and to do his old pal's celebrated vowels full justice enriched his own. '*The snakes, you say, were all inserted Mr Paragraph?* is what she hits him with on that first night.' He twirled a comic eye to give the patrons of the Ship Inn the cue for a mass gasp at Athene Seyler's gaffe. 'But young Guinness has great things before him and he barely falters, stressing both his verbs: *They were Madam, and as I COPIED them myself in a feigned hand, there can be no suspicion whence they CAME.* They stand unmoving, Snake and Sneerwell, face to face down centre. For the best part of a minute, silence reigns... until, with Snake clasped to her corset and soundlessly convulsing, Sneerwell sinks slowly to the floor. The curtain, seconds later, does the same.'

Lummy gave a little bow with one hand on his wig, before himself subsiding in a chair to round the story off. 'They tried again, poor loves, but got no further than, *The paragraphs, you say...* before the next collapse, which turned out to be terminal for the production. Young Guinness had to wait to make his name as Prince of Denmark at the Old Vic. I forget the year.'

Crazily, I wondered through the laughter if I was brave enough to share with them my own two horses' story of humiliation and disaster, but luckily was saved from more of it by Crispy Flake's compulsion to perform. 'Fasten your seat belts folks it's going to be a bouncy night,' he cried wildly from the bar. 'If we're talking of fluffed lines, you should have been at Drury Lane, folks, when I took on the lead in Andrew Markham's *Counsel for the Defence*. It was a millstone in my career.'

'Too true.' Miss Hayes stared heavenwards. 'I saw it sweetheart; *simply grinding!*'

But Blake by then was well into his monologue. 'Act II is set in the Old Bailey, and as the curtain rises you can only see the top halves of us because we've all been slotted into little wooden boxes; mine's the dock.' He slid off his stool to demonstrate with both arms to his sides. 'Well the scene begins with the Clerk of the Court, played by Jim Crawford, popping up to charge me with the murder of my wife. *Bernard Cole,* (that's my character) *you are charged on indictment for that you on the seventeenth day of November in the County of Surrey murdered Maureen Anne Cole.* Then there's this deadly 'ush onstage and in the stalls, and I stand like a hero, straight and true – to kid them all I'm innocent, you see? Jim's next line is: *Guilty or Not Guilty; how say you, Bernard Cole?* And maybe he was trained by Hunt as well, as all the emphasis is on the *SAY* – *How SAY you, Bernard Cole?* He almost has to shout the *SAY* to give my *Not Guilty* line dramatic empathy.'

'Dramatic emphasis, you cream-faced loon,' bawled Lummy Gould.

'Well I don't know, it was a first house a good way into a long run...' (Nothing short of a well-aimed cosh could have stopped Crispy by then.) 'Jim must have said the line a thousand times and doesn't have to think – or thinks he doesn't have to, which only goes to prove that you should never count spilt milk before you cross it,' Blake explained. 'But anyway...'

Playing as for panto, he awarded us a king-rat-sized wink. 'But anyway... Jim goes and fluffs it, doesn't he? *Bernard Cole, you're charged on indictment for that on the seventeenth day...* He starts well enough; so cold and stern he must have had them quaking in the circle. But when he gets to the *How SAY you, Bernard Cole* line...

'*How ARE you, Bernard Cole?* is what he gives me, twice in case I haven't heard. *How ARE you, Bernard Cole?*

'Well there's silence in the court, another deathly 'ush, and when I look across at Phillip Mason who's the judge, I see his knuckles whiten as he grips the bench. I'll be all right, I tell myself, if no one laughs I'll be all right. I think it best to close my eyes though,' Blake confided. 'But when I open them, they've *gone!* All gone – judge, jurors, everyone but me; slipped down into their little boxes to leave me on my tod.'

He did it well, I'll grant him that. Even Crispy had his moments; and however the audience in Drury Lane may or may not have reacted to it, his story saw us through to midnight closing in a cheerful frame of mind. In fact I'd never heard Mag laugh so loud. Or Auntie Bill. 'How ARE you!' she kept repeating while she buttoned her bike leathers. 'How ARE you, Bernard Cole! It's priceless!'

143

The next time the barman flicked the lights, it was for real.

I staggered to my feet to finish off my pint of Harvey's bitter and watch the queue of cast and locals heading for the door; old Lumsdon with his arm linked through Hughes-Milton's, Miss Hayes and Primme in desultory conversation, Tom Allan stooping to free Nanki's lead from where he'd wound it round a chair.

'Lining up the suspects are we?' Miss Bayliss appeared so suddenly beside me with her knitting, that I did what Mag did with her tea when Primmie told us how she'd dealt with Marilyn. I inhaled my beer.

'If you're running short of motives dear, I can give you two first class ones,' Barbara Bayliss offered. 'Just watch Tom Allan with our Abi when you next see them together, that's my advice. He once played Benedick to her Beatrice; onstage and off if all we hear is true, and with our sweet Primrose none the wiser.'

I stared at her wet-nosed.

'But I wouldn't be surprised if someone told the little wife about it later,' Miss Bayliss added, clicking past me on stiletto trotters. I felt her malice like an icy draught.

Unless it was the nasally recycled beer still dripping down my neck?

Scene 3

Which begins? Well on the Saturday, it had to be, and in my bedroom waking late. Saturdays were matinée days, with two of everything. Two Singapores, two St James's, two Antibes and '*If these shadows have offended…*'

But that was later and I've jumped the gun. It *was* that day but later…

* * *

On Saturdays Mag worked at Antoine's until mid-afternoon. I generally slept in, had brunch when I got up, and left at two o'clock to set up for the first performance – and would have done that Saturday; otherwise I would remember. I do remember getting through the matinée without any silly stunts or anything especially untoward; with the only hitch occurring in Scene 2 of the Raffles play, when old Lummy made his exit through the outside wall of the hotel. But that was normal in its way, and in the second show Miss Hayes had steered him by the elbow through the door. Martin, now I come to think of it, had broken his rule that Saturday of never coming backstage during a performance – by turning up in his red polo-neck to patrol the dressing rooms and wings for both shows in lieu of the police force, and proving a hazard in himself, by generally getting in the way and tripping over anything that wasn't screwed to the floor (and at least one thing that was).

Cordelia and I snatched time together in the first show, while she waited for her mother in the canvas booth they'd rigged up in the wings for her quick change in the St James's play. 'Abi's friend Gilly's in this evening,' she told me, a touch unromantically I thought, just after our first kiss. 'We'll be staying at her place in Lewes afterwards, to kick off Abi's birthday with a champagne breakfast in the morning. But we'll see you later on tomorrow at the picnic, won't we?' she'd added much more to the point – which in my case, as you may well imagine, was already on the rise.

'To find a way to thank me properly for singing out of tune, was what you said,' I reminded her; pressing the point in more ways than one, to feel something like a small electric current pass between us.

That was in the matinée. There were a number of rather rapid tasks we had to complete between the first two plays of the triple-bill in both performances, again with only the dimmest of blue working lights to do them by. After we'd 'gone black', as they say in the theatre, Andrea's job was to nip out of her prompt corner and push the hinged Raffles balustrade back into place. Stan moved props. Len did things with floodlights. I flapped the folded section of the St James's carpet into its original position while the revolve revolved, ran back to the effects table ready to ring the phone bell on the second bar of music – and to go on ringing when the lights came up and Susan Lee, who played the maid, walked on.

Paul thought I needed more practice with the bell, and he was right. Which would have been OK if – well Paul started the taped music; I waited for the second bar as my cue to ring the bell; then counted up to five before ringing it again for Susan's entrance. All this rather as an act of faith, because I

146

couldn't see her waiting in the darkness, and she couldn't see her way on to the set until the lights came up.

Except they didn't, did they. We'd gone down black and stayed there.

BLACKEST BLACKOUT YET

'BUGGER!' (Paul that time, not me.)

The stage electrics in those days ran through a central fuse-box in the murky sump beneath the stage, and while Len found a torch and made his way there, I did the St Edgar's thing and went on ringing the damn phone bell... on and on, until Paul hissed, 'Stop it Sam for fuck's sake, can't you!' To expose us to a restless period of non-silence, made up of muffled thuds and curses backstage and a buzz of lowered voices from the auditorium; the wind before a storm.

Then someone gripped my arm. A torch appeared, and before I really knew what I was doing, I found myself out in the dock with Len, dragging out the long reflectors we'd used one night in panto when a tree brought down the power lines – three footlight sections and two uprights, all lined with foil and socketed for scores of white wax candles packed in boxes in the prop room. It took time by torchlight to set up the candles, and long before we reached the stage with them, we heard a disembodied voice which could only have been Miss Compton's, expounding on the curse of power cuts and the utter wretchedness of Seeboard.

We saw her as we staggered downstage with our burdens, standing out in front before the curtain declaiming like a Redgrave, with Martin beaming torchlight on her face. 'So if you'll all be perfectly angelic and sit tight, my loves – within the frailty of our powers and in the winking of an eye we will go on,' she told the house. 'I promise on my sacred word that you'll be flabbergasted at how *ravishing* we'll look by candlelight!

If these shadows have offended
Think but this and all is mended,
Through the house give glimmering light;
Proceed with revels and delight!'

Not quite what Shakespeare wrote. But trust me, it produced the goods – and the audience who recognised the real McCoy in Abi Compton when they saw it, rose thunderously to her support.

I'd be tempted to tell you that what happened in the next half-hour was indescribable, if that wasn't something of a cop-out, so I'll give it my best shot.

It might sound corny to you, but looking back I think of that performance as pure enchantment; triumph fashioned from disaster. There are times when the connection between a company of actors and their audience just doesn't bond; the laughs refuse to come, the actors lose the will to live and everyone gets bored. That Saturday by candlelight it was completely the reverse. The bond was stronger than I've ever known it – and at the risk of sounding soppy, I'd say that something close to *love* flowed back and forth across the pit in the warm currents of the flames.

If the whole house that night had broken spontaneously into 'Pack up Your Troubles' or 'There's No Business Like Show Business', it wouldn't have surprised me. Because that's how it felt to be there. Candles struck reflections from waxed mirrors and acrylic window panes on the St James's set, cast dancing shadows on the canvas walls. Playing downstage almost in the laps of the front row, the actors delighted the audience with inspired new business. Shamelessly, they hammed up their entrances, exaggerating moves, shading eyes to peer at one another and introduce entire routines of blind man's bluff mishandlings and collisions. With masterly ham-fistedness they fumbled props and slopped their drinks over each other's costumes.

As for their star; Miss Compton was determined to provide them with a treat, and did so – which was no surprise. But she took things to another level. She wasn't a large woman, was actually quite small. Yet somehow she *expanded*, contriving by some magic of her own to fill the theatre from the stage door to the gods. When Tom Allan began his piece on the piano, she sauntered over to him with a lighted candelabrum, negligently concealing its true weight, to perform her part of their duet as a hilarious parody of Liberace channelling Gertie Lawrence, and conducting a masterclass in the art of improvisation. In the closing scene of the St James's piece, she brought the house down by attempting to paint her toenails with a torch held in her teeth, and ending with a long stripe of scarlet varnish from her big toe to her kneecap.

She was Wonder Woman. She was Sarah Siddons, Ellen Terry, Gertie Lawrence, all the greats (throw in Streep, Dench and Mirren if you like), and the audience just lapped her up. Not a programme rustled. No one coughed. All we heard were sighs of pleasure, loud bursts of laughter all in the right places and prolonged applause. So if the saboteur imagined they could break her, I can only say that he or she had made a big mistake.

Apparently, when Len reached the central fuse-box in the sump he'd found our joker had removed all three of the old-fashioned barrel fuses it held along with all the spares – and with the only sources of replacements being other theatres of the town, he'd whizzed off in the batmobile with Crispy Flake to see what they could find; whizzing back again in less time than anyone had dared to hope with three of the Winter Garden's precious spares. Martin thought it best to wait until after the second interval before going light.

The curtain rose on the Third Act, to blind the audience with the sudden glare of artificial sunlight, reflected off an artificial sea on to the recumbent forms of Sadie and Freddie Fawcett in their Antibes bedroom. Of course they'd all applauded loyally – although in contrast to the glimmering gold and silver of the previous scene, and without another curtain speech to warn them, the whole thing must have come to them as something of an anticlimax. There hadn't been another speech before the curtain, because from seconds after it had fallen the star and her producer were locked in combat. We could hear them shouting at each other from behind the closed door of Miss Compton's dressing room all through the second interval.

Not that the outcome of that argument could have ever been in doubt. 'Because when Abi digs her heels in, she's as stubborn as an opera diva let alone a mule,' Cordelia told me later. Her mother had warned Martin she would leave the show the very instant that the police arrived, Cordelia said, regardless of her contract – had even gone as far as taking down her telegrams and packing up her make-up before the poor man acknowledged his defeat.

***

There were no drinks in the Ship Inn for us that night. None of us could leave the theatre, we were told in no uncertain terms, until the stage cloth had been scraped clean of every last blob of candle grease and then scrubbed thoroughly with soap and water. Len rigged an extension lead for Andrea to iron the wax out of the carpets through sheets of blotting paper from the front office. We'd done it all before in panto and knew how long the whole thing would be bound to take.

Before she joined her mother for their trip to Lewes with Miss Compton's best friend Gilly, Cordelia came to find me with a scrubbing brush on hands and knees surrounded by wet lino. She waited for Andrea's second expedition to the office for more blotting paper, before asking me point blank who I suspected as the fuse thief. 'So what have you decided, Sammy? Any vital clues?' I told her what Miss Bayliss had to say the night before about Miss Compton and Tom Allan. But that was all stale news according to Cordelia.

'If all the men Abi has slept with were laid end-to-end,' she said with a short laugh, 'I wouldn't be at all surprised.'

'Well, unless they're all in it together, we can narrow down the field to Crispy Flake, Miss Bayliss and the Allans, as the only four who had the chance to switch on the revolve,' I reported. 'And Mrs Allan was onstage when Nanki-Poo escaped, remember? Which brings it down to three.'

Cordelia stared at me in admiration. 'Genius! How clever of you, Sammy.' And perhaps because I was on hands and knees still, patted me like a damp dog. 'They'll all be there tomorrow for the picnic anyway, and we can watch to see how each of them behaves with Abi on her birthday, can't we. That should help. But don't forget her card though will you, Sammy? And whatever else you do, for pity's sake don't mention *you-know-what*.'

'What?'

'The Government Top Secret.'

'What?'

'HER AGE!' But softened by the childish voice, the Mona Lisa smile. 'Her sodding age, you clot!'

THE LIGHTS SLOWLY FADE

151

Scene 4

TRANSFORMATION: As the lights come up the figures on the stage, the soap, the scrubbing brush and bucket, the deep red fabric of the tabs, the scenery, carpets, furniture and painted flats dissolve through gauze, transforming, taking substance as a sunlit landscape – as the June page of a Sussex calendar. At least that's what it looks like, being mostly white on green – white cricketers and umpires, white weather-boarded pavilion, white sight screens against a wide green ground. Across the cricket pitch, and freckled with white sheep, extends the paler parkland grass of the Hadderton estate. Beyond that, the milk-white frontage of the mansion stands against the grey-green whaleback of the downs. Above it all enough blue sky to make trousers for a whole ship's company of sailors.

To reach the cricket field at Hadderton you have to pass the main drive to the house, with its pillared gateway and squat Georgian lodge. The car park is around the corner just off the village street, with a footpath through the trees to open out into the scene I've just described – a game of weekend cricket in a noble landscape; a view so picture-perfect, so totally self-confidently English, that on first sight of it you almost had to laugh. The day was brilliant with a gentle breeze; the sort of golden summer day June promises but seldom actually delivers.

But sorry – what with one thing and another, I'm not sure how much I've said about the cricket game, apart from mentioning it that is. Did I say it was a 'friendly' match between the tenants of the Hadderton estate near Lewes and a team of Sunday players known as The Eastbourne Thespians drawn from the staff and actors of three local theatres? Well anyway, that's what it was, and how I explained it to Primmie Allan on the drive from Eastbourne; as an annual, limited-overs contest which Martin and Hughes-Milton, who were playing, had chosen as the setting for Abi Compton's birthday picnic. We'd driven up there in the Allans' sit-up-and-beg Ford Popular, with Primmie in the front with Tom, and me in the back with a malodorous Nanki-Poo and equally smelly string bag crammed with a collection of his rubber balls and plastic toys.

'But why weren't you picked to play, Tommy dear?' his wife wished to know. 'You batted so beautifully in that *Crocodile Called Clancy* film. The one where the croc ate the cricket ball, dear.'

And Tom was still attempting to convince her that it had been a stunt-double who had whacked the ball into the creature's gaping mouth, and that the ball was made of rolled-up steak, when we drove past the gates of Hadderton, and Primmie interrupted him to ask who owned the mansion. She did it again as we walked out into the open from the footpath – to ask why all the fields were full of goats. 'Actually they're sheep,' I told her. 'They only look like that because they've just been shorn.

'But look, that's Lord Southbourne over there, the chap who owns the house.' I pointed to an individual in an ancient panama and shabby blazer, deep in conversation with Lummy Gould. 'He's mad on cricket – always came to watch our First Eleven at St Edgar's.'

'Same as 'is Granfer,' a doleful voice informed us. 'Twelfth Earl 'ad 'is leg blown off somewhen at Wipers, an' still went an' scored a bleddy century agin Alciston, didn' 'e?'

'Fancy, did he really, dear?' Primmie smiled vaguely at a toothless old man wedged between two other local relics on a park bench behind us.

'Aye, 'e did an' all – an' 'ad 'is bleddy butler do the runnin' for 'im, didn' 'e.'

'How very enterprising of him, dear.'

Then: '*COOEE, YOO-HOO!*' Primmie yelled, waving madly at the Misses Hayes and Bayliss standing over by the weather-boarded pavilion – Yvonne Hayes in beads and culottes, and Barbara Bayliss in a Breton beret with her lower portions squeezed into a pair of peach-coloured Capri pants which on her looked less like Audrey Hepburn than, if I'm honest, Pigling Bland.

Our team were fielding. Martin, captain for the day, was fidgeting behind the wicket keeper in the slips. Len in his usual hunched posture was out at square leg. Crispin, typecast at silly-mid-on, was leaning forward eagerly with two-thirds of his shirt buttons cast adrift; and Nigel H-M, bowling, was in the act of delivering a ball which was pitched perfectly to strike the middle stump – or would have been, if as we watched the huge bearded batsman at the crease hadn't slashed it casually across the field, to part Crispy's chest hair in its flight, remove some paint from the pavilion, and set Nanki off into the yap-equivalent of a Thompson submachine gun.

The umpire held up both arms for the six. Hughes-Milton plunged both hands into his sandy hair, and the numbers on the scoreboard flipped up to eighty-four for two. 'That's it Tiny, knock 'em to buggery!' shouted the old gaffer on the bench; adding for our benefit, 'We call 'im Tiny Tomsett cos 'e's built so delicate. Used to be the blacksmith didn' 'e when we still 'ad the forge.' And watching the colossal Tomsett settle down to do as he was told, I couldn't help rating our team's chances of victory at something pretty close to zero.

By then Tom Allan had found a spare deckchair beside a wire waste basket full of paper bags and orange peel, and settled down to light his pipe and read the morning papers. Nanki called a ceasefire, and after complimenting Miss Hayes on her costume and charitably ignoring Barbara's, Primmie made a beeline for the Earl of Southbourne standing in the porch of the pavilion. Close-to, he looked inbred with pinkish gooseberry eyes and matching freckles, and there were moth holes round the collar of his blazer.

'I totally adore your house! It's just *too thrillingly* romantic,' trilled Primmie in the role of Lady Kitty from *The Circle* when she was introduced. 'All those generations of your family! I think heredity's *too wonderful*, don't you? I'm sure you must have a perfect fund of stories!'

'Debrett's.' Lord Southbourne tipped his hat politely. 'You'll find us in Debrett's, dear lady. Scores of Stanvilles – classic record.'

'*Lovely* dear,' gushed Lady Kitty, 'who's on it, singing what?'

'Ah, yes I see...' His lordship fumbled for a non-existent chin and failed to rub it. 'Mean we're a pretty dull lot, don't ye know – breed sheep and marry cousins. Make a point of dyin' in our beds.'

'But some of you must have been dashing, surely?'

'Sir Dickon Stanville – meant to have had a thing with Good Queen Bess.' The earl coughed modestly. 'Way we got the earldom so they say.'

'There you see, *too wonderful!*' cried Primmie, 'I knew you couldn't all be boring, dear.'

'An' then there was the heir, young Viscount Denton – took a famous whore… excuse me, a famous courtesan along with him on his Grand Tour.'

'Gorgeous! *Gloriously romantic!*' Laughing wildly, Lady Kitty all but clapped her hands.

'But nothin' came of it,' his lordship gloomily confessed. 'Got back, bred sheep an' married his first cousin. Couldn't seem to break the habit, d'ye see.' He gave another modest cough – which Nanki-Poo, who'd been snuffling round his trouser bottoms, took as a signal to bite through the threadbare fabric and gain a purchase on his lordship's bony shin.

It all happened in slow motion. Or that's the way it seemed from where I stood. On some kind of sporting reflex – uttering as he did so a series of the shortest oaths he'd learned at Eton, Lord Southbourne drop-kicked Nanki into touch. 'By heaven there's a leap!' declaimed Lummy Gould, as helplessly we watched the pekinese rise steeply from the top step of the pavilion, describe a feathery arc above the deckchairs and nosedive into the grass beyond – where he lay flattened, yapless.

'Oh dear! Poor you! Poor darling Nanki-Poo!' cried Primmie, bolting down the steps to scoop up the winded dog and clasp him to her breast. But then, having found him more or less intact, reverted instantly to Lady Kitty. 'I really can't think what possessed him. I do hope, My Lord, he didn't break the skin? I've left his toys back in the car you see. I expect that's why he chose your leg.

'I wonder if you'd be a love and go and fetch them for me, would you, Sammy dear? You can ask Tom for the key.' The eyes she turned on me were full of Melanie Wilkes-style unshed tears. 'And take poor Nanki would you dear, to keep him out of harm's way?'

I left her and the earl (by then brick red) apologising profusely to each other, to collect the car key from behind Tom's newspaper – and with a still-shocked-to-limpness Nanki under one arm, was halfway down the footpath to the car park before I dared to laugh. I'd found his bag of toys, had set him on his feet, clipped on the lead and relocked the Allans' car, when from the wings a pale grey Jaguar appeared with Miss Compton in the front.

'Bubo! Treasure!' The famous voice sliced through the passenger window. Then as the car drew level, the famous presence materialised to perfume the air for miles around. In addition to the famous smile, she wore white sailor's bell-bottoms (Dior again for all I knew), a dozen clanking bracelets, knuckleduster rings and enough gold chains to bring a lord mayor to his knees. Her blonde hair was swept back into some kind of flimsy scarf arrangement and she wore the biggest sunglasses I'd ever seen.

'Many happy returns of the day,' I said self-consciously, remembering too late that I'd left the too-pink card in Eastbourne.

'In my experience, dear heart, the last thing one requires of birthdays are returns.' She did the silvery peal. 'Well, goodbye Gilly, enjoy the lunch,' addressed to the head-scarfed driver of the Jag, as Cordelia jumped out of one of its back doors.

'Ta-ra dear, break a leg!' The other woman's voice was younger than her face, which looked surprisingly familiar. She drove off with a jaunty wave.

Cordelia mouthed 'Hello' at me behind her mother's back, and I just had time to think how pretty she looked, all in denim with her long hair in bunches like Looby Loo on *Andy Pandy*, before Miss Compton tweaked Nanki's string bag of rubber toys from my free hand, passed it to her daughter, and slipped a manicured hand through my arm. 'Much as I adore our darling Gilly, all she could talk about was her fourth husband's fling with June Aldrich,' she confided, 'which comes a little rich from a gal who feels the need to drop her knickers for any leading man who isn't a committed nancy. One's heard she made some sort of an exception of Oliver Barry as her Romeo—' (my cue to realise just *who* they'd spent the night with in her Lewes hideaway) 'although, considering the demands that Lady Barry made, the poor man simply didn't have it in him.

'Besides which, Gilly thinks Oliver's a shit,' Miss Compton added, while we watched the car containing her best pal (Dame Gillian Dashwood, only the *greatest classical actress alive!*) swing out into the lane. With bracelets jangling, Miss Compton waved away a cloud of gnats and stopped to light a fag. By then we had emerged to view the cricket field and several hundred of Lord Southbourne's sheep. 'What are those comic creatures, goats?'

'Sheep, Border Leicesters actually,' I recited. 'They look like that because they've just been shorn.'

'Which would account for their long faces I suppose? How *frightfully bucolic!*' Miss Compton's laugh immediately turned every head in her direction, on and off the field. Distaste for countryside pursuits was demonstrated for their benefit in the elaborate way she placed one high-heeled foot before the other on her walk across the grass to the pavilion, with the suggestion of a ballerina in a minefield.

They were already singing 'Happy Birthday' well before she reached them; and it was Barbara Bayliss of all people who stepped forward with a bouquet of peonies in her plump white hands, to present them with a look of acid sweetness on her painted face. Miss Compton's shades were mirrored. So you couldn't see her eyes when she pressed her palms together in a mime of helpless delight. 'You shouldn't have, you really shouldn't have, my darlings!' she exclaimed – and you can bet she meant it.

* * *

To tell the truth, I'm having trouble after all these years remembering what happened next in that long, fun-filled afternoon at Hadderton. Was it then Miss Compton made her speech?

No, not then. That had to follow the thing in the paper, surely? I think it must have been the singing, sending Nanki off into another barrage of demented yapping, which actually came next. That and what Cordelia said, and my absurd mistake.

'Kick his balls Sam,' she'd whispered in my ear – and I'd whispered that I couldn't because the wretched mutt was facing the wrong way round and anyway I couldn't see them through the hair, and she'd hissed, 'NOT THOSE BALLS, you twerp' – before it dawned on me that Cordelia meant the rubber balls we'd brought from Eastbourne in the bag – and had glanced shamefacedly at Primmie to see if she had heard – and found her looking horrified instead at something her husband Tom had just read in the local rag... Yes, all that had to come before Miss Compton's speech.

'You have to see this, Abi!' Primmie shrilled. 'It's absolutely *foul!*' Then before Tom or anyone could stop her, dashed over in the role of Hildy in *My Girl Friday*, to show Miss Compton and the rest of us what they had found.

It was in the STOP PRESS column on the front page of the *Eastbourne Gazette and Herald*:

STAR BIRTHDAY. Miss Abigail Compton, one of our most

popular and distinguished actresses, today celebrates her sixtieth birthday. She plans an al fresco luncheon party for a small group of friends and colleagues before returning to the Meads Theatre, Eastbourne, for next week's performances of Neil Craven's smash hit play, THREE SEASONS OF SADIE.

With a small decisive movement Miss Compton snapped in half the sunglasses she'd taken off to read the article and dropped them at her feet. 'How too screamingly funny,' she said, deadpan. 'We're all in stitches, sweetie-pie.'

From the cricket pitch there came the dull sound of a ball in contact with a cotton-wadded pad, followed at a hundred decibels by a banshee cry of: '*HOWZZAATT??!!*' Our team, with all arms raised, appealed to heaven for a verdict. We saw the umpire shake his head, and Tiny Tomsett flick the ball back up the pitch to a despairing H-M. The awkward silence that followed that was broken suddenly by someone speaking loudly, almost shouting. It was me. 'Miss Bayliss,' I blurted, 'it was Barbara Bayliss – we saw her at the newspaper office on Wednesday, didn't we Cordelia?' I turned to her for confirmation and she nodded.

'I don't know what you mean,' Miss Bayliss said with dignity. But by then of course we all knew what she'd done.

The truth, Gaston exclaimed. *He has the habit of exposing himself, n'est pas? Once all the facts are placed before us, mes amis, the solution he is évidente.*

But tell me really, did *you* think that it was her? In your classic thriller if the villain doesn't prove to be the least likely suspect (i.e. Primmie), they do fairly often turn out to have been one of the front-runners (e.g. Miss Bayliss as the jealous understudy, seething with resentment beneath the Russian dolly paint). 'I felt her malice like an icy draught,' was how I'd put it on the Friday.

'A tiny point of order, darlings...' Yes, *that* was when Miss Compton launched into her speech.

'Today I've reached the tricky age of fifty, give or take a long weekend – too old for Peter Pan, too young for Mother Goose. I can no longer pass for thirty-nine. My skin has softened and my arteries have hardened. But to quote the old Hollywood proverb, my darling chums, my teeth are still my own. So are my boobs – and whatever my exquisite understudy here has told the press, I'll still have to wait another decade before I qualify for a state pension.

'And that my angelic Barbara takes you off I think with a chorus of loud boos.' (The *killer line*.)

For perhaps thirty seconds Miss Bayliss remained in freeze-frame, quite still. Then drawing on technique, she rolled her knitting, turned to expose us to a double dose of peach posteriors, and bounced them off in the direction of the car park.

'I had a mother-in-law like that once,' observed Miss Compton – as if mothers-in-law came in sets; which in her case I suppose they might have. 'Jealous to the point of lunacy, ridiculous old trout.'

So that was it; a victory without a battle. Or as Gaston might have put it (if I hadn't just that moment sacked him), *The case is dried and cut, n'est pas?*

Again too obvious, would you think; another anticlimax?

Well, I wouldn't argue – was even thinking something of the sort myself, while we watched Miss Bayliss reach the trees and disappear from view. She'd shared a taxi out to Hadderton with Yvonne Hayes and Lummy Gould. Which meant she'd have to summon up another one from the phone box in the village, then sit and wait for it to drive up all the way from Eastbourne to collect her – and think about her sins while she was waiting?

One could but hope.

Scene 5

The cricket match had begun earlier than usual to allow time for the first team batting to declare after twenty overs if they survived that long, in the hope of drawing stumps soon after tea; and thanks largely to the prowess of their blacksmith, the village team had already notched up 163 for 5 by lunchtime.

Moist mountains of white sandwiches were provided for the picnic. We'd all contributed towards a cream-filled, mercifully candle-free sponge birthday cake from the Swiss bakery in Eastbourne. Martin produced a jeroboam of champagne (tasting a good bit better than Babycham, I thought, even in plastic cups, although not as good as Coca Cola). In a wicker chair provided by the earl and wreathed in cigarette smoke, the birthday girl herself held court in front of the pavilion to queues of bashful cricketers in search of autographs, which she scrawled grandly for them on their paper plates. She even signed a sweat-soaked cricket shirt the young villager inside it swore he'd never wash.

If she didn't actively encourage it, Miss Compton gave no sign of objecting to such adulation. Except when Martin attempted to express it in a speech beginning with 'Dear Friends' and ending with a tactless misquote from Antony and Cleopatra: *Age cannot wither her, nor custom stale her infinite variety!* – a line that earned him one of Abi Compton's lower wattage smiles.

I can't think anyone familiar with my history would be surprised by what I was busy planning while all this was going on. Having received another look of naked promise from Cordelia over lunch – in a furtive exploration of the scrub between the back of the pavilion and the car park, I'd found a sort of hollow in the long grass, vibrating with the sound of crickets and large enough to hide a body. Or shall we say *two* bodies lying side by side, or even better stacked? I sold the idea to Cordelia in a more eager-beaverish than suave-Bondish way during Martin's damp squib of a speech. But if that sounds unromantic, can only tell you that she bought it with the gentlest of smiles – followed by something less so under cover of my paper plate that for the moment left me with blurred vision and an open mouth.

What we decided was to wait until all eyes were on our Thespians going in to bat before attempting our own version of *Splendor in the Grass*. That was the plan, and although I'm not saying that the number of cups of bubbly I'd downed by then had anything to do with it, after years of 'preparation' shall we say, you can bet your boots that I was primed and ready! The champagne gave out some time before the Hadderton team declared, and I was on my way back to the bar with a pound note from Abi Compton to buy us all a round of something else, when I met Martin just inside the door of the pavilion.

'Ah Sam, the very man,' he said without preamble and as usual looking everywhere but at me. 'Crispin's understudy's just thrown up his sandwiches and may not be fit to play.' Forgetting the half pint of pale ale in his left hand, he mimed a Denis Compton leg drive and slopped most of it across my feet. 'So we're looking for another bat, dear boy.'

'Not me.' I meant it as a statement. But Martin chose to take it as a question.

'Yes you Sam, naturally.' He slapped me on the back to add a further splash of Double Diamond to the puddle on the floor. 'A straight bat's second nature to you public school chaps, we all know that.'

'Well perhaps.' I gave a hollow laugh. 'But I'm well out of practice, Martin – bound to be.'

'Nonsense you'll be fine.' He lost the last dregs of his beer attempting to adjust his glasses. 'Good lad; it's ten to one you won't be needed anyway.' Which suited me just fine, as the only innings I had in mind was off the pitch and over the deep cover boundary. At the bar I bought a G an' T for Miss Compton; in the absence of a Babycham, a white wine for Cordelia and a pale ale for myself.

The village team eventually declared at 176 for 6, and our opening batsmen were already on the field by the time I'd handed out the drinks and settled with my Double Diamond on the grass. Both bats were members of the Devonshire Park Theatre stage crew – first to the crease, a weedy ginger-haired lad by the name of Ben, who began with a defensive Trevor Bailey stroke straight down the line. On the next delivery he pulled back for an ambitious sky shot, that not only sent the ball up vertically, but due to an uncertain grip, the bat as well. The ball was caught at short leg. The wicket keeper caught the bat. '*HOWZZAATT??!!*' eleven players yelled. The umpire raised a finger. Someone in the outfield quacked derisively, and the spent force that was ginger Ben began his walk of shame.

Right-o, I thought, exchanging a warm-to-scorching look with Cordelia, who was sitting with her legs tucked under her blue denim skirt on the far side of her mother's chair. A light breeze stirred the grass invitingly at the back of the pavilion. Right-o, I told myself – just one more over, *then* we'll go!

'What is it do you suppose that makes men's little bums in cricket whites so *irresistibly* attractive?' Miss Compton took a long reflective sip of her G an' T as Nigel H-M strode past us on his way out to the pitch. 'I think it has to be the pads, don't you – the way they force their knees apart?' No one ventured an opinion, although a stealthy tightening of Hughes-Milton's creamy rear as he approached the crease and took his guard suggested that he'd heard. The first ball pitched outside the leg stump and H-M sent it sailing high over mid-wicket. We followed its long descent into the grass on the park-side of the boundary, and had begun to clap when, with a muffled thud and single high-pitched bleat, one of his lordship's sheep received it hard between the ears and instantly keeled over.

'There then, danged if 'e 'ent killed the bugger!' the yokel on the bench remarked approvingly, and seemed disappointed when the poor thing struggled to its feet to stagger off behind its scattering companions, listing heavily to port.

After that first six, Hughes-Milton, who was clearly better treading grass than boards, hit a single, slashed the next ball through the covers for an easy four, hooked another to the boundary beyond square leg and took three double runs off Hadderton's slow bowler; to leave the other batsman in the crease when they changed ends.

Okay that's *it!* I told myself, gulping down my beer and rising briskly to my feet.

'Think I'll just give the old legs a stretch you know, in case I have to bat,' I said aloud. 'Um... fancy a short stroll yourself, Cordelia?' Another glance between us, practically red hot.

'Darling what a perfectly *splendid* idea! Of course she would adore to help you stretch them.' Without her sunglasses, Miss Compton had to crane her neck and shade her eyes with her free hand to study my expression. 'But while you're on your feet, dear heart,' she handed me her empty glass, 'perhaps a little detour to the bar?'

While I was there still, juggling the drinks, another

deafening appeal outside was followed by an even louder cheer – and it was Len's slight figure we applauded as our next man in. The bowler he faced down the pitch was obviously from his huge shape and bushy beard the same Tiny Tomsett who'd knocked H-M's bowling all around the field. But unlike his predecessor, who barely took two steps before he bowled, the bearded giant began his run-up somewhere near the long-on boundary, looming ever larger as he charged head-down towards the wicket. He reached the point of take-off as a cross between a helicopter and a demented gorilla, to shoot the ball straight at Len's head at roughly half the speed of light.

Len ducked and lived, but was so shattered by the experience that with the next ball he committed suicide, leaping from its path to watch it, not so much scattering his stumps as smashing them to smithereens. They had to send for some more.

Our fifth man in was Crispin Blake; and while finishing my Double Diamond, I simply had to stay to witness what I was mean enough to hope would be his downfall – and wasn't disappointed. Having swaggered out on to the pitch, Crispy made a big thing of patting its already flattened mud and rearranging several blades of grass before he took his guard. Striking an heroic pose with bat upraised – trying for sardonic but achieving something closer to moronic, and absolutely *asking for it* as far as I was concerned – he waited for the ball to leave the bowler's hand. His bat was still heroically upraised, when like a thunderbolt, the ball angled in to leg, cut back to smack him smartly in the crotch with a sound like a pistol shot, then slowly rolled on into his stumps.

At which point Blake for once did shrill and ample justice to his vowels. 'Yeiiee'aaa'oooo-oouch!!

Seconds later the wider field did likewise, with another heartfelt '*HOWZZAATT!!??*'

'Middle leg before, poor chap,' Tom Allan murmured from his deckchair, as once again the umpire raised a symbolic finger. Blake, spurning ribald offers from all sides to rub or kiss it better, stomped off the field with a face (and one might assume the contents of his cricket box) as black as thunder. Pitiful, you said it – and serve him right, the git.

SO, NOW! GO NOW! I urged myself in the moment that an accidental contact with the back pocket of my jeans and the diminished Pack of Three (now down to two) reminded me of where I wished and ought and absolutely must be with Cordelia!

I looked across to where she stood behind the Earl of Southbourne who was in earnest conversation with her mother, and was about to interrupt them when Martin clapped me on the shoulder. 'Me next,' he said by way of explanation for the shrunken schoolboy's cap and tattered pads tied on with string that he was wearing. 'I'm putting you in ninth, dear – and the way that blighter's steaming through the wickets, I'd find yourself some gear if I were you. Good lad.' He dropped his bat, retrieved it, pushed his glasses up his nose and loped off unsteadily to face the demon bowler.

'Darling, how *unfortunate* for you.' Miss Compton made it clear that she'd not only overheard, but guessed far more than I'd supposed. 'That means you'll have to change and miss your little stroll with my poor Mouse here, won't you?' She sketched a smile of sympathy. 'So *desperately* frustrating for you both!'

Cordelia, half-hidden by the earl's moth-eaten blazer, moved out to let me see her face; and did I imagine it, or was there something of relief in the small shrug she gave?

Len lent me his own bat and gloves and cricket box and managed to unearth a mouldy set of pads from somewhere in the depths of the pavilion, glumly handing me another Double

Diamond while I strapped them on over my jeans. 'To put lead in your pencil, Sam boy. Christ knows you're going to need it.' He heaved a sombre sigh.

By some miracle the Hughes-Milton/Martin partnership held up for six more overs after I'd appeared in cricket togs with beer in hand from the pavilion. Upstaged this time by no one, and having given the village bowling more of the right treatment, H-M was fast approaching his century when a lucky catch at first slip dispatched Martin with a halfway to impressive score of twenty-six. Next in was the house manager from the Eastbourne Winter Garden, whom we'd been told was something of a useful bat, as it turned out with limited success. The lethal combination of Tiny Tomsett's flesh-seeking missiles and a deceptively innocuous slow left-arm bowler with a knack for deflecting balls from divots on to unsuspecting stumps, saw out the Winter Garden man and two more batsmen for a total of thirty-five more runs.

It was my chance for glory, and quite possibly (depending on the village blacksmith) death as well, with three wickets still in hand and just thirteen runs between our Thespians and a famous victory. The last man had been caught off the fifth ball of the over. So, unless the next delivery went wide and all the fielders happened to be comatose, my best hope of survival would be to score a single and put Hughes-Milton back in the crease to finish what he'd started.

My confidence back then, as I think we have established, was unreliable to say the least. But there were still times when it stepped up to the mark, and this I'm happy to report was one of them. It might have been Cordelia's thumbs-up sign, or Miss Compton's professionally supportive smile, or even Len's constrictive cricket box squeezing testosterone into my system – but was more likely to have been the four cups of bubbly and and three one-pint bottles of Double Diamond pale ale I'd drunk that did it. *A Double Diamond works wonders, works wonders...* I kept repeating the TV jingle on my way out to the crease, and having reached it asked for middle and leg. One always does. Don't ask me why.

A Double Diamond works wonders, works wonders... I planted my short, but I will say serviceably sturdy legs apart, and waited for the onslaught. At the far end of the pitch, by squinting hard to bring him into focus, I could just see Tiny Tomsett striding off into the distance before I lost him altogether. I spotted him again somewhere behind the umpire, doubling his size with every gallop. Squinting again to bring him into focus, I gripped the bat with the D D jingle looping through my brain: ... *works wonders, works wonders, a Double Diamond works wonders...* Tomsett's mighty thighs as he approached the further wicket were pumping like the pistons on a steam train... *works wonders, works wonders...* He hit the buffers with his left foot forward, releasing the ball from a great meat-plate of a hand to send it hurtling down the pitch – in a way one might have applauded if one wasn't on the receiving end and absolutely blotto.

... *works wonders, works wonders; so drink some today!* To say I followed the ball on to the bat would be a lie. I couldn't even swear my eyes were open when the leather hit the willow with a force that stung me through my gloves and jarred me to the elbows. For the match record, mine was an agricultural shot sent wide of middle stump, and although I can hardly claim to have planned it, cleared the fielder at mid-wicket, might even have gone on to reach the boundary if he'd been slower on his pins. In any case we ran – to break my duck and put us both where we belonged when the field changed over, with me safe by the umpire and H-M facing the slow bowler.

He scored another six off the first ball, and then a four.

But on the last ball of the over and with only two more runs between our Thespians and a famous victory, he tried a classic cut-shot, but ended with a thick top edge. The ball arced high into the sky, became invisible for what seemed minutes, to reappear exactly where we wished it hadn't for a straight descent into the cupped hands of the man on cover boundary. For Hughes-Milton with a total score of 125 to his credit, dismissal came as no disgrace; and when our last man in, my friend the effects man Paul, somehow chipped a single off the ferocious Tomsett, the scores drew level for a draw.

To leave me – yes, ME would you believe – to play the winning shot. Inebriated, with uncertain vision, by then dying for a pee, with Tiny Tomsett breathing fire and sensing blood, I was I knew (to use the term cricketers prefer for such contingencies) IN DEEPEST SHIT!

Of course I'd like to tell you that I *worked* the wonder, *saved* the day. But life seldom works that way I find, or not for me at least – and the end when it came was yet another anticlimax. I took my stand, watched Tomsett on his run-up inflate himself from tiny to titanic and deliver the ball as usual with the force of a tornado. After that I'm not quite sure… I think I knew the ball was short; heard rather than saw it land, stepped forward for my trademark nettle-scything sweep, and missed. Or as they put it in the match report: 'The ball missed young Ashby, but not the wicket keeper.'

He caught it while I was out of crease and flung it casually into the wicket.

Caps were thrown. Cheers were cheered, the home team hoisted Tiny Tomsett on their shoulders (it took five of them to do it); and although no one hoisted me, everyone was kind. Well almost everyone. I'd already had a 'Darling, *darling* you were *splendid!*' from Miss Compton, and a dimpled 'Bad

171

luck, Sammy,' from Cordelia, when Blake raised the bottle he'd been drinking out of, to toast me from the steps of the pavilion. 'Here's to the hero of the hour,' he sneered. 'Shame that it's not you.'

Minutes later, letting out a grateful stream of urine in the pavilion gents, and wondering if in spite of everything I still had time to slip off with Cordelia for the outstanding episode of *Splendor in the Grass* while the rest of them were having tea, I was electrified (and accidentally dampened) by a blood-curdling cry from somewhere close at hand. Zipping up and running out, the first thing that I saw was Crispy Flake clutching at his throat.

Someone else was bleating – either Primmie or a sheep. But it was Miss Hayes who seized her moment for the tag line: 'The bottle, it was in the bottle!' she projected in a high but perfectly articulated staccato at Verona amphitheatre pitch.

'Dear Lord, the poor man has been poisoned!'

CLIMAX, PICTURE AND SLOW CURTAIN

Scene 6

But he wasn't was he, poisoned I mean. More's the pity.

You might even say that Crispy's habit of not being dead was becoming slightly tiresome; in this case adding insect to injury (kick me if you must) with an angry wasp reacting as any insect with a sting is likely to when decanted from a bottle on to a human tongue.

Tom Allan removed his pipe to show the creature to us squirming in a wisp of spittle on the pavilion steps, before he crushed it with a sensibly shod foot to give us his Doctor Brooke from *Emergency Ward 10*. 'Now then, put out your tongue and keep it out until the ambulance arrives,' he told his patient sternly. Only to ruin the effect by giggling like a schoolgirl at the impromptu Maori haka Crispin was performing, with protruding tongue and starting eyes and everything akimbo. 'Hmmm, yes indeed…' The giggle merged too late into a would-be kindly smile of reassurance as Doctor Brooke informed the patient he was lucky not to have his windpipe slit open with a penknife, and advised him not to talk.

I won't say Crispin whimpered. No actually on second thoughts and while we're on the subject of schoolgirls, I think I will. Because I'm here to tell you he was still whimpering like the big girl's blouse he was, when Tom Allan asked who would volunteer to call an ambulance from the village. (Mobiles were still decades away remember, with rural calls in 1963 by courtesy of residents or the nearest public phone box.)

In the event it was the Earl of Southbourne who cleared his throat again portentously, to say he had a telephone up in the house that he'd be glad to put at our disposal. His pinkish gooseberry eyes were resting on Miss Compton as he said it – and never one to miss a cue: 'How *heavenly* of you my lord to offer! *Too spoiling, utterly!*' She caught him in the beam of an industrial-strength famous smile, then turned to Doctor Tom.

'Let me go with his gorgeous lordship, darling. I'll take Bubo with me. He's so sensible, and we'll be back in half a jiff.' Switching off the power-beam, and with a surprising turn of speed for someone in high heels, she hopped into the earl's battered Land Rover parked alongside the pavilion and beckoned me to follow.

* * *

Hadderton Place if you've never seen it is blatantly ancestral; as fine a pile as any in the land; all white stone and Georgian windows with glossy green magnolias and trellises of jasmine to soften its long horizontal lines – a mansion large enough to stun, yet small enough to look as if one might just make a go of living there, with three or four hard-working daily women, a brace or two of gardeners and a team of super-fit young groundsmen. Lord Southbourne led the way in from the drive between stone bollards, up a flight of steps and across a terrace planted with square beds of bright pink single roses hedged with box.

'*Rosa Stanvilleii*, always grown 'em, seems they like the chalk,' he told Miss Compton proudly. 'Tenth earl claimed we brought 'em back from the Crusades, although I doubt that's true. More likely to have brought back a Moslem head I should have thought.' Ushering us through a garden door into a library lined with bookshelves, he waved a freckled hand at the carved fireplace: 'Grinlin' Gibbons,' then at a naked statuette, 'an' that's a Rysbrack.'

The telephone was on an inlaid table beneath the life-sized portrait of a woman with red ringlets draped across aggressively bared breasts, identified by Lord Southbourne as the merry monarch's mistress, Barbara Palmer. 'Fourth earl's pal as well they say.' His descendant gave us a genial wink. 'Dare say our guides could tell ye' more.'

'Dyed hair and false eyebrows,' remarked Miss Compton.

Using her heels destructively on the oak flooring, she crossed it to a chair beside the portrait and with one long painted nail dialled 999. 'What's that? Yes, yes *Emergency*, we need an ambulance as soon as you can send one.' And when they put her through: 'Yes please, an ambulance; it's for a wasp sting... Where? Beside the cricket field at Hadderton... Oh, no, I see – it was the tongue; he was stung on the *tongue!*'

She put her hand across the receiver to give a shriek of genuine amusement. 'Yes, poor lambkin, drinking from a bottle,' she explained, returning to the phone. 'His tongue's already swollen dreadfully and he's struggling to... What's that? How many months? But I'm telling you my dear it's only *just* occurred!'

I saw her blue eyes widen, then her lips into a disbelieving smile. 'No, no you don't understand, it wasn't *THAT sort* of a bottle!' Miss Compton gasped, by now with both eyes closed. 'He's thirty-eight for heaven's sake! I said a *LAMBKIN*, not a *BABY!*' Convulsed, with all her gold chains clanking, she waved the phone at me – until I took it to assure the operator that we were serious, an ambulance was needed.

'Yes, *seriously!*' Despite the peals of raucous laughter in the background.

Back at the cricket field, we found the wretched Crispin with his tongue stuck out as far as ever, sprawled across a bench in the pavilion and surrounded by a group of anxious players – reduced by then from a gyrating Maori to something closer to a dying bloodhound.

'Stiffen up the sinews, Crispy darling,' Miss Compton recommended. 'The ambulance is on its way to take you into Brighton – and while that's happening we'll run the batmobile back into Eastbourne for you, dear,' she added briskly. 'I have my own space in the hotel car park, never use it, and Bubo here will drive us.'

Which was when I realised why she ordered taxis. The woman couldn't drive!

Blake's eyes were rolling madly. He tried to speak but was pure Quasimodo.

'Like all young men, he handles cars *exquisitely*, don't you Bubo, darling?' I nodded dumbly. Ignoring the blank terror in Blake's face, Miss Compton turned to her producer. 'Martin, could I have a little word, dear heart, before we speed away?' They turned their backs on us and went into a huddle.

'That's all agreed then, Bubo darling, off we go!' Abandoning a stricken-looking Martin, Miss Compton took me firmly by the arm to steer us both towards the car park.

'You sit in the back Mouse,' she told her daughter without checking that she'd followed – and I remember thinking randomly that Cordelia was the only person you never heard her call *darling*, *lambkin*, *angel*, *sweetie-pie*, or any of the extravagant endearments she showered on others. Meanwhile, I climbed into the driving seat of Crispin's batmobile like someone in a dream. The alcohol, the outcome of the cricket match, the sight of Blake's obscenely turgid tongue, had all somehow combined to give me a feeling of surreal detachment. If Miss Compton had commanded me to *fly* her back to Eastbourne, I really think I might have flapped my arms to give the thing a try – and in a way suppose I did, as we left the car park moments later in a series of ungainly kangaroo-hops.

I turned into the lane in first, ground my way up through the gears to third, then stalled at the main junction. 'Do you know my sweet, if I was an engine I think I would appreciate a little gentle *foreplay* before the killing thrust,' Miss Compton mused aloud. 'Or isn't that the way it works with cars?'

'Sorry, sorry. Here we go then.' I fumbled back to neutral, double declutched and shot up the carriageway to Eastbourne in top gear at something rapidly approaching sixty miles an hour. At least that's the way it felt.

'On the other hand dear, YIPPEE!' Miss Compton cried.

The first of us to catch her breath, with the windscreen firmly gripped in one hand and her flapping headscarf with the other, she launched into a monologue that with a minimum of interruptions lasted us the whole way back to Eastbourne. 'Now listen Bubo, I want you to do two things for me,' was how it started. 'Do you think that you could manage that, my love?' I nodded, knowing it was futile to resist. 'What I want you to do first is to stay very calm and drive us safely home. Not to panic darling, but to trust in all the years I've spent in this ridiculous profession, and do precisely what I say.'

Again I nodded, sobered up and began to sweat – and that was three things for a start.

'You know that Crispy is unlikely to be able to perform tomorrow night?' Miss Compton went on smoothly. 'His understudy's been struck down with dysentery or something equally revolting; so I've told Martin that you'll be on standby.'

'You mean?'

'I mean on standby to play Freddie for us in Antibes.'

I swerved, bounced briefly off the verge, and then

177

continued at a steady 30mph to the sound of angry hooting from a lorry just behind. 'Child's play, you'll walk it lambkin – won't he, Mouse?' (No answer from the back.) 'Good heavens above, one's had to take lead roles at practically *point-blank* notice, and you'll have simply hours to pull it off!' She felt in her handbag for a cigarette and lit it.

'But couldn't Tom Allan do it?' I would have mopped the fevered brow if both hands weren't clamped rigidly to the wheel.

'Wrong husband and too old. But trust me darling, it's a *little honey* of a part; the perfect thing to cut your juvenile lead teeth on.'

I must have felt at least as sick as Crispy's understudy – sicker I'd imagine. If I'd still had a core of any kind I would have been shaken to it, with the thing I'd dreamed of as a triumph now fast becoming hideous reality. The sweat was prickling my shoulders and running down my back. The steering wheel was slippery beneath my fingers, my feet were nerveless on the pedals – yet even while I told myself I couldn't do it, I knew that I would have to. It felt like the time they'd made me dive off the top board in a St Edgar's swimming gala. I was sure then I couldn't do it, and was red-raw afterwards for the best part of two weeks.

We took the most direct route home, along the north side of the downs through Wilmington to Polegate – where I stalled the Triumph at the traffic lights, panicked when it wouldn't start, then crossed on amber to the fury of the cars behind. While that was happening, Miss Compton told me in the sort of voice that people use for calming frightened animals how *simple* she could make it for me if I would only trust her; how *well* I'd cope, how audiences *adored* an understudy, how *wonderful* and *simply marvellous* I'd be! And while I wrestled with the Roadster's savage clutch and tried my hardest to believe her, my brain illogically became a camera snapping images at random – the image of a seagull frozen in mid-flight – a golfer with his club upraised – a woman on the seafront in the act of handing an ice cream to a screaming child.

Then we were there and parking in the hotel car park, locking up the Roadster, walking up the front steps past the doorman, sinking into carpet, rising in the lift to Miss Compton's opulently furnished, pink-shaded suite, waiting dumbly while she telephoned Dame Gillian in Lewes to explain why, 'Although it breaks my heart, my darling,' she couldn't either dine or stay with her that night.

'Right then my love, we'll sit ourselves down here and run through the whole caboodle, shall we?' She shed her chains and bracelets for a further swift transition into business-like behaviour, sending Cordelia off to order us a pot of strong black coffee before instructing her to leave us on our own (and if you've noticed as I'm sure you have, how little Cordelia featured in this recent drama, I can only say there was no part for her that afternoon; and that included mine!).

Miss Compton gestured at a pair of armchairs in the window and handed me a script. 'You read, I'll feed,' she told me. 'Let's see how well we get along before we try it blind.'

We drank the bitter coffee. She smoked two more cigarettes. I read from my script. She fed from hers, projecting the emotions I should be showing but clearly wasn't in my face. Then we tried Scene 1 without the book and found, as I had known we would, that I was less than hopeless. That was when the full horror of the situation actually struck home.

Patiently on Miss Compton's side, with mounting desperation on mine, we played the scene again with my script held at arm's length more as a reference than a crib, and on the whole it went a little better. At the end of our third reading she untied the white silk scarf affair that held her hair in place and nipped off into the bedroom for a hairbrush. 'Very well then, listen to me, Bubo. What you'll do now is walk back slowly to your digs reciting Scene 1 all the way,' she ordered while she brushed her blonde waves back into their accustomed style. 'Then get that smashing landlady of yours to hear you through Scene 2 before you go to bed. Is that quite clear? I'll ring you in the morning when we've heard how Crispy's doing in the mouth and trouser departments.

'But never fear my love, you're making strides – giant strides, and will be *marvellous*,' she said with absolute conviction. 'No earthly reason why you shouldn't be the greatest possible success!'

I did what I was told because, when it came down to it, I had no choice; pacing slowly up the hill with my script open but scarcely readable in the shadow of the wych elms.

You'll be riveted by the news that amongst those attending Saturday's masked ball at the Hotel Victor Hugo were Princess Rimscoff, the Duke and Duchess of Brentwood, with Mr Bud Solomon the London impresario. The Contessa di Castelli… Castielli?… *has recently returned to the Villa… to the Villa Rosetta? Rosina? at…* Oh God those names! I lost the rest of it. The words began to fuse and melt into the overheated runnels of my brain (do brains have runnels?). How the hell, I thought, could anyone expect me to remember all those effing names! I felt like Chicken Little with the sky about to fall, as with fevered brow I burst through Mag's chrome yellow front door.

She was in the front room on the purple settee snuggled up with Auntie Bill and glued to the *Double Your Money* quiz show on TV. 'So, Winifred my love, this question is worth thirty pounds,' Hughie Green was leering from the tiny greyish-mauve TV screen. 'What bird can run as fast as a horse and deliver a kick like a mule?'

'A robin?' the luckless contestant ventured.

In mid-hoot, Mag looked up, to take in first my ashen face and staring eyes, and then her own role in my latest crisis. Within minutes she'd pulled back the curtains, switched off the telly, sent Auntie Bill to brew more coffee in the kitchen, and seated me beside her on the settee. She read Miss Compton's part at breakneck speed with all the emphasis on the wrong words. But at least she read it, feeding me the cues, correcting me when I went wrong, then feeding them again still faster. Bill had a shift to work before their Ludo session the next evening, but dragged me from the settee first for one of her bone-crushing hugs.

'You never know what you can do until you try; you'll be a huge success Sam, SCRUMPTIOUS!' she barked into my ear. 'But wing it boy if all else fails. Just say whatever comes into your head – ten to one the punters will never know the difference.'

Scene 7

I won't make you guess how many hours of sleep I had that night, or how many litres of midnight oil I burned, reading through and endlessly repeating the three Antibes bedroom scenes until my voice gave out. I think I slept a bit at three and woke at five to start again. Cordelia rang me some time after Mag had left for Antoine's to tell me that Crispin was literally unspeakable. His understudy was still leaking from both ends, she added – so Abi said I was to come to the Excelsior at half past ten to plot the moves while we rehearsed.

Miss Compton opened the door of the Mayfair Suite herself, wearing a satin turban and a drifty sort of negligée that she clearly hadn't slept in. 'Bubo, darling *look* at you, you're positively *drooping!*' She pulled me in and shut the door. 'We'll need more coffee, lots of it, before we start – but have you eaten? Shall I send down for some breakfast for you? The Mouse and I have finished ours.'

I told her that I had, and said good morning to Cordelia on her way past to the phone. She'd been sitting at a table when I came in, cutting paper into squares. 'To stick into the newspaper you're reading in Scene 1,' explained Miss Compton, 'before she writes your lines in with the cues. For Scene 2 we'll have more stuck on to the flats behind the bathroom door, for you to read out while you're pretending to shave.' She walked me through into the suite's own lavish bedroom to rehearse Scene 2 as we would have to play it, lying on the bed. It was the scene I thought that I knew best; apart from all the bloody names which she assured me would be printed in the paper. I found that she knew all my lines in any case before I spoke them, prompting me without a script.

For the later scenes we practised in the outer suite with bright sun shining through the windows, having shifted several chairs and one of the main sofas to imitate the Antibes set. With lunchtime sandwiches in hand, we paced the moves. We read the lines, or rather I did, then ran through all the scenes without a break, with Cordelia standing in for Barbara Bayliss and my script mostly held behind my back.

By two o'clock I had begun to mumble, mispronouncing lines Neil Craven never would have dreamed of writing in the first place; walking into walls and empty of belief. 'We'll stop there now my love, you're doing quite splendidly,' Miss Compton said with iron persistence. 'But when you go home this time you must clear your mind completely. Don't speak. Don't think. Stop trying to remember – go back and run yourself a deep hot bath and *wallow* in it! Have you got that, Bubo? And while you're at it wash all that frightful gunge out of your hair, dear. It isn't Freddie's thing at all.' She placed her hands on both my shoulders, turned me round and pushed me all the way across the carpet to the door. 'I need my nap, so run along now darling. I'll see you on the set at six before the teeming hordes arrive, and don't be late my sweet.'

Cordelia came with me out into in the corridor. 'You'll manage Sam, I know you will,' she said and gave my lifeless hand a squeeze.

* * *

183

As soon as I reached home, I dashed upstairs for a rapid bout of diarrhoea, followed by the hair-wash and a soak in Mag's pink bath; or not so much a soak as a quick dip. I couldn't settle, let alone attempt a wallow, and was out and down again ten minutes later, still quite damp.

At three I tried Scene 1 again, and then Scene 2 – which went so badly that I had to stop.

At four I fried myself an egg, as much for comfort as for hunger – attempted to pull myself together, but fell apart.

At half past four I tried Scene 3 with all the moves, and that went even worse.

At half past five I trudged the fifty yards down to the theatre stage door like someone walking to his execution, opened it with nerveless fingers and heard it clang like Traitors' Gate behind me. To leave me trapped with no chance, less than no chance of escape.

The Antibes bedroom set with rumpled bed in place swung up, and then swung past to make way for the Raffles Hotel veranda ready for Scene 1, while I stood waiting in the wings. With the choice of starting a wildcat strike or hoping that Miss Compton could charm the stage crew into bringing Antibes back for us to practise on, I went on waiting. My stomach with the egg in it by then had shrivelled to the size of a small orange, and that's without the rind. Then just when I'd convinced myself she'd either overslept or forgotten me completely, Miss Compton sailed in, to wave the set back into place and whisk me through the moves of our three scenes together one last time.

The first scene as you know involved us lying side by side in bed, and was so absurdly simple I don't know why she decided to bother with the moves at all. In Scene 2, I had to scramble out of bed and stride into the bathroom for my morning shave. Scene 3 consisted of a skirmish with the Contessa di Castioni in the daunting person of Miss Bayliss – who frightened me to death by clacking onstage in her street clothes to show me how to strike the gun out of her hand without damaging her nail varnish. After that, Miss Compton assured me yet again that I'd be perfect in the role, despite the fact that by the time we'd run through Scene 3 again, I was sweating like a pig and shaking with exhaustion.

'The great thing is to trust in Neilly's lines,' she said firmly. 'It's all in the writing darling. These Method actors seem to think the silences are more important than the speeches, but that's bollocks sweetie-pie!' She met my eyes and held them for the longest moment. 'You will be marvellous, quite marvellous. Do you hear me Bubo – miraculous, but *utterly!*' She shoved me off the stage.

* * *

Half an hour later I was still sitting limply in Blake's dressing room with a copy of the script and Cordelia's doctored newspaper beside me on the dressing shelf. Tom Allan had been recruited to make me look less round-faced; and surveying the result, with shaded cheeks and highlights on my nose and chin, eyebrows strengthened, eyes enlarged with white inside the lids, tufty hair slicked down and sprayed with Rayette Aqua Net to keep it flat, I thought that I looked more like Ian Carmichael being wet and hopeless in the film of *Private's Progress* than anything approaching playboy Freddie in Antibes. Another thing that didn't help was the uncompromising note they'd slipped into the Three Seasons programmes earlier in the day:

DUE TO THE INDISPOSITION OF MR CRISPIN BLAKE, THE PART OF FREDDIE FAWCETT WILL BE PLAYED TONIGHT BY MR SAMUEL ASHBY.

I still clung to the hope the understudy might recover as the afternoon wore on, or that Blake's tongue would shrink enough for him to play – even hoped to see him burst into his dressing room to tell me to fuck off and do it yesterday. But the next man through the door was Tom Allan, popping back to let me know the understudy had bonded with his toilet, and that, when last seen, Crispy's tongue had been as turgid as a length of liverwurst and about as useful when it came to speech. 'Just be sure that you don't swallow your own words, boy. Use your diaphragm,' was Tom's advice; and to show me where that was, he punched me in the solar plexus, rather hard. 'Deliver on the breath Sam, that's the ticket, and you'll be home and dry.'

Struggling to breathe at all, I nodded at him in the mirror, without I have to say the first idea of what he meant. Nigel H-M popped in on his way back from Singapore to assure me I would be a natural. 'But move sparingly,' was his best tip, 'try not to flap about.'

Old Lummy Gould was next, to grope me with a trembling hand and to warn me to be careful with my exit in Scene 2: 'Door's a swine, dear fellow; opens in I think ye'll find or else the other way.'

Then Primmie Allan's fluffy head appeared five minutes later, to let me know that Mars was moving through Scorpio; apparently a sure sign of success.

'So lucky for you Sammy dear, and nothing's ever quite as bad as you imagine, is it? I should know dear, always quake before an entrance; positively *quake*, dear! Butterflies the size of BUFFALOS, though in the end I've always managed to go on. A pack of blessings dear – no need to say good luck... Oh *knickers*, now I've gone and said it, haven't I?' And off she rushed to swear obscenely in the stage door alley – leaving me alone to face the fact that I would *have* to manage too, basically because I had no choice.

I stared at my slicked-down, beetle-browed and unfamiliar image in the mirror to tell myself that come what may I wasn't going to die. Which didn't help much either, because I wanted to devoutly. I tried to focus on the script, to peg the lines to cues in the dim overcrowded junk room of my brain. I tried not to hear the audience applauding when the curtain rose on the St James's drawing room – tried not to listen to the confident, the disembodied voices of the Allans in the characters of Gaye Gaynor and Vincent Campion.

I tried. I did my best to convince myself and everyone who nipped into the dressing room to tell me that I'd manage; COULD do it, WOULD BE SIMPLY MARVELLOUS – that they were right and I was wrong in thinking that I WOULDN'T and I COULDN'T, then or ever in the future!

'Third Act beginners please!' blared through the tannoy suddenly to catch me unawares. And then like Sydney Carton I was walking to a certain death – hearing people who knew better defy theatrical convention to wish me luck; Cordelia and Andrea, Martin, Stan and Paul on effects; even the perfidious Miss Bayliss, knitting while she waited for her entrance with a near human look of sympathy on her flat painted face. Then I was lying in the bed beside Miss Compton. Rigid; staring at a large expanse of faded curtain, with behind it the pre-digestive rumbling of what sounded more than anything like 900 hungry lions. It's a nightmare I still have occasionally and is always just as bad.

My throat was clogged with boiling sand. My palms were wet, and so I discovered was the rest of me, soaking my pyjamas. The newspaper I held was crackling between my shaking fingers, and in spite of anything Tom Allan could achieve with make-up, I still looked underage, I knew I did. So this was it. The curtain was about to rise on the darling of the silver screen tucked up in bed beside a croaking, bedwetting teenager afflicted with St Vitus' dance!

The savage sounds behind the curtain rustled into silence. 'Use it Bubo, USE the fear,' Miss Compton told me bracingly, and did something slightly shocking with her nearside foot to make sure that I did.

Then through the warm *whoosh* of the rising curtain: 'Sparkle, sparkle darling; off we go!'

Scene 8

The curtain rises to reveal Sadie Fawcett in bed with her Riviera playboy husband, Freddie, in an ornately decorated bedroom of the Villa Bianca in Antibes. A door at the back wall leads to a passage and the rest of the villa. Another, up right leads to the bathroom. Morning sunlight streams through a window down left. Sadie has a breakfast tray across her knees. Freddie is reading from the Continental Daily Mail.

SADIE (on the same breath as the 'off we go!'): *I think I can safely say that's one of the worst nights I've ever spent. I'm black and blue from all the bits of you I had to wrestle with, not one of them remotely pleasant.*

It serves you right for being such a pest; I read as Freddie from the lines inside the paper.

Then afterwards you lay back snoring like a grampus.

What's a grampus?

Something loud and hairy one imagines, with hard knees and horny hands and an attention span of less than forty seconds.

By then and much to my astonishment I found that I was not

only ready, but positively *eager* to snap up the cues; to speak my lines and play my part. The words were from a printed script; another man's imagination. There was an audience of hungry lions out there to scrutinise our every move as we sprawled in the bed; the room we occupied was painted canvas, the sunlight through the window powered by Seeboard. Yet on another level in another world we were Freddie Fawcett and his wife; a feckless couple in a rented villa in Antibes. I felt a wave of confidence, almost of exultation. I don't suppose my words were always quite what darling Neilly had intended them to be – but near enough, I thought!

Miss Compton was there to guide me when I put down the paper with its comfortingly printed lines, faintly mouthing every line I spoke and nursing me along. It was the scene I had imagined in my daydream – and if you'll forgive me for putting it like this, you know how it is when your body tells you how to poo; when to start and when to push and how to finish off? Well that's how it felt for me in our Scene 1; almost but not completely automatic – like driving through a busy town with roundabouts and traffic lights, and finding afterwards that you've negotiated all of them without the faintest memory of doing so. A bit like being in a trance. And in my next moment of awareness, I woke to find that I had dealt successfully, not only with Sadie in the person of Miss Compton, but with a nanny and a butler, two socialites and a gentleman's valet – to reach before I knew it my final line in that first scene: *I wonder what the C stands for?*

They'd all helped me with the cues, they must have done. But I had DONE IT; got there somehow, that's the point. 'And they're right, I must be marvellous,' I thought incautiously, 'how silly of me to have doubted!'

Scene 2 was a two-hander – just me and Abi Compton, and if anything went better than the first; even better, I began to think, than when I last saw Crispy play it. Even the bit where Freddie dashes off into the bathroom for a shave. Tom Allan was behind the bathroom door, to stick a bit of bloodstained paper on my chin while I reeled off the lines Cordelia had pasted for me, this time on a canvas flat. *Ow, ow, I've cut myself on this new blade!*

Poor darling, does it hurt?

It does, it hurts LIKE HELL! And now I'm bleeding LIKE A STUCK PIG, SADIE!

'For gawd's sake tone it down a bit old lad,' Tom hissed at me while he stuck on the patch. 'You're over-egging it appallingly.'

Absurd, I thought. How could I be when the audience were clearly loving me as Freddie Fawcett; in fits at all the extra little moves and gestures I was introducing, at almost everything I said! Comedy, as anyone will tell you, is quite the hardest thing for any actor to pull off, and judging by the gales of laughter I was on the button!

There's only a brief blackout in that final play before Scene 3, which opens in the Antibes villa bedroom later in the morning, with Sadie at her dressing table and Freddie pulling on his socks.

'Perhaps just a soupçon less of Popeye the sailor man for this scene, my love,' Miss Compton suggested in a whisper judged within a gnat's wink of being audible as the lights came up. 'The object is to get the house to laugh with you, not *at* you, sweetie-pie.' Which I suppose was the beginning of my downfall, as a note of doubt, a tiny element of fear began to seep into my mind.

It was when the butler knocked to announce the Contessa di

Castione and Miss Bayliss made her entrance in the role of my rejected mistress, and declined to help me with my cues, that the all-too-narrow door into my memory quite suddenly slammed shut. It was a dozen lines or so into the scene, when Freddie panics at the sight of the Contessa's pistol pointing at his head.

HER LINE: *I've got a gun you nasty little swine, and now I'm going to shoot you!*

Help me Sadie, call her off! I cried in genuine distress.

I think it is most unlikely that she'll hit you darling, the way she's waving it about.

Unlikely isn't good enough when you're as keen to live as I am – would have, should have been my next line. But having got that far I did the absolutely worst thing that an actor can do: tried to think ahead to the line beyond the cue that hadn't yet been spoken, and panicked when it failed to come to mind.

Then give me one good reason why think your miserable life's worth sparing, Miss Bayliss in the role of the Contessa shrieked, in what I guessed was meant to be a coarse Neapolitan accent. That was when I dried completely.

It might not, didn't have to be complete disaster. The professionals could still have saved the day – if only I had stopped to let them do it. But I didn't, did I. *Sadie needs me, don't you Sadie?* was the line I somehow conjured out of nowhere in a strangely rasping voice.

Oh please! When gigolos are two a piece along the Riviera? Miss Compton unhelpfully remarked. *Besides my darling, I'm the one with all the money.*

Well I'm too young to die, I improvised. *I'm only twenty-seven and a half!*

Both ladies laughed, in what I could only think was some kind of an unholy alliance *not* to help. So did the audience. *I haven't even had a shot at sex yet*, I added suicidally.

Yes really – I really did commit that absolutely *Freudian* gaffe; to make nonsense of Freddie's age, of his profession as a gigolo, of the scene, the play and my performance in it! Out of the corner of my eye I could see Andrea leafing wildly through her prompt script, and heard a wave of laughter from beyond the footlights. Yet still the frightful voice, my voice and sounding properly pathetic, went on and on – babbling nonsense... more about my unconvincing virgin status. Anything to fill the void.

Time ground into slow motion, with every minute, every second, fantastically prolonged. I was a drowning man pretending he could swim by treading water frantically beneath the surface, but sinking anyway. I threw a look of desperation at Miss Compton sitting at the dressing table. But all she did was tip her head to smile her famously lips-parted smile at me over one green-pyjama'd shoulder.

By then I'd drained my reservoir of words – had finally run out of anything the least attentive member of the audience could possibly construe as sense. Wittered into silence.

More silence followed, then intensified. It can you know.

In retrospect, I don't suppose it lasted for more than say half a minute. But from where I stood half-wittedly with mouth ajar, it seemed to stretch for hours – before another flat and totally deflated voice, which only after it had spoken I identified as mine, appealed to the cool figure at the dressing table: *Help me Sadie!*

H E L P ME, I repeated; mouthing it at her silently with my back to the audience.

Well if I were you, my duck, I would stop advertising your physical ineptitude – a pause for knowing laughter from the stalls, while Miss Compton rose without apparent effort to pat her red wig, adjust her bright green spectacles and nonchalantly strike the gun out of Miss Bayliss's plump hand with one of Freddie's socks wound around her own.

That led, to my intense relief, to further adlib dialogue between two actresses whose well-known dislike for one another only seemed to energise the interplay between them – with Miss Compton commandeering all my lines, until eventually I found the courage to break in with the, by then nonsensical, *Thank you for having me* line from the script. To put us back on track again and keep us there – all the way to Abi Compton's tag line: *In my view the devotion of a true admirer can never be misplaced.*

Afterwards I stood beside her behind the curtain, feeling like someone who'd just survived a major trauma and couldn't quite believe that they were still alive – too shaken to know if I'd succeeded in the part or failed. Staring at a sea of faces when the curtain rose. Waiting for the boos. Then being overtaken, overwhelmed and swept away by the applause when it came crashing in across the footlights.

'Trumpets and drums, my darling – simply blissful!' Miss Compton was magnanimous between the second curtain and the third, and after that had come to rest, turned to kiss me shamelessly in front of the whole cast (though thankfully again without the tongue).

Dazed, shattered, weak-kneed, humiliated and triumphant all at once, and still in something like a trance... well you wouldn't think I had it in me would you to return Miss Compton's public kiss, enthusiastically, square on the lips and with her daughter watching from the wings?

What can I tell you? Can we just say I did, and leave it there?

I mean – look, if you'd been through what I'd been through those past two days – the lows, the highs, the feats of memory and otherwise – the trials and terrors of performance, on the cricket pitch and on the stage... if you'd been swept away by the applause, then dropped into the well of silence that's an empty auditorium, I think like me you would have *lost it*. Like me, you would have lost all sense of what to feel or do, or what they all expected of you next.

Like me you would have left the theatre. That's what I think.

CLEAR

SHORT INTERVAL

ACT IV

Scene 1

Then again, you may be right and I expect you are. Probably I should have stayed; should have gone to see Miss Compton and Cordelia to thank them both for all they'd done to see me through; should have thanked Tom Allan for the make-up – should have thanked them all, but didn't. What I did was to take off Freddie's make-up then his costume, switch off the lights in Crispy's dressing room and slope off back to Mag's.

What I had forgotten until I saw Auntie Bill's Harley-Davidson parked outside her cottage was that it was Monday, wasn't it – bloody Ludo night! So then of course they had to hear how it had gone; the best of it from me, and then the better still from Len, when he trudged in to tell it as it really was and make them both laugh even louder.

After that I lost the will to go to bed – just sat to watch them play; to drink pale ale and then drink more, while every thought I'd ever had evaporated in the smoky air of Mag's front room. The phone rang halfway through the second game, with my cousin as per usual in the lead.

'Now who the hell can that be?' Muttering about some people's cockeyed sense of time, she stomped into the hall to take it. 'What? Who? Yes, if you like – what's left of him if he can make it to the phone.' She held out the receiver. 'It's your precious girlfriend, Sammo.'

I staggered past Mag on her way back to the game. 'Sam?'

Cordelia's voice was breathlessly excited. 'Dame Gilly came backstage after you had gone, and now she's taken Abi off to Lewes with her for the night.'

'Hath'she?' The words came out like that because by then I was completely sloshed. Pissed, plastered, blotto, take your pick or add them all together; you know how it is.

'So I'm here in the suite alone,' Cordelia paused to let the penny drop, 'all night.' (Another heavy-breathing pause, at my end of the phone this time as well.) 'And Sammy, if you're up for it… she has a queen-size bed.'

Believe me I was already up for it despite the alcohol; no longer drained but instantly recharged – and back to panto as I saw it, with Cordelia cast as the good fairy, pointing to the Highgate milestone with her magic wand: *Turn again, trusty Dick, and you shall be first citizen; Lord Mayor of London!*

'Juth poppin' alon' to Excelsior then, forra nightcap ata-bar,' I announced from the hall doorway a nanosecond later, with one hand casually concealing my own state of excitement. 'Take m'key; there'th no need t'wait up.'

'You'd better change first, you're an object,' Mag said without looking up.

'And if you can think of doing anything we wouldn't, Pimpernel,' Auntie Bill bawled up the stairs, 'come back and show us how, lad!'

* * *

By the time I came to pad across the deep pile carpet of the Excelsior's vestibule, I was dressed I thought extremely smartly in a navy shirt and needlecords; still three sheets to the wind but with clean socks and pants on – and with, you may believe (to use another cricket term), new balls. They'd long since called closing time in the Starlight Bar and switched off its sparkly ceiling. The rest of the ground floor had settled into a luxurious gloom which made one realise that the night porter at the reception desk was rather nicely lit – then notice he was beckoning.

In any other circumstance, such marked attention from someone so implacably superior would almost certainly have fazed me. But that night with so much ale inside me, I decided he was there to do my bidding, and not the other way around. Unless the Excelsior had some kind of rule to put the bedrooms out of bounds at this late hour? ALL GUESTS TO BE IN BED BY MIDNIGHT. NO VISITORS OF EITHER SEX. NO TALKING AFTER LIGHTS-OUT. With upper lip prepared to curl, I wove my way unsteadily towards the desk.

'Excuse me Sir, would you be Mr Ashby?' the night porter enquired.

'I am indeed,' I told him grandly – although it came out as *am indee-eeth*, detracting slightly from the grandeaur.

'Mayfair Suite Sir, second floor, you are to go straight up.'

You may or may not be surprised to hear I was already on the rise, if not as yet straight up – and aimed myself in the direction trusty Dick was pointing, towards the lift. The second floor when I emerged, smelled like the hall downstairs; like everything in the Excelsior, of expensive woollen carpeting and Dulux paint. The door into the Mayfair Suite was off the latch.

'Cordelia?'

Hearing nothing, I lurched in through it hitting both the jambs, although with just enough remaining sense to hang out the DO NOT DISTURB sign before I closed the door and locked it. A pink desk lamp across the room lit what I knew to be the main bedroom door, which also stood ajar. 'Is that you, Sammy?' Cordelia's voice invited from the blackness on the other side. 'Come in and leave the light off. It's better in the dark.'

Blimey! Or BLOODY HALLELUJAH, to be fair.

Anyway… I did as I was told of course, deviating slightly to bang my knee on something painful; drunker than I'd thought and intoxicated still further by her mother's all-pervasive perfume. *JOY* EVERYWHERE – it filled the room. 'Sure you're sure sh'won' come back?' I muttered thickly, as Cordelia's arms reached out to pull me down towards her in the bed. I could feel her long hair spread across the pillow and would have liked to stroke it. But she was in a hurry, already plucking at the buttons of my shirt to make it clear romantic hair-stroking was out.

In circumstances well beyond control, I struggled to pull down my needlecords while fumbling in my wallet (yet again) for one or other of the two remaining Durex. All I could hear was the heavy thumping of my heart. She must have caught the sound of ripping foil though, because her voice cut through the darkness like whiplash: 'I'm on the pill you jerk!'

It wasn't possibly the best thing to say to someone needing more than a stiff upper lip to be of useful service. But as I was shortly to discover she already had things well in hand. Both hands in fact. Invisible in the darkness, so close that she was more a scent, a marvellous sensation than a person, she played me like a one-armed bandit, spinning up rows of cherries and bananas.

'I love you! LOVE YOU!' I might have shouted or just gasped it at the payout; knew only that the words sprang out of me spontaneously – and wouldn't be the only thing to do so. Something else was clenching, clamouring for release. With both my own hands in Cordelia's hair, fingers, buttocks, sphincter, prostate, perineum… anything remotely capable of spasm, *SPASMED!*

At the moment, in the instant that with dawning horror I felt her hair – *I felt Cordelia's whole scalp move backwards on the pillow…*

Aaaaarrgh!!

My nerves short-circuited! I leaped into the air – exploded, and went on exploding at two second intervals in all directions!

'Legend has it that Zeus came to Perseus's mamma in a shower of golden rain – and it's too sadly obvious to me now what *that* was all about,' Miss Compton's voice remarked. 'I think you'll find you've missed your entrance darling, one way or another.' And she switched on the bedside light.

Wrong character, was all that I could think of; *wrong character in the wrong play!* Miss Compton, in full make-up, with her hair tucked into a pink nylon cap and the long wig from the Raffles play crouched like an evil blonde tarantula beside her on the pillow, was smiling broadly – worse, trying not to laugh. With my own back to the nearest wall, I felt (and am aware that it's a crass way to describe it) – I felt, if you must know, like a bottle of champagne that's popped its cork. It's true and shame on you for laughing.

'But why did you pretend to be Cordelia?' I demanded as I'm pretty sure you would have done in my shoes – and yes, I had them on still.

'Bring on the drama darling if you like, but please not melodrama; and do try to keep your voice down, Bubo,' said Abi Compton. 'God only knows who the Mouse imagines I've got in here, and I think we'd rather that she doesn't find out, wouldn't we? So pop back into bed now, there's a dear – and bring some Kleenex will you darling; I feel as if I have been caught in a typhoon.'

***

It's always seemed to me that at most crises in your life you're faced with two choices, seldom more; as if you've reached a junction in the road and only ever need to choose the left fork

205

or the right – with one of them in this case leading onwards, and the other back the way I'd come. (Sorry, could have phrased that better.) So what would you have done, I won't say in my shoes this time because by then I'd pulled them off along with all the rest of my damp clothing. Which way would you have gone? Backwards to attempt some kind of dignified retreat?

Naked? Are you *serious?*

In what for me had turned out to be some kind of bedroom farce, I think we can assume that dignity of any kind was off the table. Which should go some way to explaining why and how I came to fetch the box of Kleenex from Abi Compton's dressing table as she'd asked, and perch self-consciously beside her on the bed.

The eiderdown still bore the horrid evidence of my catharsis and smelled powerfully of Ajax scouring powder. (Another bitter irony for men I think you will agree, that at such times of *virile inspiration* shall we say, we have to smell no better than a household cleaner used for scrubbing scum off baths!)

'I chose not to take the starring role my sweet because, let's face it, you never would have dared approach me of your own free will,' explained Miss Compton. 'Naughty of me darling, but I do so disapprove of rape. Besides, I wanted to surprise you and would seem to have succeeded,' she said, busy with the tissues, 'beyond my wildest expectations, dear!'

'But did Cordelia tell you? I mean, how did you know that I was coming?' (I'd say to let that go this time. But actually it made her laugh, and even meant I had to turn away myself to hide a shamefaced grin.)

'*Dame Gilly came backstage after you had gone, and now she's taken Abi off to Lewes with her for the night,*' repeated Abi in a perfect imitation of her daughter's childish voice. I stared at her, unable for the moment to decide if I was shocked or secretly delighted at the lengths she'd taken to deceive me. But by then she'd finished with the Kleenex, had lit a cigarette and lain back inhaling deeply – just as they did in those old movies when sex was hinted at but smoking was still graphic. These days it's the other way about. She lay and smoked. I sat and wrestled with my hardly stainless record; although not in either case for long.

'Now you've perked up so beguilingly... I mean, good heavens darling!' Abi contemplated my topography and stubbed out her cigarette. 'What would you say my love to running through that bedroom scene again?'

Which technically you could say offered me a choice.

Scene 2

If it's all the same to you I think I'd rather leave the details of the next scene off the record – perhaps just mentioning that rotten dress rehearsals very often lead to great first night performances – possibly observing that if Abi proved to be an expert in the field, she found in me a ready learner with reserves of energy I scarcely knew that I possessed – and finally pointing out without I hope undue conceit that if the upshot (stop it!) was what you might call a howling success, the howling wasn't necessarily all mine. In other words, against all odds I'd found another thing that I was really rather good at.

Afterwards, while I lay like a frog on its back with faintly moving fingertips and a wide amphibious grin, still vaguely hoping that too much would prove to be not quite enough, when Abi thought to tell me by way of light relief that Crispy Flake had rung before she left the theatre to say that he was better.

'So is all set to let you off the hook dear for tomorrow – but good lord it's not tomorrow is it?' She pointed at the bedside clock. 'It's *tonight* that we go on!'

'Good morning then,' I murmured from my warm cocoon of bedclothes and post-copulatory endorphins.

But Abi was already busy with a cleanser and a mirror. 'I do wish that you could manage not to look so young, and smooth, my dear; it makes one feel so corrugated at this early hour.' She put down the mirror for a moment to remove my bedclothes, and with an elegantly well-placed foot to roll me off the bed. 'But now my angel, much as I adore you I'm going to have to throw you out; *detestable*, but there it is.'

My cue to retrieve my clothes from points north, south, east and west, to crawl round the bed and underneath it, put on my socks and shoes – and repeat a line of Freddie's dialogue from the Antibes play, to thank Miss Compton very much for having me.

I left the suite the way that I had come, tiptoeing past the connecting door into her daughter's bedroom. Not that I felt any sort of guilt about Cordelia – just didn't think it fair to wake her up, that's all. The downstairs vestibule was silently off-duty; which was a shame because I so much needed to tell Eastbourne and the wider world, starting with the Excelsior's night porter, how I'd leaped the age-gap to play Antony to Abi Compton's Cleopatra. Troilus to her Cressida. Bottom to her Titania if you must, in a midsummer revelry that even in the light of day was anything but a dream.

How young I was still, looking back, to think the wider world could care.

Viewed from the front steps of the hotel, the sun was rising like a waking goddess shaking off her veils. The lawns above the promenade glowed with the promise of another glorious summer day; and with Pisces very much in the ascendant I ran their full length to the No Vehicular Access sign above the line of beach huts at the cliff end of the seafront.

From the head of the Pinnacle stairway I watched the cloud banks fracture into smoky streaks of pink and gold and apple green, gilding everything in sight. The tide was in. The sea swelled seductively, and with my clothes behind me

209

on the shingle I stood nakedly triumphant – absolutely male and every inch the hero. Perhaps a fraction less so when I hit the ice-blue water, and several inches less again as I emerged goose-pimpled and genitally-shrunken, to dry myself on my forbearing y-fronts. But by then the sky was clean-washed, boundless, glowing, just like me! Inspired by the fine morning, I began to whistle the 'Oh What a Beautiful...' song from *Oklahoma* for the climb up from the beach; whistled past a brace of paper boys on my way through the village, past a chinking milk van and someone sneaking out of someone else's house, and felt a warm affection for them all.

Mag's gleaming yellow door was locked. So having left my door-key in the attic, I rootled in her garden shed to find a hoe and put in an hour of honest toil in the allotments; with a bright-eyed robin for a companion and my wet pants spread beside me on the dewy grass. The bird world was singing its collective head off. The sun shone on rows of perfect lettuces and world-class beans. The peas were dazzling, the spinach fabulous I thought, and had just awarded all of them a beatific smile, when a window in Mag's cottage shot up with a loud report and its tenant's orange head appeared, with Auntie Bill's, blue-chinned as Desperate Dan's, a curler's length behind it.

'Sam, what the bleeding hell do you think you're up to?' my cousin demanded. 'Do you know what time it is? It's half past bleeding five!'

But all I could think of doing was to kiss an earthy hand at both of them and tell them both they looked sensational – absolutely *gorgeous!*

When Mag opened the cottage door in her quilted dressing-gown, the one with the tulips and gingerbread-man buttons down the front, I knew from the expression on her face that further stabs at conversation, bright or otherwise, would

210

be rash in the extreme. Which was again a shame, because I wanted desperately to tell Mag how I'd lost my L-plates, passed the test (if not unscathed then fabulously scathed) to become at last a signed-up, bona fide man!

As things stood, I sidled past her quilted, tulip-spattered form in silence with the wet pants held behind my back. Mag slammed the door and stamped upstairs, leaving me to rinse them in the kitchen sink. At breakfast, after Auntie Bill had scorched off on her Harley, she was more forthcoming. But the world by then had turned a notch or two and I'd decided on discretion. 'Who were you with last night then, Sammo?' The question was for me. But Mag, who already thought she knew the answer, made sure that Len and both the Allans at her kitchen table could feel themselves to be included.

'I'm sure that we don't need to know, dear.' Primmie nudged her husband, who looked up from his *Daily Mail* for long enough to wink. 'It's entirely your affair, dear, and Cordelia is the sweetest child I've always thought – Aquarius like me dear, truthful and unspoiled.'

I smiled in a knowingly evasive sort of way, which I hoped they'd take as a confirmation of the fact, while underneath it I was crowing, positively *crowing* with delight! Aha, I thought, *aha!* – if you only knew who I was *really* with last night, you'd be amazed. You would, you'd all fall over backwards if you knew – right off your kitchen chairs!'

But Mag hadn't finished with me yet. 'Is that why you're looking like the cat that got the cream then, Sammo?' she said largely for the others' benefit. 'Got the part and got the girl; turned into Roger Moore, is that what it's about? Len thought you looked quite like him in the play,' she added kindly, 'until he saw you out of bed and standing up, that is.'

***

211

I'd scoffed my Weetabix, was halfway through my second cup of coffee when the doorbell rang. It was one of those tinkly ice-cream-van affairs which played the first sixteen notes of 'Dixie', and then repeated them until everyone went mad – apart from Nanki-Poo, who went mad on the first note. 'Who's that then?' Mag stalked off to see, and after some kind of a kerfuffle in the hallway, Cordelia shot through into the kitchen to take me by surprise.

'So who the hell were you with last night, Sam?' she demanded in a ruder version of my cousin's question – and honestly, it was Mag's face behind her that made me smile rather than the accusing look on hers. Cordelia must have heard us through the bedroom wall was all that I could think.

'But you telephoned him from the Excelsior, dear.' Mag for once was at a loss. 'You called last night to offer him a drink; at least that's what he said.' She turned to stare at me with orange eyebrows hovering around her vivid hairline.

'Ah no, well it wasn't actually Cordelia who rang.' The knowing smile had gone and I was floundering – onstage again without the lines. 'As a matter of fact it was Abi who telephoned,' I said, 'to tell me Crispin Blake was better...' I glanced at Cordelia, standing beside the cooker with glittering eyes and both hands on her hips, to see how she was taking it. 'But Abi still wanted me to come over and rehearse you see, in case... in case he had some sort of a relapse. Perhaps you heard us through the wall? I think we might have been quite loud.' And not bad, I thought, not bad at all; it covered all the bases.

Except: 'You called her *Abi!*' Cordelia burst out, so suddenly and loudly that everybody jumped. 'You called my mother *Abi*, and you said it TWICE!' Which was pretty sharp of her you must admit, to have picked that one word out of all the flannel. Not that it could have proved a thing – or

212

wouldn't have, if my wretched teenage body hadn't chosen to betray me by turning a high-gloss shade of crimson.

'Bloody Abi! Bloody men!' Cordelia shouted on her way out through the hall, before slamming the front door behind her in a way that for an Aquarius wasn't sweet and didn't seem unspoiled, but obviously was truthful.

Nanki went berserk and Primmie looked upset. But Mag just said mildly, 'Temper, temper,' viewing me across the kitchen table with the sort of look a mog has on its face when it's about to eat a vole. 'Let's have it Romeo then, shall we?' She reached out to pat me on the cheek soft-pawed, then pounced. 'Who *were* you with last night?'

I looked at Primmie, who looked at Tom, who folded up his *Daily Mail* and took Len by the scrawny arm. 'Cue end of scene,' he said benignly, 'exit all but principals stage left.' And it was only when he'd closed the door behind them that I was able to explain to Mag what really happened, in an expurgated version of events which omitted anything actually explosive.

I was I have to say a trifle disappointed by her thank heavens for small mercies remark and the calm way she handed me the breakfast plates to dry, from where she stood to wash them in the sink. I did notice she was smiling though, which is normally unheard of for my cousin any time before nine-thirty.

***

It seemed a long wait for that Monday night's performance. So I took myself for a lengthy walk around the valley in the downs above Meads Village that they call 'the horseshoe'. To feel the sun and listen to the skylarks, to watch the butterflies and grazing sheep and get my feet back on the chalky turf where they belonged. As if I could – walking as I was on air the whole way round, seeing practically nothing. Thinking of nothing but Abi Compton, and how and when I next could hope to get her into bed!

Back in the theatre, I'd checked every prop on the Singapore set and winched up the iron, and was chatting to Trevor-on-the-stage-door when the First Act beginners started to arrive. Miss Hayes and Lummy Gould came in together – then Abi, looking stunning in a biscuit-coloured linen suit with a crimson headscarf and sunglasses (new ones every bit as large). She took them off to step in from the sunny street and hear me say 'Hello' and see me waiting for the reminiscent smile, the roguish wink, the touch that lingered just a fraction to acknowledge what we'd shared and what still lay between us.

But, 'Hello Bubo darling. How's tricks?' was all I got, as she swept past me in the corridor and exposed me to the full force of Cordelia's accusing stare. That's when my feet came back to earth in its most concrete form.

We'd long since had the half-hour call and were waiting in the wings for the beginners, when I was shaken out of my self-pity by the sound of my own name. 'Sam! Sammy, Abi needs you. Can you come?'

Cordelia of all people was beside me, no longer hostile but white-faced and apprehensive. 'She's lost her contact lenses, someone's taken them – and you know that she's completely *blind* without them!' I didn't know, had no idea she even wore the things. 'It's that bitch Barbara, must have been!' And as she said it something in me snapped.

I think I've mentioned that I saw myself as an easy-going sort of fellow at least above the waist; liked women as a sex and always had done. But now I'd had enough. We'd reached the end; the Gaston moment, if you like – and yes I'm reinstating him in time for the dénouement.

'But where are you going? Abi needs to see you *now* Sam!' Cordelia almost shrieked it. 'She can't go on without them!' But by then I was already halfway up the concrete stairs, taking them three steps at a time.

Luckily, the door into the dressing room Barbara shared with Yvonne Hayes wasn't locked and didn't stick, or else I might have done some damage. Miss Hayes was on her feet and fully dressed, made-up with a pale strip down her nose to make it look less beaky. Barbara, in a dressing-robe, was in the act of reshaping her straight upper lip into an artful little cupid's bow with one of the moist rouges.

'Where *are* they?' I yelled at her, infuriated. 'What have you done with Abi's lenses?' At first she didn't answer and while we waited, the final strains of 'Moonlight in Mayo' sounded through the speaker in the corner of the room.

'Ye gods, I'm on!' Miss Hayes rushed for the door.

'Come on, where ARE they?' I repeated rudely after she'd brushed past. 'I asked you what you'd done with them, you stupid bloody cow!'

Unruffled, with a steady hand, Barbara was delicately edging her reconstructed lipline with medium blue to hold its shape under the lights. 'Lawks a'mercy,' she offered straight-faced, replacing the blue liner and taking up a white one to begin the process of enlarging her small eyes. 'Can't you see, you moron? If anyone has taken Abi's lenses it's her darling, delinquent daughter.'

'What? You can't mean Cordelia?' I said blankly. She awarded me a stare Medusa could be proud of, before asking who the fuck I thought it was. But still I didn't get it; still refused to wither. 'You,' I told her, floundering. 'You had her wrong birthday printed in the paper – it's you, it has to be.'

Miss Bayliss smiled the smile that she reserved for halfwits. 'Well you're the only one who thinks so, petal. Who else do you suppose had access to her mother's wig or necklace? We've all known who it was since Bournemouth, you poor sap, including I may say the Goddess Almighty Star herself; the great and glorious Abi Compton. Ask her if you don't believe me.'

Et voilà! That's when I took the bullet she had spared me in the Antibes play as the revengeful Contessa di Castioni. That was when the ten-ton cartoon weight crashed through the ceiling to flatten me completely.

Mon Dieu, I am the imbecile. Gaston has been blind! BLIND! Miserable aveugle that I am, I saw nothing! The Corsican super-sleuth peels himself off the floor to strike the little grey cells beneath his lacquered scalp another stunning blow. *I have been stumbling in a darkened room, mes amis. You give me the cock and balls story that is false. But now parbleu, the light it penetrates. The truth is clear – the case it is complete!*

Cordelia! It was Cordelia, the one person I had never seriously considered despite the fact that as her mother's dresser she was and always had been ideally placed to sabotage her costumes, break her mirror, creep about when nobody was looking to tamper with the props and lighting, fetch Nanki from the attic wardrobe, steal the fuses, start the stage revolving.

All of it behind the childish voice, the khaki eyes, the Mona Lisa smile.

Scene 3

OK I know I've cheated, deliberately misled you back in Act I, by giving you a false list of suspects when the real culprit was offstage all the time. But be fair, red herrings are traditional; and anyway I'm not Dame Agatha, so who says we have to play by her rules?

No melodramatic dénouement after all then. No *Mesdames et messieurs*... no ring of guilty faces, each one accused in turn and then dismissed. *Voyez, mes amis, we will not beat about the shrub. This farce reveals to us the culprit. Qu'est ce qu'il y a? La Souris qui rugissait. You say the Mouse who roars, n'est pas?*

But were you as totally gobsmacked as I was at the time, or did you see it coming? Was it obvious to you from the start? I'd be interested to know.

* * *

I was still staring at Miss Bayliss in her dressing room imperturbably making up her eyes, when over the tannoy we both heard Abi Compton's resonant stage voice in the Raffles play introducing Hughes-Milton as her husband to Lummy as the stuffed-shirt Colonel Westgate.

ABI: *This gorgeous man is Max, my husband. Don't you think he's perfect?*

LUMSDON: *I might if I was any judge of masculine attraction. It's my wife here who's the leading expert.*

I pictured Cordelia standing in the wings, acting out her role as daughter-in-distress; waiting this time for her blinded mother to blunder through the wall of the hotel – and held the picture in my mind as like a mad thing I leaped down the concrete stairs, to find Cordelia's tote bag where she always left it tucked behind the pier glass in the star dressing room. It was made of canvas with a big pink daisy stencilled on the front; and when I tipped its contents out into a small heap on the floor, there under a hairbrush, a scuffed leather purse, a bunch of safety pins, a tube of Polos and a Biro, I found what I was looking for – a small enamelled box wrapped in a hanky. Inside it were the lenses: Exhibits A and B, nestled like birds' eggs in two little plastic nests. A dunnock's or a whinchat's eggs, because they were bright blue. I had already guessed Miss Compton's lashes must be made of nylon; now realised that the legendary, impossibly blue eyes had been just that, impossible. It was my day for shattered dreams.

I walked through the wings to drop the lens box on to Andrea's open script in the prompt corner. 'Miss Compton's missing contact lenses; I found them in her daughter's tote bag,' I told her shortly. 'See that she gets them, will you Andie, as soon as she comes off.' And walked off myself before she could reply.

It was a cowardly, ignoble way to do it. But by then I'd lost all interest in dénouement and didn't want to be there when it happened – although of course I heard it in the interval, even from the prop room. We all did.

I came back in time to watch Miss Compton waiting in the wings in beads and fringes for her St James's entrance, and could see from her intent expression and the way she held her head that she had her lenses on by then. Cordelia wasn't there, and wasn't there again for the quick change, which Andrea had to leave her script to help with. Poor Andrea. I took her place in the prompt corner, and helped her in the longer interval to take the tea around – which was when I saw Cordelia for the last time, and I mean the last. I suppose it hardly matters any of it now. But it did then.

I was on my way up from the prop room with the tea tray when Martin hustled her along the dressing-room corridor and past us to the stage door. I'm not sure if Cordelia saw me, really hope she didn't. But the glimpse I had of her will stay with me for ever. Hers was a face that no one, *no one* should have seen; tear-stained and swollen, abject with humiliation. I stopped and looked away until she'd gone, then ran down to the lavatory to be very sick.

For the second interval I'd arranged with Andrea to take in Abi's tea myself, in her own cup with sugar on the tray and a couple of the bourbon biscuits that she liked. I knocked, listened for a moment and went in.

The star dressing room looked as if a crowd of drunken football fans had hit it – with water and face powder everywhere, cracked photographs, a chair on its side with one leg broken, a waste bin full of flower stalks and sodden greeting cards. Absolute and total chaos! Half the light bulbs round the central mirror had been smashed, with the broken stubs of Abi's paint-sticks heaped to one side of her dressing table. The rest of them were streaked and smeared across its triple mirrors in frenzied strokes of colour. A fresh set of make-up, borrowed I supposed, had been set out amongst the desolation on a clean white towel. Only Abi's costumes on their hangers appeared to have survived undamaged; five sheeted witnesses to her dresser's ultimate defeat.

Abi Compton was already in her green pyjamas with

a muslin scarf tied round the bright red wig she wore for 'Autumn in Antibes'. They'd cleared a window for her in the central mirror through the mad abstract of the grease. 'Bubo darling, how *very kind*,' she said, smiling at me through it. Her eyes without their lenses were bloodshot round the blue, looking tired and far from young. 'Just think how utterly unbearable our lives would be without the cheering cuppa.'

I set the cup and sugar gently down beside her. But she didn't turn around. 'I'm sorry. I am so sorry, Abi.' I had to say something, and that was all that came to mind.

'Lamentings in the air, my sweet.' Her hands were lightly clasped, her body held erect; although I couldn't help but notice that one foot kept tap-tapping underneath the dressing table. 'I won't sob on your shoulder, attractive as it is.' She smiled again. 'But do you think you could spare a moment darling? I'm so tired of everybody hiding from me behind the props.'

I found a small armchair with the full complement of legs and shunted backwards into it. 'If only I had known or even guessed,' I said, 'perhaps I could have helped?'

'My poorest Bubo, *what* a woeful face!' She moved a little to one side to let me see it in the mirror. 'A dismal matinée for *Murder on the Nile* out in the sticks on a wet Wednesday in November. That's how you look my pet. But if you're asking – no, I doubt you could have helped. It might have helped if the Mouse's useless father had thought to wear a rubber johnnie on some part of him before we spawned her in the trap room of the Abbey Theatre; and I suppose I might have helped her by being a worse actress and a better mother all these years.' She spooned in the sugar and began to stir her tea. 'But then again I've never gone in for wailing, and can't begin to think how one would gnash one's teeth without appearing totally unhinged.'

She paused to take her first sip, gingerly to save her make-up. 'In the end life must go on, dear heart – and that's a line you may be sure crops up in half the weepies that were ever written. Which what the hell, could even mean it's true.' She set the cup back in its saucer, dabbed her mouth with a spare tissue, caught me looking at her tapping foot and stilled it. 'I don't remember much about the Mouse's birth, I think they must have knocked me out. But the pregnancy was dreary utterly, the living end. I was pea green all through *The Millionairess* and had to give my Desdemona up at Stratford in a sort of vast tulle tent. No joke to manage I can tell you, when it came to being smothered!'

Pause for laughter... from force of habit I suppose, and I felt dreadful when it came; disloyal somehow to poor Cordelia.

'Then quite soon after she was born I did a thing called *Rose Without a Thorn*. You're too young to remember it; a costume piece with these excruciating corsets reinforced with planks. Really darling, *wooden planks*, you can't imagine what they felt like. Look, could you be a perfect angel and fetch that towel?' She interrupted herself to show me where Cordelia had flung it, then how to drape it round her shoulders for the powder. 'I never seem to get the hang of marriage, darling. Can't cope with husbands rushing about and trying to make one *listen* to them all the time. Never found the time for other babies either; isn't that *too* tragic?' She made a rueful face at me through a cloud of blending powder and took a last sip of her tea.

I found it hard, impossible to know if she was really suffering, or simply acting her idea of how it looked to suffer. 'I'm good at all this nonsense darling, but not at real life, not really,' she said as if she'd read my thoughts. 'But you mustn't think the Mouse was in any way neglected. I bought a place

221

in Blackheath with a nursery and a nanny; with every size of teddy bear that Harrods stock and a *simply gorgeous* rocking horse with Kenny Williams nostrils. Then later there was Denis...

'No *Derek*, that husband was called *Derek*.' She smiled apologetically. 'Nondescript you see, but really very sweet. It was Derek, must have been, who found the house for us in Ealing near the studios, with hydrangeas and a lawn for the Mouse to run on. I believe he kept it on when we split up and had the Mouse there for the holidays; even built a tree house for her, bless his cotton socks. He was easily the nicest of my exes,' she added with a sigh. 'So I expect that's where she'll go, don't you? To Ealing and to Derek what's-his-name, as her port and happy haven do you see?'

I said I did. I said I felt it very likely that she'd go there. But, *will you take me somewhere then, where we can be alone to try again?* was what I was remembering. At the centre of the great enchantment a young girl, damaged and in pain.

'I'm sorry Sammy darling, but I rather think that Denis... I mean Derek, is the only man our little Mouse can bear.'

'But who will dress you if she goes?' I asked her in as normal a voice as I could manage.

Abi smiled into the greasy mirror, examining the damage to her lip rouge. 'My pet, my angel, heart of my desire, how absurdly typical, how *gorgeous* of you to care!'

With only minutes left before Last Act Beginners, she'd had to cram the rest of Cordelia's sad little story into the time it took to make her last repairs. 'The poor child never really settled after that divorce, kept pinching things at boarding school and pretending that she hadn't.'

'But why?'

'Oh I don't know.' She gave a little shrug, 'I suppose she did it for my *attention*, darling? It was the reason she left school early to come to me in Rome; the reason why I've been expecting this from her, or something like it, all along. I knew that she was up to her old tricks you see almost from the start of this benighted tour. All that cloak and dagger business with the filters up in Oxford, or was it Birmingham; too juvenile – too very much her line of country darling to be anything but obvious to those with ears to hear and eyes to see. But even then I thought that when she saw it didn't work, she'd settle down and let us both get on with what we do. It was the only way that I could play it; the reason why I couldn't let dear Martin blow the whistle on her. But darling, something tells me, I have this sneaking little feeling that she will be back for the first night in London, though heaven knows I could be wrong.'

'No I'm sure you're not,' I lied. 'I think she will be back. But why do you think she had to drag me into it, when there was nothing I could do to help her?' I added louder than I meant to.

'Oh but of course you *did* help her, my tenderest piglet-in-the-middle!' Having finished with the Max Factor Clear Red No. 1, Abi untied the muslin scarf and made some small adjustments to the wig. 'You helped *immeasurably*, my dear, by listening to her, bless you; by playing Buttons to her Cinderella – by being someone she could hide behind and lie to as part of the charade.' Abi's foot began to tap again beneath the shelf. 'Although of course you do know, don't you Bubo, that she is frigid, *pathologically!* That's why I had to hijack you, my dear. However far you thought you'd got with her, she never would have given you what you so needed; never could have done what *I* did for you, sweetie-pie. Not without an anaesthetic.'

'But she did, we almost very nearly...'

I got no further, because that's when the tannoy crackled into life to call Miss Compton for the final act. We both got up and automatically she handed me the towel. 'I mourn in spirit darling, couldn't loathe it more – but even this is not the worst of it, you see; the worst thing is that I am bound to find all this negative emotion *useful*. Isn't that the absolute rock bottom? The way we actors use our feelings to turn dross to gold? Shaw says all artists have a duty to be selfish, and I believe he may be right.'

She sighed again melodiously, already thinking of the stage. 'People seem to want to come to see me, watch me doing what I do. I'm open to the public darling, and however cockeyed it might seem to you, or to my poor Cordelia, I simply *cannot* let them down.' On her way across the room she brushed my cheek with one long varnished talon, then kissed the air beside it to preserve her make-up. 'But if you're thinking serpents' teeth and thankless children, darling; deplorably I've never been maternal – never should have had a child, much less a daughter.'

Then for her exit from The Painful Scene: 'It's probably a cliché sweetheart, without a script to hand we do tend to them in the profession. I know I'm thoroughly unprincipled, but have to say that women really *aren't* my favourite sex.' She kissed the air again and left.

It was beautifully done.

Scene 4

I wonder if I'm going to be able to do full justice to that last performance of 'The Three Seasons' at the Meads four days and five shows later? It was a little like the time we left St Edgar's, but sadder, like the feeling of nostalgia that you get in autumn sometimes on those damp, misty days when everything smells of leaves. As if something magical is coming to an end.

The wings that night were crammed with actors, staff and management jostling one another for a final chance to catch a show they knew was bound to pull out all the stops. I was with Paul for one last shot at bell effects, and wasn't helped with it by Miss Bayliss's clicking needles just behind my head, or by her caustic comments on the action. In spite of all I'd said, she treated me no worse than usual, with cool indifference, to bring it home to me between the pings just what a sad and friendless sort of person she must be. I was too busy with the bells when Abi made her exit for the quick change to pay her much attention. But as she passed me on her way back to the stage and touched my hair with one long-fingered hand, I scented *JOY* and felt the thrill of contact.

Otherwise whenever I was free to do it, I squeezed in with Andrea for a prompter's view of the performance. For Abi Compton and the way she played the stalls, the circle and the gallery, Stanislavsky might never have existed. For her there were no fluky performances and no bad houses.

She acted and her audience reacted; everyone was happy – and by the time on that last night of the provincial tour she came to speak the final tag line: *In my view the devotion of a true admirer can never be misplaced*, her comeback was assured.

There was a small wild party in the star dressing room after the show and another, smaller and less wild, in H-M's room. But those were for the actors. For us there were still inventories of props to check, curtains to unhook, carpets to roll and skips to pack, before the stage crew could begin to strike the set to make way for the Ballet Rambert company, and we were free to celebrate ourselves.

At 1a.m. the theatre manager, Eric Benson, sent a car to whisk Andrea, Stan and me along the seafront to his flat in Cavendish Place, and join his party as we were: dishevelled and exhausted, and dying for a drink. The flat was large and opulent with crimson walls and white plaster mouldings round the ceiling – which was almost all that we could see of it above the throng. The whole place seethed with people, shouting to be heard across each other's shouting voices; all of them (apart from us of course) well dressed, and very few as far as we could tell connected to the theatre.

I fought my way through to a small bar faced with buttoned leather, extracted a stiff whisky from a Spanish barman, and because she was alone and looking bored, struck up a conversation with someone's Swiss au pair girl. Her name she said was Trudi. She had brown eyes, teeth even bigger than Monroe's, and long dark plaits wound tightly round her head. She liked the seaside she was keen to tell me, but not the stony beaches which were *horrible*. Eastbourne was a boring town, she said, as anyone could see, and English people: 'Rude they are, yes *horrible*, especially the children.'

Trudi wanted very much to go back home, she said, to

Basle where people were polite and never rude. I said I thought she should, which prompted her to tell me I was *horrible* as well. 'I say what is wrong in England. But you, like all the English a rude man are. You look behind me and not listen. You see woman *mit dem Lila Hose*, not Trudi who is talking.'

It was astute of her, because my mind *was* where she thought it was, across the room with Abi Compton. I'd picked her out as soon as we came in, standing with her back against the crimson wall beneath a bracket light that gilded her fair hair and picked out the colour of her outfit in dramatic contrast. She'd changed into another snazzy trouser suit, this time in an adventurous shade of violet, with great hoops of ostrich feathers dyed to match around its neck and cuffs.

'Go then, why not? You see she smiles at you,' offered my companion sourly. 'Join your English club, be *horrible* to Trudi.' So I took her at her word – to give the girl the satisfaction of being proved right yet again about the rudeness of the English, and to find Abi with a cigarette in one hand and a glass of brandy in the other.

'Darling, you're filthy, *totally abhorrent!*' In spite of which, she tucked me cosily beneath her smoking wing beside her handbag before introducing me to a man with a tight collar who looked like a borough councillor or successful butcher. 'Here's someone, Mr Booth, you simply have to meet. His name's Sam Ashby and he's *far* too sensible to be an actor. A total pet; the kindest man since Jesus!'

I could see that Trudi, watching me resentfully across the room, thought otherwise and once again was right. I leaned out from the vibrant plumage to shake hands with Butcher Booth, but was not released. 'We absolutely owe our *lives* to this young man and his stage management. No really Mr Booth dear, that's no exaggeration,' Abi assured him, exaggerating madly. 'But for our darling Bubo these past weeks, I swear

we'd all have leaped off Beachy Head like suicidal lemmings!'
This time she was plastered for a change and I was sober. But
the voice, the perfume and the scarlet fingernails massaging
my arm, gave me the courage that I needed.

'Can I talk to you Abi,' I beseeched the artificially blue
eyes. 'On our own I mean?' She laughed, the silvery cascade.
'For you the world my darling on a bed of roses! We'll nip
into Eric's bedroom shall we? Then Mr Booth here can tell
everyone we're at it in there like ferrets in a bag.'

We left the poor man flushed around the gills – and as
Abi steered me off towards the bedroom, I caught sight of
Primmie Allan peering at us from the protective bulwark
of her husband's shoulder, and guessed from some sudden
movements in the press around them that they'd brought
Nanki-Poo along. The bedroom when we reached it was a
gleaming mausoleum of burgundy mahogany, with a king-
sized, red satin-covered bed that went some way to explaining
Eric Benson's single status.

'Macabre isn't it, too vile!' Abi made for the dressing table
with its red top and redder stool, consigning her half-smoked
cigarette to a convenient ashtray, putting down her glass and
fishing in her handbag for a compact – while I stood watching
her reflection in the mirror. Always in the mirror like the Lady
of Shalott.

I took a breath. 'May I come on to you tonight?' I asked
as steadily as possible. 'At your hotel?' Then as I watched her
face change: 'Please Abi?'

''Fraid not darling,' she said lightly, '*terribly unwise*;
a) because I'm sloshed, b) because you look too shattered
to do either of us justice, and c) well what's the future in it
darling, when I'm... let's just say *mature*, and you're – what,
seventeen?'

'I'm nineteen.'

'How splendid for you, sweetie-pie!' She leaned forward to the larger mirror, to scrutinise some defect that she'd spotted, in a way that I imagined she had done so often it was automatic. 'Besides,' she went on smoothly while attending to the problem, 'I really think it might just do my daughter's head in if she heard about it later. Or have you forgotten our poor crazy little Mouse?'

To my shame I had.

'When you're a little older darling and I'm beyond repair, you'll see our little *mésalliance* for what it was; a single crazy night, dear, in circumstances that have changed.'

'But I love you,' I blurted at her in the mirror.

'Yes, there's that... although my darling *what* an awkward line – as I remember thinking when you positively bludgeoned me with it the last time we did the bedroom scene. When you imagined I was someone else entirely, Cordelia as it happens. I'm sorry, Bubo darling, but I don't believe it's love you feel or ever did.' She turned around to study my reaction. 'It's lust again my dear, impure and simple – and you can't say that I didn't warn you about my morals, sweetie, because I well remember that I did.'

The mirror should have cracked from side to side. 'The curse is come upon me,' Abi should have cried. And in a way she did. 'What is it that you see in me? A noble character?' she asked, 'a youthful body? Legendary kindness, Bubo?'

'The truth is I see beauty,' I said quietly.

'Ah truth, but IS there such a thing?' She turned back to indicate her own reflection. 'Let me tell you what you see, my love. You see a set of moderately regular features in all their usual places; in my case flattered by some of Max Factor's finest work. Glitter darling, glamour, razzmatazz and fancy dress – far more to do with artifice and presentation than anyone's aware.'

She raised a hand to her own face. 'Do you have any concept of the work that the directors and costumiers, the hair stylists, make-up artists, lighting people and film editors put into our screen legends? Do you know why Garbo will never risk a comeback? Not because she can't perform. She can and always could act all of us off the screen. It's because the poor dear hasn't anyone that she can trust to show her literally in the best light. Look at Marlene if you don't believe me. That woman's photographed these days through so much cheesecloth, they say her fan club's almost totally made up of rodents. Look at Vivien, look at Flo Girton – look at me, my darling. You see the shining surface of the Lovely Lady but miss the emptiness inside. Isn't that the line? Deep down our beauty's superficial, painted like the scenery with nothing much behind it.'

'It's not, that isn't true!' I cried, remembering the taste of nicotine and brandy, the feel of warm receptive flesh. But I cried it silently because it would have spoiled the scene.

'We're used to working with illusions. I'm mistress of them all, and certainly should be, considering how much I've practised since I ran away to join the circus. I'm a mimic, like a magpie, darling – or a starling is it, I never am quite sure.'

Abi used her smile as punctuation for a longer speech. 'Some actors work by stripping off the layers to show the raw emotions underneath, but that's not me. What I do is to paint them *on*. I base my characters on other people's traits and mannerisms, ways of speaking, moving, looking, dressing. I can act onstage or for the camera, learn the lines, play anyone but Hedda Gabler, or Mrs bloody Alving. When I look back on my career I see Estella, Lady Teazle, Vanessa, Portia and Viola. All those faces, wigs and voices. Not one of them my own. *Tem-per-amen-tal in-exac-ti-tude*,' she stressed the consonants. 'That's part of a speech exercise, and is sadly, darling, all I have to offer. I know precisely how to be and how to feel and how to look when I'm in character. But when I peel off the layers and pack away my sad old box of tricks, I don't know who the hell I am.'

She snapped her compact shut and dropped it back into her handbag. 'So then I dress up again in this or something like it.' Abi made a downward movement with her hands to brush the surface of her violet tunic in one of her most telling gestures. 'Another pretty costume to help me play the famous fucking star! Do you know what Noël Coward said of Gertrude Lawrence?' She raised her painted eyebrows in the mirror.

I shook my head. Knowing that she wasn't looking, knowing she was talking to herself.

'They'd been together all their lives, and yet he said of Gertie that apart from seeing that she ate and slept and acted beautifully, he never really knew what she was like or what was true of her. I doubt that she knew either,' Abi added bleakly, 'or could tell if it was Monday night or Christmas when she wasn't in the theatre.' She sought my eyes and held them. 'Here then for your delight the painted clown.'

And for the briefest instant, two seconds nothing more, I saw what she intended me to see reflected in the mirror; a woman, middle-aged, emotionally spent, with sagging skin beneath her jaw and blue eyes lifeless as the glass that coloured them – a performance in itself. And I was six again and terrified, staring at the ruins of my grandpa's butchered face. Then it was over.

'So what now?' I said shakenly, unable to believe what I'd just seen.

'What now? We go back to the script, dear: *Our revels now are ended*, is all I think we need here. No need to signpost or prolong it: *Our revels now are ended*. CURTAIN.'

She rose to take three measured steps towards the door, and because there wasn't actually a curtain, continued speaking. 'There'll be a comp ticket waiting for you at Her Majesty's for the opening on Tuesday. It'll be up in the gods I fear. But don't waste it will you?' She closed the famous open smile to indicate finality. 'Sparkle, sparkle darling, rise above.'

The noise of a faint cheer followed by a burst of laughter sounded from the room beyond. I waited, needing her to turn back in the doorway. But for once she went for the Swift Exit. To leave me with nothing but a single violet feather dancing in the draught.

On top of everything she had begun to moult.

***

Abi had already left the party when I emerged from Eric's bedroom some minutes later. So I left it too and walked. I thought that the fresh air would help. It didn't.

There's a bit in *Room at the Top*, if you've ever read it, when a forlorn and woebegone Joe Lampton leans against a lamp-post because he can't go on. That's what I did when the ache inside me felt too heavy to be borne; stopped to lean against a wall and then push back until the flints that it was built of cut my hands. These days you'd call it channelling one's inner masochist, with pain a substitute for tears. I went on leaning against walls and lamp-posts all the way down to the seafront.

Then I was on the beach, crunching over shingle with the wind full in my face. A moon shone mercilessly silvering the water. But someone had put the stars out. I couldn't *sparkle, sparkle*, had sunk too low to rise above. The pain was worse I was convinced than anyone had ever felt, and I mean ever! If I'd had a soul, I would have lost it. If I was Elvis I'd have

232

sobbed the length of Lonely Street all the way down to Heartbreak Hotel.

If I was a hound-dog I'd have howled.

Scene 5

Have you ever had a morning when you wake up in a pool of dribble with a head like suet, step out of bed on to a hairbrush, bristles-up, wet your pyjamas in the bathroom with a delayed follow-through of urine, then walk into the wardrobe door?

I know I said that I loved summer mornings, but these things take their toll.

It was Auntie Bill's bike roaring off to work that woke me; the rain skiffling the grey pane of my attic window that prevented me from me dropping off again; and the sound of Mag crashing about downstairs that finally got me up. My tongue felt and looked like moist grey flannel, and in the kitchen I was barely able to unstick it long enough for a 'Morning Mag' in my cousin's rough direction before I sank into a chair. The news on the radio was bad. More rain was due apparently with frequent showers, as if there was a difference – and in response to my glum greeting, Mag turned on me like a mauve-overalled rattlesnake with curlers clashing.

'I warn you mate,' she growled. 'I've had it up to here with Abi Compton this, and Abi bloody Compton that, and what she did to you and what she didn't, and how she's wrecked your sad pathetic life!' She dropped another egg into the sizzling pan as the shipping forecast gave way to the new Beatles in-your-face hit single. Ironically, 'She Loves You'!

'Considering the state that you were in last night,' Mag

raised her voice above the *ooos* and the *yeahs*, 'I don't suppose that you remember Billy lugging you upstairs? Or cleaning up your puke, Sam? Or putting you to bed?' I shook my head and told her I was sorry. It had become my middle name. 'So you bloody should be! She's a saint that woman. More than you deserve – or I do for that matter.' Mag flipped the egg on to a plate mounded with fried bread and bacon from the oven, and slammed it down on to the table. 'So do us all a favour will you, mate? Sit down. Shut up, and eat your bleeding breakfast!'

There were times, I thought morosely, when you could sympathise with Abi Compton's views on the sexes – which one was favourite, and otherwise.

***

I wasn't needed for the Ballet Rambert that week, not until the Thursday, and was still in a state of semi-suicidal gloom as I boarded the train to London. I'd put on a collar and tie with a suit (my one and only from the January sale at Bobby's). Mag told me, scowling, that I looked a dog's dinner in it, but hoisted my tie for me and gave me a brisk workout with a clothes brush, before digging out an outsized Philip Marlowe mackintosh of Auntie Bill's from the hall cupboard and insisting that I put it on. It made me look like Mr Noah from the old wooden ark at the Bury Farm, and its collar chafed my neck where the latest boil was starting to erupt.

'Now don't you dare go backstage and get involved again,' Mag called after me outside the station. 'Theatricals – do you hear me Sammo; they're nothing but plain trouble!' She wound up the car window with the sort of fierce expression which I knew from long experience was the nearest that my cousin ever came to affectionate concern.

In those days you didn't have to take a mortgage out to buy a day return to London. There were no loudspeaker announcements on the platform to tell you not to travel if you thought it likely that you'd die in transit. No one was interested in detonating unattended luggage, or clinching business deals with iPhones clamped to their ears; imagine that. Undisturbed and unmolested, I was rattled through a green and saturated landscape all the way to London – or anyway until we reached its suburbs, where the rows of houses swooshing by were grey, dispirited and ugly, and stayed that way for the longish walk from Victoria to Her Majesty's Haymarket, where 'The Three Seasons' was to open.

It was raining hard by the time I left the shelter of the station. Water trickled down my neck to lubricate the throbbing boil (so yes, I still felt bloody awful, but nice of you to ask). I looked up to see a million raindrops pelting from a leaden sky, looked down to watch the tops of my black lace-ups marching one behind another across the gleaming tarmac, looked out to see the pavements crowded with pedestrians under wet umbrellas. Hurried and incurious, single or in couples, none of them remotely fabulous to me. I saw them as humanity, if not exactly at its worst, then at its most depressing – while I felt sadder than the saddest; a pincushion without its sawdust, a hole without a toad.

Back then my knowledge of the great metropolis was limited to a series of discovered islands linked by the tunnels of the Underground. In my mind's eye I still saw Baker Street as brown and Oxford Circus as bright red and Leicester Square as black. (I also pictured Mayfair as dark blue, but think that was more to do with Monopoly than the colours of the tube lines.) I'd found a battered London A–Z Street Atlas of Auntie Bill's in her mac pocket, which helped me plot a course down Buckingham Palace Road, through Green Park and St James's to join up my Victoria and Piccadilly islands for me, like dropping four new pieces into an enormous jigsaw.

If you know London well, as I expect you do, you might have trouble understanding how oppressive it could feel back in the 1960s to a country boy like me. Everything I passed looked doleful, drably nondescript; walls, pavements, pigeons and policemen. Through endless streams of traffic, double-decker busses lumbered nose to tail, like grimy elephants beneath a leaden sky. The streets were lined with what looked like rows of town halls cast in dingy concrete and topped with sooty chimneys. Bronze statues of old men struck attitudes in cloaks; or else to look more virile and less podgy, sat astride proud stallions with big balls. I found it hard to imagine that there could be earth, real earth beneath it all – even in the park, which looked as false to me as a giant roof-garden with painted trees and imitation grass.

Or was that just the way I felt?

I'd actually walked past the stage door twice before I found the entrance to Her Majesty's Theatre, looking self-consciously ornate beside the soaring block of glass and steel which was New Zealand House. Outside it, beside a HOUSE FULL notice, Abigail Compton's three-times-life-sized photo beamed starrily at me through the airbrushing. Inside the foyer, the theatre's Victorian actor-manager, Herbert Tree, glared morosely from his portrait in the role of bad King John – and the man in the box office did much the same, as if he disapproved of anyone as young as I was qualifying for a first night complimentary ticket. Even in the gods.

False though she be to me and love, I'll ne'er pursue revenge. For still the charmer I approve, though I deplore the change. That's what I wrote on the card the girl provided in the florists round the corner in the Royal Opera Arcade, and had to write it small to cram it in around the Good Luck message.

'From Bubo? But how *sweet* of him,' she would exclaim with just the right amount of touched amusement in her voice. False blue eyes unblinking in the glass. That's what I hoped.

After I delivered the extravagant bouquet of salmon-coloured gladioli at the stage door (it cost me £3.10s.) there was still an hour or so to kill before the opening. The rain had stopped. So I bought a hot dog from a stand in Lower Regent Street and ate it sitting on Bill's folded mac on a damp park bench in St James's Square (the *real* St James's), between the statue of another fat old king on horseback and a row of Georgian mansions. A blue plaque by the steps of Number 15, the office of the Clerical, Medical & General Life Assurance Soc., declared it to be the home of David Stanville, Ninth Earl of Southbourne. A serendipitous link with Sussex which I found comforting somehow.

The previous Sunday I'd gone home with Mag for a visit to the farm that was long overdue, and was surprised at how affectionate they'd all been – even Dad, who'd given me a hug before we left. And funny that he'd done that, I thought afterwards. I mean just when I needed it the most.

On either side of the stage door of Her Majesty's, blank poster frames were ready for the first night critics' predictably rave notices: *Scintillating, glorious, enthralling, utterly bewitching, riotously funny, limitlessly entertaining, critically acclaimed, miraculously daring;* interchangeable phrases waiting to be shuffled into order under an appropriate headline: SMASH HIT! TRIUMPHANT COMEBACK! STAR PERFORMANCE! A computer could have done it, even then.

By the time I reached the gallery street entrance, a steady stream of climbers were already panting up a stairway that quite literally was not for the faint-hearted. Nor one would have thought for anyone with vertigo or a tendency to altitude sickness. You could snatch a breath of oxygen from a small window on to Charles II Street at some sort of base-camp landing at the top of the sixth flight; and from the summit were rewarded, once you felt strong enough to raise your head, with a near view of the theatre ceiling, a distant prospect of the orchestra pit, and with the stage in miniature some eighty feet below. My seat was near the front and I was luckily long-sighted.

I fumbled for the change to buy a programme (another 1/6) and sat down feeling – not simply breathless from the climb, but breathlessly excited. People all around me were rustling their programmes and chattering about the show – about Neil Craven and Flo Girton and the world famous Abigail Compton. *My* Abi Compton! As if they'd bloody known them all their bloody lives! And suddenly I felt the urge to shout them down; to stand up on my seat and shout that this was not their show but MINE. To tell them that I'd acted with Miss Compton, that I'd shared her curtain call, had BEEN TO BED WITH HER, for fuck's sake! To tell them I knew everything about the show and everyone behind that curtain; had been a part of it, was still a part of it, that I was one of *them*!

Except I wasn't, was I?

'This is going to be a treat,' a man beside me said to no one in particular. A man so ancient that I wondered how he made it up as far as base-camp, let alone the gods. I forced myself to read the programme. (I still have it in a drawer somewhere, that first night programme, and have read since as I read then that Abi Compton had been born in India as a daughter of the Raj – had first appeared onstage in Delhi at the age of six as Prince Arthur in King John.)

She would be putting on her wig now, examining her make-up in a mirror with a full set of lights, applying a last

239

lavish squirt of *JOY*. But who to stand behind her, check for powder and remember not to wish her luck? 'I have this sneaking little feeling that the Mouse will be back for the first night.' Was that how she'd put it? And might she, could she possibly be right?

'House lights!'

A feeling of expectancy as the house lights dimmed. The people round me settled in their seats; several cleared their throats. I'd thought that I had no excitement left in me, but once again and typically was wrong. My heart began to beat so violently that I could feel it pounding in my temples.

'Stand by... *curtain!*'

And up it went without a sound.

Scene 6

As the curtain rises the orchestra is playing the 'Moonlight in Mayo' waltz (and sounding so much better than on Paul's tape). The stage is empty for a moment, then Sadie Swanson dances out on to the moonlit veranda of Raffles Hotel in Singapore, before returning to the embrace of her young husband, Max. They are both still in their twenties and waltz divinely, despite their youth.

From where I was sitting in the gods, she looked tiny; a white moth fluttering ahead of Nigel H-M out into the moonlight (Len used Steel Blue filters for the effect). She fluttered back into his open arms, and together they danced a circuit of the stage through fresh storms of applause.

'Lordy, will you *look* at her?' a raspingly American and female voice demanded from behind me. 'Sixty, has to be, and see the way she moves!'

I clenched a fist deciding that not only man is vile. But before I could persuade the beast in me that it wasn't nice to smash a woman's face in, I realised that Abi had introduced another piece of new business before the kiss, and had to see how it played out. She'd disengaged herself from H-M for the last few bars of 'Moonlight in Mayo' and was pirouetting slowly down centre, Ginger Rogers fashion, out on to the apron – another of her masterly illusions; another character too perfect to be real.

That's when she caught her left heel in the hem of the white dress, and the whole thing became a series of jerky strobe-lit stills. There was no net or stage extension, nothing to impede her. Her follow-spot by definition followed her – and in my memory I can still see her plunge backwards, still hear the audience's horrified and horrifying indrawn breath, and hear the perfect word she found to fit the situation: '*SHIT!*' projected crisply through the auditorium to reach us in the gods.

She hit the harp on her way down and took it with her slap into the kettle drum – followed by the crash; a terrible confused percussion mingled with the harpist's screams.

As 1200 members of the audience rose to their feet, I stumbled blindly for the exit. Down the endless stairs and out on to the wet pavement.

FINAL CURTAIN

Producer's notes

Thank you, ladies and gentlemen – all back onstage then please to hear how that Suddenly Last Summer year of 1963 changed everything for me for ever.

If that's how personal histories work?

Abigail Compton's unexampled exit far down centre might well have marked the end of her illustrious career. In the fall she might so easily have broken an arm, a leg or collar bone or any number of ribs. Barbara Bayliss might have seized her chance to prove that lack of physical allure was no obstacle to a sensational performance, or achieving stardom at the age of forty-five. But in fact the only thing that Abi broke in her descent was the taut membrane of the kettle drum; and after an interval of no more than twenty minutes for repairs to wig and make-up, and the application of some arnica to a large bruise on her backside, she limped back onstage – not this time to waltz divinely despite her youth, but to apologise to a capacity audience for using a four-letter word.

'I can't think *where* I can have heard it,' she'd told them with a conspiratorial version of the famous smile.

I read afterwards in Bernard Levin's rave review for the *Daily Mail* that she had turned disaster in his estimation into an artistic triumph, to give the comic performance of her career. In other words, the show went on to become a sure-fire success, and so did Abi Compton.

Three Seasons of Sadie opened at Her Majesty's early in July of 1963, and ran for eighteen months before transferring to The Palace with Mollie Raye in the lead role. By then the triple-bill had not only revived Miss Compton's stage career, but also its author's. On the strength of its success, Neil Craven was persuaded to leave his beach house in the Virgin Islands to direct a series of revivals of his best loved comedies, and in due course to collect a knighthood from the Queen. In later years he called it his *renaissance*.

The rest of Abi Compton's story is embedded in the history of British stage and television drama for the latter part of the twentieth century. If you Google her as I did just the other day, you'll see from Wikipedia that despite her reputation as a light comedienne she enjoyed personal successes with a number of classically distinguished roles, in Shakespearean tragedies with the RSC as Cleopatra and as Gertrude. She triumphed as Blanche Dubois, as Eleanor of Aquitaine and Mary Stuart. She sang and danced again in *Charlie Girl* at the Adelphi and hammed it up in *No Sex Please We're British* at the Strand – appearing later as The Dame of Sark, in a fluffy white wig as Miss Marple in the *Thirteen Problems* TV series, and going on to win the Society of West End Theatres Award for a lifetime's contribution to the British stage.

'People seem to want to come to see me, watch me doing what I do,' was what she'd told me. 'I'm open to the public darling, simply cannot let them down.' She wasn't like Jean Simmons, who lived long enough to play Estella *and* Miss Havisham in *Great Expectations*. But like Canute she'd bravely faced the tide, in her case of the sags and bags and wrinkles that eventually attend old age. In 1986 I saw her in the BBC2 production of *All Passion Spent*, and was surprised and moved to see the depth of feeling she put into Lady Slane and her memories of a misspent life. The *Guardian* critic called it 'stunning' and 'exquisite', and went on to hazard that: '*Abigail Compton played it with an emotional transparency that is the hallmark of a truly great actress.*' So not something you would think she could dismiss as temperamental inexactitude, or fish out of what she once described as her tired old box of tricks?

I wondered then and wonder still if she was after all a much more complex character than anyone, including her daughter, had ever suspected; and an even better actress than we'd thought? In all those years I saw her in the flesh perhaps a dozen times, but always from the safe side of the proscenium. She never returned to Eastbourne or tried to find me. As she'd told me when she thought I was seventeen, what would have been the point?

I've often thought though about Cordelia, and wondered if she ever came to terms with Abi's latter-day successes. She was never mentioned in her mother's biographies or interviews; so I guess they must have gone their separate ways. By now she would be seventy-one, if she's alive still; a rather frightening thought. Abi Compton died at the age of ninety, appropriately enough in her dressing room at Chichester during a limited run of Noël Coward's *Blithe Spirit*, and what turned out to be her farewell performance as Madame Arcati. I read in her obituary that after her sixth and final divorce from the head of drama at the BBC, she'd lived on her own in a flat at Wimbledon – not quite alone, because she left a little dog, a Scottie. Which I must say came as a surprise. For family, the obituary acknowledged 'one daughter'.

So no one but a little dog to love her in the end, and apparently no husbands for the Mouse.

They gave Miss Compton a memorial service at St-Martin-in-the-Fields attended by all the theatrical knights and dames. Ken Branagh's eulogy for the occasion paid tribute to her

245

artistry and limitless capacity for being loved. At some sort of gala later at the University of Southern California, they ran her screen test for *Great Expectations*, followed by a digitally restored version of *Maytime in Mayfair* with Michael Wilding – and the great and good, the luminaries of the movies, came out in droves to be filmed weeping when it ended, whether they had known her personally or not.

As for me, she was proved right in her assessment. I never was cut out to be an actor, although I don't think that had anything to do with kindness. For me that summer of 1963 was made up of great expectations, and of moonshine if you like – began and ended with them; so serious, so tragic at the time but never really real. I don't believe on more mature reflection that my long-postponed initiation into sex, or love or both, made any fundamental changes to my character. If Abi Compton's inevitable rejection, or the knowledge of Cordelia's unhappiness upset me for a while, I think I must have recognised my 'love' for them to be no more when it came down to it than a projection of libido. I was too young besides to be depressed for long. At most it took me three months and a chance encounter with a down to earth Glaswegian nurse to restore my confidence and cure me of my morbid fear of long straight hair.

The next summer, on the beach at Seaford, I met a gorgeous, uninhibited Danish girl who'd never heard of structured underwear and offered no resistance to an English version of splendour in the grass. She was willing, I was able. But by then I needed something more than sex, I'm happy to report. Ingrid and I embarked on our relationship in mutual understanding and delight. Our love was all-absorbing and complete.

Wait until I tell you.

Reader, I married her without a trace of sadness or nostalgia on one of those misty autumn days when the world smelled wonderfully of smoke and leaf mould – standing in the village church at Sellington with my sister Caro as our bridesmaid, both the Allans in the congregation and Nanki yapping madly in their car outside. (This following an impromptu stag night with Hughes-Milton and Tom Allan at a Soho strip club, where I was photographed in an untoward state of excitement with my y-fronts on my head. I have destroyed the image since.)

We honeymooned in Dorset two weeks before it dawned on either of us that Ingie was already pregnant, and then came back to what I'd always known I would, to farm up on the Sussex downs.

If you remember what I said back in Scene 1 of my personal history – that I have always been in love with Sellington and the Bury Farm and would be to the day I die. Well that's proved true also. I think I may have mentioned that the valley these days isn't quite so peaceful, with the sound of traffic from the main road so often carried on the wind. But the old place is quite as beautiful as ever, with its gabled farmhouse, its byres and barn, its outbuildings and hanging woods. Ingie and I have two grown-up children and five grandchildren now, all living with us in the Bury complex; all working one way or another with the rare breeds on the farm. You'll find us, did I tell you, with the other leaflets in the Sussex tourist centres, described as 'Ashby's Ark'.

Grannie, Grandpa, both my parents are all long dead – ghosts, all ghosts, their spirits melted into air. Mummy lingered in an increasing state of vagueness almost to her century, painting seascapes which became so abstract there was nothing in them but blue lines. Caro married an American and lives in Baltimore. And you'll be pleased to hear I know that now all obstacles to the convention have been removed, Mag has married her faithful Bill – who in old age has swopped her Harley-Davidson for a Scout Spitfire 3 mobility scooter, but still wears leathers when they're out shopping, and now sports a super white moustache.

And looking back? Was Ingie after all what I deserved? Or, considering my verging-on-the beastly attitude when I was in my teens still, much *more* than I deserved? I only know that I'm content – contented Sam at last. It's generally agreed that one of the advantages of a long life is that its youthful disappointments no longer hurt. Or not at least as much. Speaking for myself, I tend to see my early years as strips of picture postcards; brightly coloured memories which can be concertina'd, folded up and neatly stored from view.

And the card for 1963?

When I look at that rudely coloured image, do I ever wish I'd never met the glamorous Miss Compton or her mixed-up daughter – never let them use me, bruise me, educate me in the way they did? How could I, when some part of me has never left that time. Or to view the thing the other way about, when an aspect of that time and of the embarrassing self-centred teenager I was in 1963 has never left the adult me completely.

***

Meanwhile, with box sets of her TV series and DVDs available for all of her old movies, Abigail Compton has achieved some kind of immortality. The other day, as a Sony Movies Classic they showed the 1932 version of *Great Expectations*; the one with Lewis Hayward and the young Abi Compton as the leads.

Lines, costumes, lighting, music, beautifully presented; the taste of nicotine and brandy, the sensation of receptive flesh –

none of them at this distance I should say more real than any other. I watched the old film with my granddaughter, Amelia, right through to the final frame.

'Grandpa, you're not *crying?!*' Melly stared at me in disbelief.

Estella, Estella! Oh my God, Estella!

As the titles rolled up through the moonlit sky cloth... well yes, I will admit I wiped away a surreptitious tear. Absurd at my age.

Credits

Three Seasons of Sadie started life as my first novel, drafted more than a half-century ago when I was still in my twenties and memories of adolescent frustrations working as an ASM and bit-part player at Richmond Theatre in Surrey were still fresh in my mind. The story served a useful purpose in finding me a literary agent, but at the time was thought too lightweight for publication. A Hutchinson reader considered it an entertaining read, but wondered if it could overcome that period's bad track-record for comedy thrillers. 'But at least the author is well worth encouraging,' she wrote; kind woman.

I've revised the story in this latter day updated version, and in the process altered it a good deal more than I anticipated – not only as a means of tying up some trailing loose ends from my previous sequential novel, *Chalkhill Blue*, but also out of a certain nostalgia for my misspent youth. From my point of view there is a kind of symmetry in the idea of converting my first attempt at fiction into the fifth of my Sussex stories, as if I've turned full circle.

The village of Sellington and the Bury Farm, which appear in two of my other novels, are fictional but set in the real landscape of the Sussex downs between Friston village and the sea. The Hadderton estate, which also features in my medieval and early nineteenth-century stories, *The White Cross* and *Painted Lady*, is based loosely on Firle Place near

Lewes. The Cosmopol and Maxims were both real coffee bars in the Eastbourne of the 1960s. But there wasn't a St Edgar's, a Wimborne House or an Excelsior Hotel there. None of the Meads cottages have attic bedrooms so far as I know, nor was there ever a theatre in the Meads – although there are or were four others in the town, three of them Victorian.

A number of the events I've described really happened during my time in rep. at Richmond and on tour – such as the brown pancake make-up in the public baths, the intense Ludo games in theatrical digs, the magic candlelit performance, the old ham actor who tended to dematerialise through walls, and the tales of theatrical disasters in the pub. The shrinking jeans fiasco also happened, but to a flat-mate rather than to me. The character of Abigail Compton owes something to the glamorous musical comedy star, Evelyn Laye, whom I encountered backstage at Richmond where her husband was performing, but perhaps more to an actress I won't name, who shocked me backstage with a far ruder rendition than the cabbages and peas song and later gained celebrity in a TV soap. Nor were the other characters in this piece drawn entirely from my imagination – but let's not go into that.

The stories of Sim's four-letter-word experiments, and of mine in the double-back-seated cinema are also true, as is the *School for Scandal* story involving Alec Guinness. The stung tongue/wasp-in-the-bottle and cross-purposes conversation with the hospital happened to me at my own eighteenth birthday party. My Eastbourne Thespians cricket team are based on a genuine weekend cricket club of actors and associates: the Occasional Harry Baldwins, for whom my son Rob still plays. (And I'd also recommend as a thoroughly good read and comic account of their activities, *Fatty Batter* by the well-known actor, Michael Simkins; published by Ebury Press.).

My heartfelt thanks are due as ever to my wife Lee for her unfailing patience, and to Margaret Furley for her encouragement through the script's meadering development. More thanks to Debbie Sear and Carole Haggar, who've both raised funds for St Wilfrid's Hospice in Eastbourne by bidding in auction for the right to name two characters in the Three Seasons company (the married actors Tom and Primrose Allan), and have waited patiently since then for me to finish the story.

For additional help I am indebted to Clare Christian, Heather Boisseau, Anna Burtt and Lizzie Lewis of RedDoor Press, to Carol Anderson and Rosemary Ross, to Rob Masefield for advice on cricket, to Jenny McEvoy, Chris Whitehouse and Gabrielle Bryant for shared experience of the 1960s, to Faye Craddock of the very excellent Ship Inn in Meads Village, and to Stephen Bamber of Techmedic for nursing me through computer hiccups along the way; and then last, but certainly not least, I'm grateful to the incomparable Noël Coward for his repertoire of *Tonight at 8.30* one act plays, which were in many ways the inspiration for my triple-bill.

Richard Masefield's
SUSSEX NOVELS

Three Seasons of Sadie is the final playful episode in Richard Masefield's quintet of Sussex novels. Between them spanning more than eight hundred years of English history, the five stories follow the fortunes of two local families from their homeland in the Sussex Downs to far flung locations across the world; from crusade sieges in medieval Palestine to the early settlement of New South Wales; from the Grand Tour of Europe to the battlefields of the First World War. Each story is a romance and an adventure in its own right. Each is meticulously researched to bring the period in which it's set alive – each calculated to surprise the reader before they reach its final page.

THE WHITE CROSS: 1175–1198

Bringing something entirely new to historical fiction. Set in the late twelfth century at the time of King Richard I's crusade to recover Jerusalem from the Saracens, *The White Cross* is a vividly descriptive novel that captures the sights, sounds and the very smells of medieval living; one that blazes with colour and pulses with life. Whilst engaging with timeless issues – the moralities of warfare and religion; humanity and inhumanity and flawed ideals, it is also the passionate story of Garon and Elise – of love and separation; of a young husband's journey to self-realisation, and a woman's battle for justice and recognition in a brutal man's world. A captivating story unlike anything you will have read before.

'Brilliant! Really brilliant! I am now very enthusiastic to read more of Masefield's novels.'
GOODREADS

BRIMSTONE: 1770–1805

A story of ambition and temptation in the Georgian world of Sussex contrabanding and convict transports to New South Wales. The novel's two heroes are brothers bound by love, but separated by opposing characters which come to represent the two faces of eighteenth century England – its brutality and its enlightenment. Ellin Rimmer, daughter of a 'fire and brimstone' preacher, marries one brother to escape the loneliness of life in a parsonage, only to find herself hopelessly attracted to the other – and to be compelled through him to an impetuous decision that will have drastic consequences for all three.

'A brilliant evocation of the eighteenth century world.'
MELBOURNE ADVERTISER

PAINTED LADY: 1807–1861

A delightful, romping adventure that introduces an unforgettable new heroine to historical fiction. As a prostitute in Regency Brighton, Sary Snudden has no faith in love between a man and woman, until she meets Lord David Stanville. Caught up in a passionate affair with the heir to a great Sussex estate, she and her lover cross the Alps in a perilous journey by coach and sled to the excitement of a popular revolution in Turin and an erotically charged idyll in the Italian lakes. But the question of how she'll bridge the greater gulf between her humble origin and the noble status David seeks for her, remains for Sarah the central problem of her life.

'Jane Austen below the waist!'
CAMPAIGN MAGAZINE

CHALKHILL BLUE: 1889–1925

An epic story of war and peacetime, a descriptive novel of tremendous scope and a must read for anyone with a taste for the authentic and the unusual.

From the parched landscapes of Queensland and the Andes to the chalky scarps of the Sussex downs; from the Victorian heyday through the cataclysm of the First War to the uncertain new world of the 1920s, the novel follows the lives of two very different women who have dared to flout the rules of their society, and those of the men they choose – the double strands of a remarkable love story with a heart-stopping double-twist in the tail that makes it unforgettable.

'Beautifully and lovingly brought to life, with a warmth that makes it linger kindly in the mind long after the book is closed.'
THE LITERARY REVIEW

About the Author

Richard Masefield and his Australian wife Lee have been married for more than five decades, with three children and seven grandchildren to their credit. Although his father and both his brothers made careers in aviation, Richard always spent as much time as possible outside with animals, or indoors scribbling. As a cousin of the poet, John Masefield, he decided early that he'd farm and write, preferably both at once. In fact, it took him years to get there. After school he travelled abroad, tried acting and stage management (the subject of this latest novel), gave radio talks and spent ten years as an adman in a London office before he could afford to buy his own small dairy farm in Sussex. For one exhausting year he rose at four-thirty to milk the cows before commuting for a working day in London and returning for a second session in the milking parlour after dark. He continued working with a milking herd and later with beef cattle, whilst venturing into fiction and being employed for a number of years as a care manager and teacher for a special needs school near Haywards Heath. Eventually retiring to cross the border into Kent, he remains devoted to the English countryside, its wildlife and its agriculture, and is keen to help preserve as much of it as possible for future generations.

Find out more about RedDoor Press and sign up to our newsletter to hear about our **latest releases, author events,** exciting **competitions** and more at

reddoorpress.co.uk

YOU CAN ALSO FOLLOW US:

  @RedDoorBooks

  Facebook.com/RedDoorPress

  @RedDoorBooks